THE
VIOLET
HOUR

—◆◆◆—

ALSO BY DANIEL JUDSON

✦

THE
VIOLET
HOUR

Daniel Judson

MINOTAUR BOOKS ⚏ NEW YORK

This is a work of fiction. All of the characters, organizations, and events portrayed in this novel are either products of the author's imagination or are used fictitiously.

www.minotaurbooks.com

The Library of Congress has cataloged the hardcover edition as follows:

Judson, Daniel.
    The violet hour / Daniel Judson.—1st ed.
       p. cm.
    ISBN 978-0-312-38357-2
    1. Hamptons (N.Y.)—Fiction. I. Title.
PS3610.U532V56 2009
813' .6—dc22   2009016659

ISBN 978-0-312-38358-9

First Minotaur Books Paperback Edition: October 2010

10 9 8 7 6 5 4 3 2 1

for Schwegel

THE
VIOLET
HOUR

PART ONE

October 30

MISCHIEF
NIGHT

─◆◆◆─

One

———◆———

During the final week of October, on a clear but moonless night, the last train from Manhattan pulled into Bridgehampton, a solitary female passenger disembarking and heading straight for the nondescript black Ford sedan waiting at the far end of the station parking lot.

She was tall—this much her long overcoat could not conceal—but beneath the coat was the body of an athlete, lean and strong, which was something of a miracle, considering where she had come from, the childhood she'd endured and, at last, escaped. A head of curly black hair, the dark skin of her South American mother, all of twenty-six years old now but confident—something else her overcoat could not hide. She walked steadily, without once looking around, and reached finally the sedan. The glove compartment was to contain directions to her final destination, and under the passenger seat she was to find a two-foot-long Maglite flashlight. Once inside the vehicle, she retrieved both items and laid them beside her, then waited behind the wheel till the train began to pull away from the empty platform. When it was gone, she surveyed the lot, particularly its several shadows, looking for anything that might indicate she wasn't alone. Seeing nothing suspicious, she removed the key from over the visor and turned the ignition, beginning the last—and, hopefully, the briefest—leg of her night's journey.

The directions looked simple enough, only a handful of turns, and in the end it took her less than ten minutes, which pleased her; a long late-night train ride meant she wasn't in the mood for difficulties. The building sat on the edge of a two-lane road called, according to the paper beside her, Montauk Highway. Hardly a highway at all, she thought, at least not as she understood the meaning of the word, but that was English, wasn't it? Of all the things she'd learned in these past few years—all the things she'd been taught to make her what she was now—it was the English language that had given her the most trouble.

Her instructions tonight were to pull around to the back of this building, and as she did, following the curve of the gravel path, she caught sight of the unlit neon sign hanging above the darkened front door. HOTEL ST. JAMES. Maybe once, she thought, long ago; now, though, it was just a two-story building with all its windows boarded over, little more than a dark shape standing silent and still beneath the dark night. Her home for the next few days, but she'd known worse places than this, suffered through hardships greater by far than a few nights in some abandoned hotel at the end of the known world.

She parked the sedan at the rear driveway's edge, out of sight of the main road. No need to worry about leaving tire tracks or footprints, or so she'd been told; still, she kept to the gravel as she approached the back door.

Using the flashlight to find the key that had been placed for her under the second of three stone steps, she entered the building through its
kitchen, instantly sensing all around her an absolute stillness. This was
a dormant and forgotten place, cold to the point of being raw—that
kind of chill that is only found inside, never outside. Stagnant, like a
cave. As always, she carried with her only what she needed, deriving
for herself a deep joy from *limited possessions*. Maybe it was simply a
matter of her enjoying the fact that it was by choice, *her* choice, as op-
posed to the times in her life—the first twenty years of it, trapped in the
slums of São Paulo—when having nothing was not a choice at all.

Her few possessions—clothes for a handful of days and various
tools of her trade—were packed into a small canvas shoulder bag, a
tank mechanic's bag, according to the man at the army surplus store.
Though compact, it held all that would be required to live till it came
time for her to act.

The room in which she was to wait for the call—in the only part of
the building with running water and electricity—was on the second
floor, at the far end of the hall. Looking for the stairs, her flashlight the
only source of illumination, she left the kitchen and entered a dining
room, stepping from there into a large and echoing foyer beyond which
stood the main stairway. Wide, curving, its ornate banister all but lost
to rot. She made her way to it and started up, testing each plank before
she dared to place her full weight upon it.

The room at the end of the hall was as cold as the rest of the hotel.
She found a light switch on the wall just inside the door, flipped it on,
and looked around for a thermostat but found none. Beside the bed,
which had been made up for her with fresh linens and several heavy
blankets, was a small electric heater. She plugged it in, her face already
numbing, and switched the power on, watching as the inner coils went
from black to orange.

As the dry heat began finally to rise, she placed the mechanic's bag on the foot of the strange bed. Still in her overcoat, she looked around this bare and indifferent room, studying each wall and corner, bracing herself for the long days of solitude, and the even longer nights, ahead.

Inside her still, despite what she was now, what she had become, was that child he had found, the slum-flower, he had called her, who lived in fear every day of sunset.

The call came three nights later, on a Friday, at half past seven.

She sat up fast, answering before the cell phone had the chance to buzz a second time. Only Janssen had this number, so there was no reason for her to consider that it might be someone else on the other end.

"Hey," she whispered. Her voice was soft, groggy. She wished instantly that she had sounded different—*anything other than this sleepy girl.*

"I woke you," Janssen said.

She moved to the edge of the mattress, looked toward the one window that wasn't boarded over. It offered a view of the rear driveway and a backyard of overgrown grass, but all she could see now was the top of the line of half-bare trees that bordered the property.

"No."

"Daydreaming, then?"

She nodded. "Yeah."

"Good things, I hope."

"Yes," she said. It was a lie. To cover it up, she said quickly, "Are you home?"

"I am."

She closed her eyes, thought of his place—*their* place, he insisted.

"If all goes well tonight," he said, "you'll be back in time for breakfast."

Hearing that pleased her. The sooner she was out of there—*too much time to lie around and remember the past*—the better.

"I can be out the door in a half hour."

"We have time, so no need to rush. Do what you need to do first. According to our man on the inside, he should be in place some time after ten. It shouldn't be difficult at all for you to get next to him. I'll text you the details."

"Okay."

"If for some reason he doesn't show tonight, we'll try again tomorrow night."

She closed her eyes at the thought of another day spent sleeping till she could sleep no more, then lying still on that worn and musty mattress, waiting for the night to come. She decided to focus on him instead. Significantly older than she, his hair already gray, he was nonetheless a *vital* man. Tall, strong, kind, patient. The touch of his hand all but paralyzed her, brought her joy instead of torment. His was the only hand to ever do so. Of course, all she had of him at this moment was the sound of his voice—deep and resonant like a cello. It, too, had an effect on her, but it wasn't enough, not now.

"We'll go away after this," he offered. "Once it's done we'll be free to go anywhere we want."

"I'd like that." She paused a moment, then said, "I miss you."

There was no hesitation from Janssen. "I miss you, too, Evie. Get this done and come back to me. Okay?"

"Yes."

Before she could say anything more, the line went dead.

◆◆◆

The transformation didn't take long at all; she was good at making this change, so much so that the woman who made her way down the dark hallway a half hour later was, for all intents and purposes, not the woman who had entered it three days before.

A wig of thick auburn hair—straight, with long bangs—masked her dark curls, and her eyes, which were green—*covetous eyes*, he called them—were sharp blue now, made so by the contact lenses he had provided. High heels and a padded bra changed not only her over-all shape but the way she carried herself—no longer simply tall, she was now statuesque; no longer athletic, she was now curvy. Eye-catching, provocative, she—not *she*, not Evangeline Amendora, Evie to him, but rather *this woman*—would no doubt stand out in a crowd, which was a necessity. *Have them looking for this auburn-haired woman while a woman with dark curly hair was slipping out of town.*

A black evening dress that hugged her curves—natural and otherwise—completed the transformation from who and what she was to who and what she needed to be. Even her overcoat, held closed against the stagnant chill of the dark hallway, couldn't hide the woman below, not *this* woman.

The text he had sent her was thorough, as always. Directions to the location, a restaurant in the nearby town of Southampton. He had also sent several photos of the target and her best route of escape, should it come to that. In that case, she was to make it to a train station a mile to the north—directions to it and the times of the last few trains for the night were, of course, included. Though she expected nothing less, she was grateful for his attention to detail; as good as she was, a num-ber of things could still go wrong. She had to always keep that in mind.

Reaching the end of the hallway, she climbed down the rotting stairs, needed to move with more caution than before now because of the heels. Making her way to the empty kitchen, she exited through the back door and started toward the sedan. Cold out tonight, windy, dead leaves scuffling across the gravel driveway. That, and the sound of her footsteps, was all there was for her to hear.

Heading westward, into strong winds, it felt at times as if she were driving against the current of a rushing river, but the glass and steel of the sedan protected her, and the heater, set on high, blew an endless supply of warmth that was nothing less than exquisite.

Twenty minutes later she was in the town of Southampton, found the restaurant easily enough—in the heart of that village on Main Street—its facade a long row of tall glass doors, its interior lit by soft yellow light. She rode past it, slowly, studying the place, then turned around at the end of the block and passed it once more before driving north, through a residential neighborhood to the train station. From there she could catch the train west, take it back to the city, leaving the sedan to be picked up by whoever had left it for her.

On her way back to the heart of town she took note of the storm drains, where she would ditch her various elements of disguise as she made her escape. Again, only if things went wrong.

She passed the restaurant one last time, then parked a half block down from it but remained behind the wheel, taking a good look at her surroundings. She saw shops and boutiques and a number of other restaurants—upper-scale places, every last one of them. The shops were all closed, so the restaurants were the only signs of life tonight. A street somehow both lit and dark. A wealthy town, no doubt about that. She sat still, felt nothing but a steady calm now. Poised to strike. No one better at that than she.

At ten she took one more look at herself in the rearview mirror—cold blue eyes all but obscured by long auburn bangs—then got out and walked toward the restaurant. Her heels sounded hollow on the old brick sidewalk, the echo somehow both following her and out in front. Steps from the restaurant, she felt her stomach suddenly tighten. Not nerves or fear, simply an anticipatory response, as deep and raw as a sexual urge.

He lived only a few blocks away, on a street called Meeting House Lane; she, of course, knew this, knew, too, that he walked home from this restaurant, more than likely to avoid having to drive his brand-new car while drunk. It was a walk that would take them, at best, ten minutes, and as she sat next to him at the bar and drank, holding her own with him, she counted on those moments in the cold night air to clear her head, knew that she could drag the walk out longer if she needed more time.

Control was crucial, always.

Her mark was a big man, but she wasn't at all intimidated. In his midthirties, handsome enough, in that polished but rugged way—short dark hair, perfectly tousled, a square jaw shadowed with a few days' stubble, a midlength leather jacket, wornout but still shiny, well-fitting jeans and motorcycle boots. Militich was his name, though he was known by another here, had used it, as she knew he would, when, after several drinks, it came time finally for them to exchange names.

She added time to their walk to his place—arm in arm, so obvious, to him and those who had seen them leave together, where exactly this seemingly chance meeting was leading—by stopping at shops to look in their windows at things that were on display, things she otherwise had no interest in. She giggled and laughed, pretended to almost fall over now and then—an exaggeration of her inebriated state that was for him and anyone who might be watching them. Each time she almost fell, he'd pull her to him, hold her close. There was a youthfulness to his power, but she had no interest in that, either.

His apartment, three small rooms on the top floor of a two-story house, looked exactly like the hideaway it was. Sparsely furnished, bare walls, little that couldn't be taken quickly or, if needed, left behind. He kept the lights off; the streetlamps outside were more than enough. Plus, she knew, a woman was more likely to be uninhibited in dim light.

She stood by his front window, still wearing her overcoat, looked down at the narrow side street, lined with modest homes, and asked if he had something for them to drink. It was, at last, time for her to act. He went into his kitchen and came out with a bottle of cheap tequila and two tumblers—thick glass with heavy bottoms, square shaped, the words SOUTHAMPTON PUBLICK HOUSE stenciled on three sides. She sent him back into the kitchen for some ice, then added, once he was gone from sight, a clear liquid to his glass, expertly pouring it from a mini flask that she then returned to her overcoat. Back from the kitchen, he dropped a handful of ice into her glass, and she handed his to him. They drank, the contents of both glasses gone in single gulps. This alcohol wouldn't hit her system for a while, wouldn't negate her efforts to keep in control, at least not immediately. The effects of what she had added to his drink, however, wouldn't take long at all to manifest.

He stayed with her by the window, facing her, standing close and touching her shoulder with his right hand. He was, it seemed, in no rush, was maybe even waiting for her to make the move, be the one to initiate their inevitable shift from strangers to lovers.

She told him she needed to use the bathroom first, made the point of softly emphasizing the word "first." *Let him believe he was just moments away.*

In the tiny room off the kitchen she ran the cold water, splashing her face with it. She would need every possible scrap of clarity now.

Drying her face and hands, she looked at her reflection in the mirror above the sink, told herself what she always told herself in the moments prior to a kill.

Men were now the prey, and she was the one with the power.

She returned to the living room, saw that he was seated on the couch, slouching, his eyes closing and opening sluggishly. When he realized that she was standing in the doorway, he looked at her, said softly, "Hey," and got up, or at least tried to. He managed to stand, but it took him a moment to do so, and even when he was at last upright, facing her, he swayed just a little.

She felt no sadness for him.

He took a step toward her, stumbled, caught himself, then stood perfectly still, as if he were afraid suddenly of moving at all, in any manner or direction. She remained where she was, watching him. There was nothing left for her to do now but wait. *Just moments left.*

"I don't feel so hot all of a sudden," he muttered. He took another step, staggering now, bumped the coffee table with his shin, wavered a moment, then slumped down to one knee. She immediately thought of his downstairs neighbors—the street-level apartment, she had noted as they entered his place, had been dark, but it was late, its occupants could have been asleep. If that were the case, would they still be now?

He started to get to his feet again, and knowing he would certainly fall once more and make even more noise, she quickly moved to his side and grabbed hold of his arm. It took all of her considerable strength to keep him up.

"What the hell?" he muttered.

"It's okay," she whispered.

Steering him back to the couch, she eased him down onto the cushions. The knife was in her overcoat pocket. A Spyderco Scorpius, three inches of Japanese steel, the single-edged blade serrated, each tiny ridge and valley razor sharp. She reached for the weapon, but before she could remove it, something happened that hadn't ever happened before. Her victim was looking up at her—his eyes fluttering, his breathing growing labored—with nothing shy of a clear understanding of what was going on.

He grasped her wrist with his right hand. Despite his condition, there was power in his grip.

"What did you do?" he demanded.

She didn't answer, just looked at him.

"What did you *do*?"

"Just relax," she told him. "It'll be better if you just let it happen."

"He sent you."

"You should just relax."

"He sent you, right?"

She pulled her hand from his grip—it was easier than she had expected it would be; his strength, too, was fading as the drug tranquilized him. Free of him, she took a step back—just in case, this one was full of surprises—and reached again into the pocket of her overcoat. In its deep bottom was the knife. She grabbed it, took hold of it, but didn't yet remove it.

"Listen to me," he said. "He doesn't want me dead." It was a struggle for him to speak. "It won't go well for him if I'm dead."

He tried again to stand but made it only as far as moving to the end of the cushion, then slipped off the couch entirely and slumped to the floor. *Enough noise already,* she thought. Removing the knife from her coat pocket, she held it behind her back, out of his sight. He was attempting yet again to stand, but it wouldn't come to anything, she knew, not now. The drug was doing its work, was well into his blood at this point.

"You should call him right now . . . tell him that he doesn't want this." He removed his cell phone from his leather jacket and offered it to her.

She refused to take it. Shaking her head, she said only, "Quiet now." Any second he would succumb, and she'd walk to him, ease him down to the floor and roll him onto his stomach, then pull his head back, exposing his throat. One long slashing motion—from the left to the right, the serrated blade cutting through arteries and tendons and muscle, slicing down to the bone—and it would be done.

Like those before him.

She waited for that complete surrender. *A dangerous man,* she had been warned, so *take care.* Now wasn't the time to forget that. Instead of surrendering, he struggled once more to stand, made it to his knees, then to one foot, then the other. Rising but not yet upright, he was nonetheless close enough to it. He dropped the cell phone, had both hands firmly on the arm of the couch now, wouldn't have been able to come this far without it there to support him. He was looking straight at her, his eyes no longer sluggish but wild, grimly determined.

He was the first to move, lunging for her clumsily, lumbering like a drunk. Still, he was much faster than she had expected would have been possible. He had grabbed his empty glass, the tumbler with the heavy bottom, was cocking his arm back, ready to bring the solid, inch-thick base down upon her skull, had the presence of mind for that much at least. She opened the knife with one hand, felt the solid jolt of the blade clicking into place, gripped the perfectly shaped handle tight. She had already begun to move the instant he had—to intercept his charge, her movements nothing less than swift and precise.

Muscles coiled but relaxed, center of gravity low, feet directly beneath her, where they belonged, her stance never wider than her shoulders. *Years to make her like this, so little chance of her forgetting any of it.*

All she needed was one good swing of the razor-sharp blade, strike at him with one good killing *sting*.

Once that was done, there'd be no one left to come between her and the life she'd been promised.

Back at the hotel, in her room, she removed the bloodstained overcoat, placed it into a plastic garbage bag, did the same with the wig, the torn black dress, the high-heel shoes, padded bra, and panties—everything, even the contact lenses, had to go. She had shut off the heater before leaving, and the cold air against her bare skin was unpleasant. It was, she knew, nothing compared to what awaited her.

In the bathroom, she paused to look at her face in the mirror, saw the bruise beneath her left eye and the long scratch along her cheek. Deep, it oozed blood. With a trembling hand she started the shower. She knew not to expect anything close to warm water; still, she wasn't prepared for the utter cold that hit her as she stepped under the drizzling stream.

She washed away the blood, her own and his, and whatever traces the dress she had worn might have been left upon her waxed skin, was shuddering by the time she was done, barely able to breathe. Drying herself off in all-out convulsions, her core temperature dangerously low, she quickly redressed—jeans and a heavy knit turtleneck sweater, socks and leather boots—then grabbed the garbage bag and flashlight and left the room, hurrying down the long hallway and rotting stairs to the lobby, through that to the kitchen and out again into the windy night.

Her still-wet hair froze instantly, but there was nothing she could do about that. In the trunk of the sedan the only thing that passed for a digging tool was the tire iron. Through the bordering trees, at the edge of a field, where the dirt was softer, she scraped out a hole deep enough to take the garbage bag, then covered it over. The effort had begun to warm her up, but only barely—she knew she had a long way to go yet before the cold within her would be gone.

Back in the room, she stood by the electric heater, removed a first aid kit from her mechanic's bag, and tended to her wound. She worked without a mirror, didn't want to see her reflection again. When she was done, her hands still shaking, she removed the cell phone she had taken before leaving Militich's apartment, flipped open its lid, and saw by the digits at the bottom of the screen that it was after one o'clock.

She didn't care about that, though, and began right away to scroll through the list of recent calls. She had managed to cut her mark before he got away, a deep enough cut, she knew, even in all the confusion, that it would be necessary for him to get somewhere and have it taken care of as soon as possible. Where else would a wounded and drugged man—a man who was on the run to begin with, living in hiding—go except to a lover, if he had one, or, if he didn't, a friend? Hospitals were of course out of the question. So were the police. He had left on foot, but close to an hour had passed, so if he hadn't bled out first, he must have gotten somewhere by now.

He was out there, then, possibly dead or dying, or maybe being put back together. Whatever the case, she needed to find him, had to *know*.

It didn't take long for her to determine the number he called most often because there was only one number in any of the phone's contact lists. Odd, perhaps, but this made her job easier. She knew his names—his real name and the name he went by now—but she would ask for his fake name; there was no reason for her to think anyone here would know him as Militich.

From her mechanic's bag, Evangeline Amendora removed a pre-paid cell phone and turned it on. As she waited for it to power up, she took out the snub-nosed Smith and Wesson .357, studied it for a moment, felt its weight, the solidness of its walnut grip—so assuring, so powerful—then returned it to the bag. She preferred a revolver to a semiautomatic. Revolvers didn't eject bullet casings; semiautomatics did. The marks left by a gun's hammer on the shell's primer were nowadays as good as a fingerprint.

Leave no trace.

When the phone was powered up, she punched in the number. Pressing the button marked TALK, she brought the phone to her face.

Her ear ached from the cold—it felt as if someone had smashed it with something hard—but she ignored that. She wondered how Janssen would react to the bad news, which of his many sides this would bring out. She had never failed him before, was, at this moment, in unknown territory. Without him, what would become of her?

She needed to ignore this, too. It was chatter, born of fear, spoken in the voice of that little girl lost to terror.

Trying to focus, she counted the rings as she waited for her call to be answered.

One, two, three, four . . .

Two

❖

On a back road a mile or so north of Bridgehampton Village, in the moments just prior to the fall of full night, Caleb Rakowski, a mechanic, stepped out of the auto repair shop in which he worked and, walking to the edge of the gravel driveway, looked west for a glimpse of what might remain of the sunset. It was a ritual of his, making a point of quietly observing the day's end like this, but he was, at the age of twenty-two, nothing if not obedient to the careful schedule that carried him each day from waking to sleep.

He saw tonight only the slightest inference of color along the length of the western horizon, a fading slash of violent red, nothing more, really, than a stain in all that gathering darkness. Maintaining his silent vigil despite a chill wind that at times buffeted him like a crowd, he watched till the last remnant of daylight was gone—a transition that didn't take that long—and then turned his attention to Scuttlehole Road below, looking for any indication that Lebell was in fact on his way back.

He hadn't kept an eye on the time, was too busy concentrating on the engine he was in the final stages of rebuilding—a '62 Mercedes-Benz 300SL, nothing short of a work of art. But he was certain that Lebell had been gone an hour at least, maybe more. Having finished the fender replacement on the '58 Citroën in the next work bay around six, Lebell had offered to make Cal's end-of-the-week supply run—there were only two quarts of oil on the back shelf, he had pointed out, and Cal would need five. He should have been gone for a half hour at the most—ten minutes to get to the store just east of Bridgehampton Village, ten minutes to grab the needed items, and ten minutes to get back—but Lebell wasn't exactly known for always doing what he should.

No sign of the guy didn't necessarily mean anything, then; he could have run into someone he knew or decided to take the long way, or both. Cal was just a little too aware, though, of how quickly things can happen—terrible things, life-altering things. More importantly, he was aware that word of such things often took time to reach those who were most affected. If anything bad *had* happened to Lebell— swerved off the road, or been part of a head-on collision, *anything*— there was the chance that Cal would be left to wait for the news to make its way to him. How many hours—or, like before, days—of looking and listening like this, of *not knowing*, would he be required to endure this time around?

Foolish thoughts, he knew that. Lebell had simply taken the long way back—any excuse to put his Mustang through its paces, and no better place to do that than the winding back roads of Bridgehampton no-man's-land. Even the most remote of possibilities was a possibility, and though it had been four years since his life had last been changed by an untimely death, Cal didn't completely trust that it wouldn't happen again.

Taking one last glance down that dark road, Cal turned and faced the garage. It was a clapboard structure, a decade or two shy of a century old—three work bays and an adjoining office with an apartment above. The dark panes of the upper-floor windows told him that Heather was still asleep. She usually lay down for a nap in the late afternoon, but he couldn't remember her, in the two months since she had arrived, ever sleeping this far into the evening. Still, he wasn't surprised; she lived these days, as she put it, like a housecat, rarely leaving his apartment, at times doing little more than staring out windows for hours on end, waiting with a patience that bordered on detachment as each day of hiding passed.

He paused one last time, took in a deep breath of the clear, bracing night air, and looked once more at the place in the sky where the sun had moments ago been. It wasn't the completion of this ritual, however, that sent him finally back to the shelter of the old garage. It was, instead, a sudden gust of wind, colder than any so far and almost hostile in the way it rushed at him. Slender—lanky, even—Cal, caught off guard by this burst, had to shift to keep his balance. An unpleasant feeling, being shoved like this, even if only by an autumn wind.

Crossing the narrow gravel driveway, he stepped back into the first bay—the pale blue glow of fluorescent light spilling from its row of small windows was the only illumination visible for miles—and resumed the work that awaited him there.

Moments later he heard the sound of a car approaching, knew by the pitch of its engine, though, that it wasn't Lebell's Mustang.

Wiping his hands with a cloth rag he always kept in the back pocket of his coveralls, he stepped to the bay door and looked out just in time to see a Corvette rolling past. An unfamiliar car, but that in itself wasn't uncommon; on occasion passersby, mainly summer tourists, mistook the dilapidated garage for an actual filling station, especially after dark.

Of course, it wasn't exactly summer anymore, was it?

Cal moved into the unlit office and looked through its large storefront window, expecting the driver of the Corvette to realize his or her mistake and drive off. Instead, the vehicle stopped. Cal could see the thing clearly now—not just any 'Vette, it was a Stingray, from the early '70s, in mint condition, its competition orange paint job visible even in the limited light. *Maybe a customer's dropping it off,* he thought— the shop did specialize in classic and collectible vehicles—but almost all of what he worked on was foreign made, European for the most part, the toys of the wealthy and status-minded. Anyway, drop-offs as such were scheduled, and there was nothing due in, that Cal knew of, at least till after the weekend.

He glanced at the panel beside the office door, making sure that the alarm system was activated, which of course it was. *A ritual of his, setting it every time he entered and exited.* The garage, though old and falling apart in many ways, was up to date in at least one: its alarm system was state-of-the-art, needed to be to ensure the safety of the vehicles, some priceless, that were stored here at any given time. Cal knew that no one hoping to get his hands on any or all of the three vehicles currently in the work bays would arrive to do so in a Corvette Stingray—painted orange, no less. Still, anything out of the ordinary was of concern to him, and the presence of a strange car at seven o'clock on a Friday night was out of the ordinary.

He looked through the large window again, thought then of his other concern, his *real* concern, the possibility that this 'Vette was in some way connected to Heather's husband and that behind its wheel was either the man himself or someone who worked for him. Her husband had made it clear, according to Heather, that he would never stop looking for her, and as careful as she was—rarely going out, her BMW permanently parked between the rear of the garage and a crowded line of covering trees, out of sight—there was no guarantee that she hadn't left some kind of trail, something that a man with more than enough money to hire the best would eventually discover and follow. Again, though, would such a man—Heather's husband or someone he might hire—arrive in a vehicle as notable as a Stingray?

Stranger things have happened, Cal thought.

He watched as the 'Vette's headlights went out. The left-hand door opened, and the driver swung his feet out, one at a time, placing them on the gravel. Cal needed only a glimpse of the white snakeskin cowboy boots to recognize the owner.

He entered the six-digit code into the keypad, disarming the security system, then switched on the office lights. The single long fluorescent bulb hanging above flickered and then came on. Opening the door, Cal stepped back out into the chilly night and watched his boss, Eric Carver, approach.

A tall man, athletically built, Carver was dressed, as always, in expensive clothes—European jeans, designer-label black sweater, Belstaff leather jacket. He owned not just the business but the building as well, made his money, though, in construction; the shop was simply a means for him to network with the kind of men who had the money to spend on such costly toys and, by extension, the means to finance an addition on an existing home or, better yet, build a brand-new one. Teardowns were his specialty: purchasing modest homes for the lots on which they stood, then promptly demolishing them and constructing would-be mansions—McMansions, the newspapers called them—in their place. Only in his midthirties, Carver already owned a home in

Southampton, was on his second wife, and, perhaps most important to the man, had a collection of close to a dozen cars, some new, some classics, all of them, though, clear indications of, if not his status, then at least his desire for it.

Carver spotted Cal in the doorway and instantly smiled that smile of his—a boyish, knowing grin that was a combination of both pride and sheepishness, meant to communicate that he had not only done something he shouldn't have done but was finding joy in having done so. Cal had seen that smile many times before, knew by it that Carver more than likely had just recently—possibly even moments ago—bought the 'Vette.

"So what do you think?"

Cal nodded. "What's not to like? When did you get it?"

"I just picked it up." Carver, several steps from the door, stopped to look back and admire his new pride and joy, to see it, Cal knew, from this particular angle and linger for just a moment more with the feeling the mere sight of it stirred in him. "I probably shouldn't have, but I just couldn't resist."

"Who could?"

"It's only money, right? You can always make more."

Cal said nothing. He didn't understand those who sought to fill their lives with chaos. Emotional, financial, sexual, it didn't matter; it was, to him, all the same nonsense.

Carver paused a moment longer, then finally resumed crossing the remaining distance to the garage. He was still grinning, his perfect teeth, catching the light spilling from the doorway, showing bone white against the darkness behind him.

"You're working late."

"Lebell wanted to finish up the body work on the Citroën, so I just kept plugging away on the Benz."

"Actually, I wanted to talk to you about that. How's it coming? Everything's okay, no major problems?"

"No, no problems at all. It's just taking the time these things take."

Nodding, Carver thought about that. He looked past Cal, through the office and into what could be seen from where he was standing of the work bays. "Is Lebell still here?"

"He ran out to get some oil and stuff."

"We're out?"

"Of oil?"

"Yeah."

"Just low."

"How many quarts do we have left?"

"Two."

Carver glanced toward the dark road. He seemed to Cal to be pre-occupied by something.

"Is he on his way back now?" Carver said.

"He should be, yeah."

"I'm going to need the quarts we have back there. I think my work truck is burning oil."

He stepped past Cal and into the office. Following him inside, Cal noticed that there was something else about his boss tonight that was odd—the man seemed to be just a little breathless, winded, even, as if he had very recently exerted himself in some manner and had yet to fully recover. His eyes, too, now that Cal could see them clearly in the office light, possessed a kind of wildness, like the eyes, maybe, of a man who had found himself suddenly on the run from something. Though Cal was only twenty-two and had lived since he was eighteen in the apartment above—alone, till recently, his days and nights all carefully structured to prevent any semblance of trouble from ever finding him—he knew enough of the world to know what the effects of certain illicit drugs looked like. His older brother, dead now, had been drawn since they were kids to one dangerous crowd or another; never completely belonging to one, Aaron Rakowski had instead existed on the edges of several. Cal had, then, seen enough of every type of abuser there was to recognize certain signs when they were right before him.

"Listen," Carver said, "I want to ask you something before Lebell gets back." He glanced at the road again, had to look past Cal and through the open door directly behind him to do so.

"What's up?"

"The owner of the Mercedes is breathing down my neck. He wants it back, says we're taking too long."

"It's a total engine rebuild, Eric. They take as long as they take."

"I know that, and you know that, but he's a rich fuck, doesn't care, wants it done. I know you probably have plans tonight, but do you think you could maybe stick around and finish it up?"

Cal said nothing. There were advantages to the setup he had— thirty bucks an hour off the books; steady, year-round work; the apartment above, rent-free and all utilities paid. To a young man—a gifted mechanic but uncertified—this was the deal of a lifetime. The only real disadvantage was that he was, in effect, beholden to his boss—how could he, really, say no to anything the man asked of him?

"You were going to go out with Lebell tonight, I assume," Carver said.

Every Friday night after work they made the rounds in Southampton. LeChef, Red Bar, Barrister's, Fellingham's, the Driver's Seat, ending up always at 75 Main. Usual places, familiar faces, a way to mark the end of the week.

"Yeah," Cal said.

"If you have just a few hours left, maybe you can knock it out and catch up with Lebell later. I'd consider it a favor."

"I'm a little burned out. I've been at it all day."

"The thing is, I don't want to piss this guy off, 'cause he can get me a lot of construction work."

"How about I get Lebell to help me? Together we can finish it up fast and still go out."

"No, I gave this guy a deal, so we'll be lucky to break even. I can only afford to pay you."

It was odd, Cal thought, for Carver to think responsibly like that, but the man was hardly as rich as he wanted people to think. There were times, in fact, when Carver claimed to be completely without cash, anxiously awaiting some big payoff that was on its way. It was possible that Corvette had left him once again cash-poor.

"Please, man. I really need you to do this for me."

Cal shrugged, glanced at the clock on the wall. It was just past seven, which meant he'd been at work for almost twelve hours so far today. What, though, could he say?

"Yeah, all right."

Carver seemed relieved—tremendously so, actually. "Thanks, man. I'll call the guy when I get home, tell him to pick it up at, what, noon?"

"Okay."

"You'll be here?"

"Yeah."

"I'd come by myself and meet him, let you sleep in, but I'm leaving town for the weekend."

"No problem."

Carver checked his watch. "Listen, would you mind grabbing the oil for me?"

The shop floors, narrow wood planks long since softened by years of use, were stained with layers of motor oil. Carver only came to the garage about once a week, and then stayed for only an hour or so, however long it took him to go over the bills. He never came anywhere near entering the work bays, even while wearing the Timberland boots he brought out for visits to construction sites. He certainly wasn't going to walk through them now, dressed as he was in his beloved snake-skin boots.

Cal headed through the first two work bays to the third. Beneath the plank stairs leading up to the apartment was the shelf where they stored the oil and antifreeze and transmission fluids. Grabbing the remaining two quarts of oil, he headed back to the office. Carver was standing by the large window, watching the stretch of dark road beyond. He turned suddenly, as if startled, when he realized Cal had returned.

"You okay?" Cal said.

Carver smiled his quick smile, but there was something false about it now. "Yeah."

"You sure?"

"Yeah."

Cal held out the two quarts, and Carver took them with hands that were trembling slightly. He looked closely at Carver's eyes then—glassy, pupils dilated. On the man's brow, despite the brisk night, were a few beads of sweat.

"I'll make sure the Mercedes is picked up at noon," Carver said.

"I'll keep an eye out for him."

It looked for a moment as if Carver were about to say something more. Cal waited, watching the man's face. Eventually, shaking his head slightly from side to side, Carver dismissed whatever it was he was thinking of saying. Instead, in a flat voice, he said, "Remember to cover up all the windows."

A precaution, to be taken every time Cal worked late, as much to keep the vehicles parked within away from potential prying eyes as to conceal the fact that this building housed a less than legitimate business.

"Have a good weekend," Cal said.

"You, too, man."

Crossing the gravel to the 'Vette, Carver was in a hurry now. Cal watched through the window as his boss placed the two containers of oil in the trunk, then, glancing once more toward the unlit road, climbed in behind the wheel and took off.

He headed west, toward Southampton. *Like a man getting away.* Despite the wind, the sound of the performance motor lingered long after the vehicle was gone from sight.

Finally, though, all trace of it faded to nothing. Flipping off the fluorescent light, Cal stepped into the open doorway for a moment, wondering as he stood there what, if anything, he should do.

There was, of course, nothing he could do. He had built a good life— a safe life—around a series of consistent habits, one of which was minding his own business. He saw no reason at all to alter his behavior now.

He was about to swing the door closed and reactivate the security system when he heard off in the distance the sound of Lebell's Mustang. A distinctive low and throaty *rat-ta-tat* rising above the sound of the wind, coming from the west, the Southampton side of town—the long way back indeed.

He closed the office door and moved through the garage to the third bay door, figuring he'd help Lebell carry in the cases of oil and fill him in on the change in plans in the process. Removing the two locking pins and releasing the center lock, he lifted the third door, its casters sliding noisily along their metal rails. He thought of Heather asleep above, was certain this noise would have awakened her. Stepping across the gravel to wait for Lebell, he glanced over his shoulder at the windows of his apartment.

Still dark.

He imagined Heather in her bed, stretched out in one of his shirts—she had come to him, more or less, with nothing but the clothes on her back. He didn't think of her like that for too long, though; there wasn't any point in it, and anyway it wasn't appropriate.

He needed, of course, no more reasons than those.

"You're killing me, man, you realize that, right?"

Lebell had parked his Mustang in front of the third bay. Even with that door open all the way, the light that strayed from inside the garage had little influence on the surrounding darkness. Lebell handed Cal the first case of oil, then leaned into the trunk for a second, shaking his head as he repeated, "Seriously, man, you're killing me here."

Cal shrugged. "What could I say?"

"It seems to me this was one of those rare occasions in life when the truth would have actually worked nicely."

"He knew I had plans, but he's in a jam."

Balancing the second case on his knee, Lebell closed the trunk. He was taller than Cal by an inch or so, with a thicker build, standing more to the brutish side of athletic while Cal, at best, was somewhere off on the sleeker side. Older by more than a decade, Lebell had taken it upon himself, pretty much from the day he first showed up a year ago, to take Cal under his wing, in every way imaginable.

"Without you, this place would fall to the ground, you know that, right?" Lebell said.

Hoisting the case onto his right shoulder, he headed into the third work bay. Cal followed, waited as Lebell placed his case onto the shelf below the plank stairs, then slid his on top of it.

"Maybe, but he is my boss."

"I just hate seeing you get taken advantage of, that's all."

"It's what he pays me to do—and pays me well."

"Yeah, he pays you well, and half what he'd have to pay a certified mechanic."

Lebell crossed to the other side of the garage, where, mounted on the wall, was a large metal sink. Opening the two taps, he grabbed the bar of soap from the basin's rim and began scrubbing his hands. The water falling from the spigot wasn't much more than a trickle. Little in this building, upstairs or down, was up to code—electrical outlets weren't grounded; most of them, uncovered, showed frayed and brittle wiring. That, combined with this wooden floor—layered with oil, saturated in spots with gasoline spills—made the place nothing less than a fire trap.

"How much work do you have left?" Lebell said.

Cal pulled the heavy bay door closed. The racket of the casters sliding down their rails made him think again of Heather. If she hadn't awakened before, she was certainly awake now.

"Four hours or so, if it goes well."

"We could still go out," Lebell offered. "You could get up early, work on the thing then, have it done by noon, easy."

"Yeah, but if I run into a snag, I'm screwed."

"I'll help you, then."

"Carver says he can only pay me."

Once more, Lebell shook his head disapprovingly. "Man, I love it when that guy cries poverty."

Cal reinserted the lock pins through holes in the rails, then spun the center lever, locking the door. He made his way through the three bays, pausing at each door to lower the makeshift curtains—pieces of heavy black fabric secured to the wood with thumbtacks. Joining Lebell at the sink, he began washing his hands, watching the swirl of blackened water circle into the drain.

"Did you pass that Corvette on your way here?"

"Don't tell me."

"That was him."

"You're kidding."

"Nope. He just bought it."

"Jesus."

His hands clean, Lebell stepped away from the sink and pulled a long piece of paper towel from the nearby dispenser. He began to dry his forearms first. "Listen," he said, "I've been thinking. Maybe you and I should go into business together."

"What do you mean?"

"We could set up a little two-man shop. You practically run this place by yourself. Why work for someone else, right?"

"What kind of shop?"

"I was thinking we could specialize in motorcycles. There isn't a place like that anywhere out here. We wouldn't need that big of a space, so that knocks down the overhead right there."

"You think there's enough business out here for us to make a living at that?"

Lebell shrugged. "It's worth looking into. We could repair bikes, maybe even customize a few and sell them on eBay. I knew a guy once who made a living rebuilding old Indian Chiefs. To be honest, it's probably not the smartest thing for you to put all your eggs in one basket, especially when a guy like Carver's the one holding the basket."

Cal thought about the signs he'd seen tonight, wasn't sure if he should say anything about them; in the end, though, he didn't have to.

"The talk around town is that our man's in a real downward spiral," Lebell said. "The word is he overextended himself on some property deal recently—one of those old places he buys to tear down, only now the town is giving him shit, saying it's a historic landmark and he can only restore it. And from what I understand wife number two is ready to bolt, just like wife number one did. If all that isn't bad enough, he's supposedly started hitting the coke. Hard."

"Who told you that?"

Lebell crumbled up the paper towel, tossed it into the nearby trash barrel. "Who hasn't?" he said. "Listen, I just don't like to see you being so loyal to a guy who'd screw you in a second if he had to."

"How could he do that?"

Cal turned off the taps, stepped to the dispenser, and tore off his own piece of paper towel. "I wouldn't put it past Carver to do something stupid if it meant getting his hands on some quick cash. It might be more than him just hitting the coke, if you know what I mean."

"You think he's dealing."

Lebell pulled down the sleeves of his thermal shirt. His forearms were thick, powerful. "I wouldn't put it past him. I mean, I've always kind of wondered if this place was just a front for laundering money. It certainly has all the telltale signs of that. The thing that worries me is that, whatever's going on, it probably wouldn't take much for you to look like an accomplice."

"What do you mean?"

"If he got busted, I could see him trying to make a deal for himself by implicating you."

"How exactly could he do that?"

"I don't know. I once knew a dude who kept a friend around just so he'd have a fall guy in case if he ever needed one."

"You think Carver is doing that with me?"

"Like I said, I wouldn't put it past him. Especially after hearing the things I've heard lately. Listen, if George is working tonight, I'll ask him what he knows."

George was a career bartender, a local fixture in Southampton. He currently worked at 75 Main and had—or liked people to think he had—the lowdown on everyone in town.

"Don't worry, man," Lebell said, "I'm looking out for you."

Cal said nothing.

"Listen, if you finish early or change your mind or whatever, you know where to find me. I'll be making the usual rounds."

Everyone, in one way or another, had a routine.

"Okay."

"I wasn't going to say anything till I knew more. Who knows, maybe his buying the Corvette means he found a way out of this jam. He always seems to save his ass at the last minute."

Cal nodded. Again, though, he said nothing.

Lebell reached out and placed his hand on Cal's shoulder. "I'll ask around, see what else I can find out tonight. If I hear anything I think you need to know right away, I'll call you. Otherwise, I'll check in with you in the morning, see if you need help with the Benz."

"Thanks."

"What are friends for, right?" Lebell said. He read Cal's expression and offered a smile that was meant to reassure his friend. Lebell was a handsome guy, had the kind of looks to which women, or at least certain women, were drawn—rugged, unpolished, a *bad boy, you want to know in what way exactly, why don't you come over here and find out?* The opposite of Cal, who was at best still boyish and at worst almost . . . pretty. *Beautiful boy,* Heather used to call him back when he had first started working for her in the restaurant she and her husband had owned. He was all of fifteen then, a lowly dishwasher, and the nickname had made him blush. It did still, when, on occasion, and probably for old times' sake, she said it.

Despite his older friend's smile, Cal didn't feel all that reassured.

"Don't worry," Lebell said. "I shouldn't have said anything."

"No. It's better to know, right?"

"I've always thought so."

"It's just, you know, a few minutes ago things were pretty set."

"Like I said, it's probably not the smartest thing to put all your eggs in one basket."

"You really think Carver would do that? Leave me holding the bag?"

"I think the guy's out of control, and it's pretty obvious that he only cares about himself. People like that are always dangerous. If he's up to something, I'll find out, I promise. I'm pretty good at this, actually."

Cal didn't ask what he meant by that. What Lebell had done prior to his arrival a year ago was something they didn't discuss. Cal had tried, initially, of course, but he knew evasiveness when he saw it and simply stopped asking.

"I'll see you tomorrow, bro," Lebell said. He grabbed his leather jacket from its hook on the wall, put it on.

"Yeah, okay," Cal said. "Take it easy, man."

Lebell exited through the office. Cal waited till the sound of the Mustang faded, then stepped into the adjoining room, locked the door, and armed the security system. Moving through the work bays, he double-checked those locks and shut off the lights. His nighttime routine, darkness following him in stages till the entire garage was in complete blackness.

The only entrance to the apartment above was the plank stairs against the far wall of the third bay—there was no outside stairway, no fire escape, nothing at all. An old building, yes, but as secure as a fortress for those people and things occupying it, upstairs and down.

Cal made it the rest of the way through the garage by memory. At the bottom of the plank steps he looked up and saw a thin line of soft, dancing light coming from beneath the door above.

Heather was at last awake. He checked his watch, saw by its luminous dial that it was now just past seven thirty. His routine was shattered, for this night anyway, but suddenly that was the least of his concerns.

Three

He smelled her the moment he opened the door, that mixture of jasmine and rose oil, a vial of which she kept next to her candles and deck of worn tarot cards on the bureau in her bedroom.

Closing the door behind him and locking it, he heard from the far end of the apartment the sound of water running. This, and all the burning candles, told him that Heather was taking her nightly bath.

The top floor of the building, intended as a storage area, had been hastily converted by Carver into a living space; a large room originally, but makeshift walls of unpainted Sheetrock had been erected in one half of it, creating two small bedrooms and, between them, a narrow bathroom. A raw, bare-bones place, it was nonetheless all that Cal needed. The other half of the room—a sparse kitchen and what served as a living room—had been, with the exception of a counter, left undivided. A wide open space, hot in the summer, cold in the winter, it was tonight a place of drafts that at times caused the candle flames to dance, some even sputter, on the verge of being blown out.

As he stepped from the kitchen and into the living room area, he could see Heather through the half-open door of the bathroom. Her long back to him, she was sitting in the claw-footed tub that stood in the center of that room. She had just shut off the water and was leaning back, submerging herself up to her neck. Her hair—dark, thick, straight—was fastened into a loose bun, a few strands hanging free here and there. She must have thought the sounds of all those doors closing downstairs, followed by the racket of Lebell's Mustang racing off, meant that Cal had gone out for the night; otherwise the bathroom door would have been shut completely. Respecting such privacies and avoiding any semblance of impropriety were rituals both she and Cal were always careful to observe.

He returned to the kitchen, opening the refrigerator door and grabbing a container of leftovers as loudly as he could. The refrigerator, at least four decades old, had a heavy door that shut with a sharp bang and a metal latch that caught with a loud click. Certainly Heather would hear all that and realize that he was home.

Then, right on cue: "Cal? That you?" There was no concern in her voice; there was no chance that it was anyone but him.

"Yeah."

"I thought you'd gone out already."

Cal placed the container on the counter next to the refrigerator, his back to the bathroom. "Change in plans."

"You can turn on the lights if you need to."

"No, it's fine, I can see."

"I'll be out in a minute."

"Take your time."

He grabbed a clean fork from the dish drainer and stabbed through a chunk of chicken, catching also a little bit of pasta. Hungrier than he realized, he shoveled the first forkful in, then quickly shoveled in another. He was normally fed and showered by now, either playing cards with Heather in the living room or out with Lebell. There was for him no ignoring the sense of, at this moment, being just a little astray.

"I can't believe I slept so late," Heather said.

A deep plunk followed by a long trickling sound told Cal that she had stood to get out of the tub.

"You must have been tired."

"Oh, yes, I've had a terribly busy day," she joked. "You know, in a few more months, I'm probably going need you to help me get in and out of this thing. Or maybe I could just live in the tub, have you bring my meals to me, wait on me hand and foot. You'd do that, right?"

"Of course," Cal said. "Whatever you need."

"Such a good boy," she teased. She was out of the tub now—all watery sounds had ceased. Standing on the bathmat, then, drying off. "Why the change in plans tonight?"

"I need to finish up the car I'm working on."

The bathroom door opened all the way, and he heard the sound of bare feet padding on the plank floor.

"I'm decent now," she said.

Chewing, he looked over his shoulder. She was wearing a kimono-style robe that he had found for her at the thrift shop in Southampton. Black, faux silk, sleeves that stopped just past the elbow, an embroidered hem that was several inches above her knees. Unwilling to leave his place, and having arrived with close to nothing, Heather was dependent on Cal to get things for her. Over time he had collected a number of essentials, and he kept his eye out pretty much everywhere he went for items he thought she might need.

Her hair was still up, the loose strands, damp now, clinging to her sleek neck. She was taller than Cal, statuesque—and, at forty-three, nearly twice his age. Her face was oval shaped, her features delicate, precisely arranged. A dancer in her youth, then briefly a television actress—guest spots, mainly, dramatic roles in a handful of cop dramas. She had given it up—probably had been asked to—when she married Ronnie Pamona. Cal's brother, Aaron, had worked for her in the restaurant she and her husband owned, a place in Wainscott she'd named Helenbach's—her mother's maiden name. She had often quietly joked that the name was also fairly descriptive of her marriage, which was like going to "hell and back." *One of life's funny little synchronicities,* according to her.

Aaron, a prep cook, had gotten Cal a job as a dishwasher. They had worked for Heather for almost four years, becoming, as was often the case with restaurant people, as close as family. Working six shifts a week—doubles on the weekends—will do that. Aaron had a habit of coming up with nicknames for people, names that fit and often stuck. Heather was *Heatherlicious.* Cal and Aaron—the Rakowski boys, Heather liked to call them—had rarely addressed her by anything else.

Cal glanced at her stomach, at the bump that could no longer be concealed by even the loose-hanging black kimono. Getting larger and rounder by the day now. Four months pregnant when she had arrived, carrying the child of a man she had finally come to hate—a man she vowed would never see her again and, more importantly, never, ever meet his son—she was now six months along. On her left wrist still was the cast that had been newly applied by an emergency room doctor the night she had driven herself to Cal's place. He had offered, when she had called, to have a friend drive him to the hospital so she didn't have to drive with a broken wrist, but she had refused to let him do that—refused, even, to let him call her a cab and leave her vehicle in the hospital lot for now. *Too dangerous,* she had said. *There had to be no trail for anyone to follow.*

Crossing the length of the living room, she moved past Cal standing at the counter and entered the makeshift kitchen. Having yet to apply her jasmine and rose oil, she smelled simply of damp hair and clean skin.

"You should sit down when you eat, Mr. Fix-it," she said.

One of her nicknames for him—he could fix anything; he'd had, since he was a young boy, an innate mechanical aptitude.

At the sink Heather rose up on her bare toes and grabbed a plate from a shelf. Placing the plate on the counter between them, she took the container and fork from his hands, scraped the remaining pasta and chicken out and onto the plate, then handed the fork back to him.

"Sit down and eat like a civilized man," she said.

He pulled up a stool, sat on it, and resumed eating.

"Would you like anything to drink?"

"Water's good, but I can get it."

"It's okay, I'm right here."

She turned to the sink, filled a glass from the tap, turned again, and placed it in front of his plate. Taking an opened bottle of red wine from a cupboard beneath the counter, she poured herself a half glass. She stepped back and leaned against the sink, looked down at her stomach, and began to run her free hand over it, a gesture both absent and loving.

"I laid down at, what, four?" she said, "and didn't wake up till a few minutes ago. Jesus. I've got three more months of this ahead of me."

"We must have awakened you when we brought the oil in. Sorry."

"No, believe me, a three-and-a-half-hour nap is more than enough." She focused on her stomach for a moment, took a sip of her wine, then said, "I had this crazy dream." Her voice was low, soft.

"What about?"

"It was nighttime, and really windy, like tonight. Almost . . . Gothic. Blustery. I must have heard the wind blowing as I slept." She glanced at the kitchen window. "Anyway, I was holding this candle that I needed to keep from going out. I don't know why, but it was very important that I kept it burning. I was outside, somewhere, and suddenly someone was behind me. I couldn't see who it was, all I saw was this shadow looming, but I knew it was a man, and I knew he was up to no good."

She stopped there, then took another sip.

"So what happened?"

She shrugged, then said, "I kept trying to lose him. One minute I was out on this English moor, and the next I was in this old city, in these winding back streets. Then I was out on the moor again, then back in another city, running, hiding, looking back every time I stopped to see if he was still there. All the time I was doing this, I was trying to keep this little goddamn candle from going out. It barely gave off any light, was always flickering, but it was all I had. I mean, I could barely see my own hand in front of my face half the time, and it was probably only making it easier for this shadow to follow me, but I knew it had to stay lit, no matter what."

Cal listened closely, thinking about everything she had said. He had once spent the night with a woman who devoted what felt to him like hours the following morning to explaining the dream she'd had when they'd finally gone to sleep. That was tedious, uninteresting; this wasn't, not at all.

"Did you finally get away?"

She squinted a little, trying to remember. "I don't know. I guess I woke up before it got to that. I mean, in the dream I was being chased for hours and hours, it just didn't end. Through town after town after town, miles of nothingness between them. I remember being so exhausted that I was ready to give up. I actually remember getting pissed—I mean really pissed—and coming very close to turning around and telling whoever it was behind me to just fuck off. I was still pissed when I woke up."

"Weird." He wasn't sure what else to say.

"Not really, I guess. Pretty straightforward stuff, if you think about it." She took in a breath, let it out. "All right, Mr. Fix-it, I've told you my dream, now tell me one of yours. The most recent one you can remember."

"I don't really have any," he lied.

"C'mon, every one dreams."

"I guess I just don't remember mine."

"That's a damn shame. I'd be interested to know what goes on in that noggin of yours while you sleep."

He felt a blush start, looked down at his plate in an attempt to hide it. "So I take it the man in your dream was your husband," he said. He'd stopped eating to listen to her; he resumed now with the little that was left.

"Maybe. Or maybe not."

"Who else could it be?"

"It could be me running away from my own bad-ass self."

"You said it was a man following you."

"Yeah. My shadow is my opposite, so it would make sense that in a dream it would be a man."

"So there's a part of you that's up to no good."

"I think maybe there's a part of me that's afraid of getting up to no good. Of having no *choice* but to get up to no good. I know for certain there's part of me that's wishing no good would befall a certain someone."

This someone she spoke of was, of course, her husband. Though the man had played no part in running the restaurant, he had come in often, usually with friends or business associates, run up huge tabs and made it known to everyone that this was his place, that when he snapped his fingers, people all around jumped. A large man, a former professional football player, he was proudly short-tempered and capable, obviously, of a kind of brutality Cal couldn't imagine.

The only person who hadn't ever seemed afraid of him was Aaron. He'd been a celebrated wrestler in high school, freakishly powerful for his size and amazingly fast. At times it was obvious that he was actually going out of his way to displease the man.

Protective of his kid brother, but, too, protective of Heatherlicious.

The heroic thing to do, if not the smart thing—but that was Aaron, or the way Cal liked to remember him.

"He's out there looking for me," Heather said, "and he's got all the money in the world to burn. That's what he used to say every time I threatened to leave." She paused a moment, then continued. "I'm starting to realize that I can't hide forever. I mean, in three months this darling little brat inside of me is going to need to come out. All Ronnie has to do is wait till my due date and pay someone to keep an eye on the hospitals. Or do it himself."

"It's not like he can walk in and grab your son and walk out. Right?"

"You don't understand, Cal. I never want to see his face or hear his voice ever again. I want him to never have any contact with this child. He's going to grow up to be a good boy, just like you. Once I give birth, all Ronnie has to do is have someone follow me when I leave the hospital, find out where I am, so he can file a lawsuit. Can't sue someone if you don't know where they live. Once the suit is filed, he'll drag the whole thing out till the little money I managed to squirrel away is gone. Can't run and hide without money."

Pamona was a ruthless businessman, there was no doubt about that. The list of business partners he had "screwed" was long. The man had, in fact, behind Heather's back, sold the restaurant that she ran and loved to some South American gangster two years ago. Word was, according to Lebell, Pamona had recently bought the restaurant back from the bank after that gangster mysteriously disappeared and the property went into foreclosure.

Cal tried to think of the best thing to say to Heather right now, but all he could come up with was, "So we've got three months to figure something out."

"That's not much."

"We're both pretty smart. I'm sure we can come up with something."

He was just a kid, he knew that; what could he hope to do against a man like Ronnie Pamona? Or the kind of men Ronnie Pamona could afford to hire? At the same time, though, what else was there for him to say to her? He was grateful to be able to offer her a place to stay that was safe, and there had been no sign at all of her husband—or hired men—in the two months she'd been here. Wherever the man was looking for her, it wasn't above a ramshackle garage out in the no-man's-land of Bridgehampton.

"Let's talk about something else," Heather said. She'd put the wineglass—half of her nightly ration already gone—on the countertop, was touching her stomach with both hands. "Someone else's problem always cheers me up. What's this jam your boss is in that's keeping you from a Friday night on the town?"

"Some rich guy he needs to impress wants his car tomorrow."

"I see. A matter of life and death."

"Exactly."

"I could get dressed, come down and hand you tools."

Cal, chewing his last mouthful, grinned. She was, of course, joking, he knew that. The image, though, had its appeal. "That's okay, but thanks."

"I think I'd look cute in a pair of your coveralls, don't you? I could wear a little cap, put it on sideways. My glass of red wine in one hand, me handing you tools with the other. C'mon, it'd be fun."

They laughed. A small distraction, for her, but she'd take what she could get.

"Okay, suit yourself," she said.

"So what's Heatherlicious up to tonight?"

"Oh, you know, my usual big plans. The bath, my doctor-approved half-glass of wine, a few dozen or so games of solitaire. Then, of course, some much deserved sleep."

Cal stood, gulped down his water, then carried the glass and his plate and fork to the sink. Heather remained where she was, watching him as he began to clean up after himself.

"Did you have enough to eat?"

"Yeah." He glanced at his watch. "I'm going to wash up, then chill out for a bit before I go back down and finish up. I was thinking maybe I'd hang around up here till ten."

"We could play a few hands."

"Sure."

"It feels like a gin rummy night to me."

"Whatever you want. Anything for Heatherlicious, you know that."

She smiled, amused and pleased and, too, just a little proud. That nickname, even after all these years, never failed to evoke this very mix of responses from her.

There was no shower in the bathroom—what would be the point, anyway, with the water pressure as bad as it was?—so Cal took a bath, needed to scrub away the smell of oil and gasoline from his face and body so he could relax for the few hours that he had. Normally, prior to going out, he would shave, was definitely in need of one, but there wasn't any reason for him to bother with that now.

In his bedroom he put on a clean pair of jeans and a T-shirt; he would wait till he was about to go back downstairs to put on the same coveralls he had worn all day. Combing his hair, he looked at himself in the mirror above his bureau. The glass was smudged, his reflection hazy, but he could see himself well enough. A lesser version of his brother, in more or less every way, but he'd always be that, wouldn't he? Nothing at all of his father—of what he remembered of his father—so his looks had certainly come from his mother. Not much that could be done about that, though. Unshaven, as he was, only seemed somehow to emphasize the boyishness of his looks—a youth in a man's mask of scruff. His only recourse was to wear his hair just a little long, let it hang into his eyes and hide his ears. This was a look, of course, that actually required a degree of effort, and he was working on that, trying to find that fine line between *carefree* and *mess*, when he heard the sound of Heather's cell phone ringing.

She hadn't gotten a single call since arriving, had, as part of her careful escape from her husband, she'd told Cal, secured a new cell phone without her husband's knowledge, opting for paperless billing and having the monthly charges paid automatically by an account she had set up for herself just prior to fleeing. By the way she carried the phone everywhere she went—from one room to another, keeping it near during her bath and as she slept—Cal had always assumed she was expecting it to ring at any moment.

And now it had.

His first thought was to step out of his bedroom, and he moved toward his door with that in mind, but then he decided he'd better not—they were, the two of them, after all, about privacies and boundaries. Maybe the call she had been hoping for was from a long-lost lover, and, if so, that was her business, had nothing at all to do with him. Returning to the mirror, tending to his appearance, he tried not to listen, but Sheetrock wasn't much of a barricade to the sound of a voice, particularly one that quickly escalated to urgent.

He waited, feeling a sense of dread move through him. Could it be her husband? Could he have somehow, despite all her efforts, finally tracked her down? If he was calling from outside, he would not get in, that much was certain, and a call to the police would easily take care of him—but then what? Cal suddenly realized that calling the police was something of a problem since the business wasn't exactly aboveboard. Carver dealt only in cash, the apartment was illegal, and the building itself didn't come anywhere near being up to code. Bringing the existence of this place to the attention to the police was to risk the setup Cal had for himself coming to an abrupt end.

Yet *anything for Heatherlicious. Right?*

A moment passed—Heather said only a few more things—and then Cal heard nothing else. Tossing his comb onto the bureau top, he walked to his bedroom door.

She had, as she always did, settled into the living room for the night—her glass of wine, her playing cards and tarot cards, all within reach on the table at the end of the old couch. Normally her cell phone was among those items, but she was holding it in her hand, tight. Standing by the couch, facing Cal, she said, "I need to go to Shelter Island."

Her concern was impossible to miss.

"What?"

"I need to go out to Shelter Island. Right now."

"What's going on?"

"Someone spotted Amanda."

"Wait. What do you mean?"

"At a party, someone spotted her. I need to go get her and bring her here."

"Hang on a second," Cal said. "I'm lost."

Amanda was her half sister. Not much older than Cal, she had worked as a waitress during Cal's last summer as dishwasher. Heather had mentioned shortly after arriving that she didn't know where Amanda was, but Cal hadn't thought too much of that; Amanda did that now and again, disappeared for weeks or months on end, staying with friends or some guy she thought loved her, always, though, showing up again eventually, either heartbroken or broke—or both. Cal hadn't realized till now that this was the reason why Heather carried her cell phone with her everywhere she went.

"A few years ago she fell in with a bad crowd," Heather said. "She started using all kinds of drugs. When she used to disappear, it meant she was with a new boyfriend or had taken off with some friends to India or Thailand or something like that to study yoga. Those days are over, it seems."

"Jesus, Heather. I didn't know."

"I figured we had enough to worry about. When I knew I was about to bolt and got my new number, I tracked down the one friend of hers I could find, told him to call me if he ever saw her again. Other than you, he's the only other person who has my new number."

"Who is he?"

"Just some guy. I don't know if she dated him or what. I have a feeling he was her dealer. I'll tell you, I was lucky to be able to find him."

"And he lives out on Shelter Island?"

"No, he lives in the city. That's where she was, last I knew. Living somewhere in the East Village. He was my only possible connection to her once I took off. I mean, if something terrible happened to her, if she overdosed and died, no one would know how to reach me, not even the police. *She* wouldn't even know how to reach me."

"You should have told me this."

"Like I said, we had enough to worry about."

Cal thought about that, then said, "What's an East Village drug dealer doing way the hell out on Shelter Island?"

"He said it was some kind of party. A Halloween thing. I told him I'd be there as soon as I could."

Cal looked at her. Her wrist in a cast, six months pregnant, dressed at this moment in a cheap kimono. Then he glanced at the glass of red wine.

"Listen, why don't I go for you?" he said.

"You have to work."

"It's only a half hour to Shelter Island and a half hour back. Anyway, I don't really feel right letting you make that drive the way you are."

"I'm pregnant, Cal, not fragile."

"I mean the wine."

"I've only had a couple of sips."

He shrugged. "I know. Just let me do this for you, okay?"

"You're going to protect me from the big, bad drug dealer?" she teased.

"I guess that's it, yeah. Besides, I'm sure your husband canceled the insurance on your X3. You get pulled over driving without insurance, he'll be able to find you, right? I mean, if he's that determined, he probably has someone checking the police blotter, just in case. All he needs is to know your court date, have someone wait outside the courthouse and tail you back here."

"That's very smart of you, Cal," she said. Teasing again, or half teasing—but half proud, too.

He shrugged a second time. What could he say? He knew how

criminals thought, knew the compulsions that drove them. In fact, everything he did in his life was designed to prevent such compulsions from ever finding him.

Certainly, a tendency toward criminality was hereditary, no?

"Let me do this for you," he said. "Okay?"

She nodded. "Okay. But how are *you* going to get there? I mean, you're not going to get her on your motorcycle, are you?"

Cal didn't own a car, only a motorcycle, an old Triumph Bonneville that had belonged to—had been stolen by—his brother. He didn't really need anything more than that because he was a year-round rider, and if the weather didn't permit going somewhere on his bike, and Lebell wasn't around to take him, then he simply didn't go. Whenever he needed groceries or supplies, he waited till he test-drove one of the vehicles he was working on, ran his errands as he did that. There were cabs, too, and, if it came to it, the trains. It was only a fifteen-minute walk from the garage to the Bridgehampton train station.

"All right, so maybe I'm not as smart as you think I am," he said. He hadn't thought this far ahead. If her BMW was out of the question, and his motorcycle not an option, then how was he going to make the run to Shelter Island? He thought for a moment, then said, "I could call a cab."

"It'll cost a fortune."

"I don't mind."

"Actually, that brings up something I need to ask you."

"What?"

"I told Amanda's friend that I'd pay him five hundred dollars. I needed to give him a reason to actually call me if he saw her. I don't have that much here. Do you think maybe you could loan it to me? Or hit my ATM on the way back for me, if you don't have it."

"I can give you that," Cal said.

"I'll pay you back, of course."

"I'm not worried. I know where you live."

"Thanks."

"No problem."

"Anyway, aside from the money, a cab isn't a good idea," Heather said.

Cal, of course, knew why. There needed to be no record of her sister being brought here, no trail that could be followed.

"So what do we do?" Heather said. "How do we get you out there and back?"

From his closet he removed his old wool peacoat and Sidi Canyon boots. The boots were leather but had a thick waterproof lining—he could stand in a cold river with those things on and his feet would remain warm and dry—and what was better for a night as blustery as tonight than a peacoat?

Boots and coat on, he stepped to the back of the closet, knelt down and removed a loose floorboard. Reaching down into the dark gap, he pulled out a small metal cashier's box.

Opening it, he took out one of the stacks of bills, counted out five hundred dollars, then put the stack back, closed the box again, and returned it to its hiding place, carefully replacing the board so it looked no different from all the others.

On last count he had saved close to two hundred grand. He made, on average, sixty grand a year, all of it off the books, which was why he didn't bother to use a bank. He had no real living expenses beyond food—and detergent to clean his coveralls. Since he lived where he worked and didn't own a car, the only gasoline he burned was what his old Triumph consumed during the handful of joyrides he took in a week. Unregistered and uninsured, so no additional cost there, beyond the occasional oil and tire change, which naturally he did himself. His only other expense was what he gave to various bartenders on his Friday nights out with Lebell.

Where else, then, would most of his money go except into this fireproof box hidden beneath his closet floor?

A compulsion, saving his money in this way, but, as far as compulsions went, not such a bad one.

Heather was waiting in the kitchen, her cell phone in her hand. As he approached, crossing through the open and chilly living room, she said, "The guy you're meeting is named Angstrom. I don't know his first name, but Amanda always referred to him as Rabbit. I already called him back and told him a friend of mine is coming to meet him instead."

She tore a piece of paper off a pad, folded it once, and handed it to Cal. "These are the directions. It's just two left turns off the ferry. You know how to get to the landing, right? It's out in North Haven."

"Yeah." He slipped the paper into the pocket of his peacoat.

"Take this, too." She handed him her cell phone. The landline to the garage, with an extension in the apartment above, was all the contact with the outside world that he usually needed.

"You sure?"

She nodded. "That way you can call me if there's a problem. Or I can call you if I think it's taking too long."

Cal took the phone and pocketed it.

"Be careful," Heather said.

It was just a run to Shelter Island and back. Like he had said, a half hour to get there and a half hour to get home again.

Still, he appreciated the concern. *Who didn't want, at least, that?*
"No problem," he said.

Downstairs, in the garage, he deactivated the security system and opened the second bay door, then paused to look at the Citroën. It was, of the three vehicles there, the only one currently roadworthy. The fact that it was a '58 DS19 meant, too, that it was the rarest and therefore most valuable. Not the wisest thing, then, taking it on an errand such as this, but there was no other choice.

He backed out onto the gravel, then exited the vehicle and reentered the garage, closing the bay door behind him. Sliding in the locking pins and spinning the lever, he exited through the office and reactivated the security system from the outside keypad. He hurried toward the waiting Citroën, looking around as he went, not really sure what he expected to see. He saw, in fact, nothing but the dark back road and the empty fields bordered by swaying trees. Still, he looked and listened; something told him to be on his toes.

He thought of his brother, the last time he'd seen him: at sundown, on a cold spring night, rushing off to meet up with a friend—or so Aaron had told him. *Nothing to worry about, be back soon.* Before Heather had given him a shot and hired him to work in her kitchen, Aaron had been a small-time criminal—stealing vehicles and breaking into homes, even running drugs now and then, whatever it took to make rent and buy food for himself and his kid brother. According to the police, though, Aaron had been killed only a few hours after leaving Cal—a drug deal gone bad, the cops had called it. Even so, his body, or what was left of it, hadn't been found for close to two days. A long time for Cal to sit and wait, to look out the window of their apartment for any sign of the only family he had left.

He knew he was thinking of this now as a reminder to himself of what he already knew so well: One's life can quickly change, and the last words spoken can easily become the last words ever spoken.

A ritual of his that he obeyed, one way or another, every time he left the safety of this place.

Climbing in behind the wheel, he pulled the door closed, pushed in the clutch and shifted into gear, then paused to look up. In one of his windows stood Heather, watching him. He knew that she would be there. Backlit by all the candles, she was nothing but a silhouette. He waved to her, and she waved back.

He took off then, crossing from the loose gravel of the driveway onto the solidness of the paved road. Above him, the Long Island sky—crowded with dark and fast-moving clouds as big as ships—was like chaos.

He kept to the posted speed limit, heading east along Scuttlehole Road.

Four

———◆———

The Shelter Island ferry disembarked from Tyndal Point in North Haven. Fifteen minutes after leaving the garage, Cal passed through the village of Sag Harbor, lit up but empty tonight, then crossed the bridge that spanned the wide inlet and turned right onto North Haven Road. He followed the dark straightaway that led down to the water's edge—a mile-long decline, gradual at first, then steep, the lights of the landing dead ahead.

Shelter Island was, at the most, a mile from North Haven; Cal could see it clearly across the choppy water, a dark shape holding steady against the rushing current and the windy night. Once he reached the end of North Haven Road he shut off the lights and the motor and waited as the ferry made its return trip from the island. For several long minutes the Citroën was the only automobile in sight, but as the ferry began to dock, the headlights of another vehicle appeared behind Cal. He watched in the mirror mounted on the driver's door as these headlights approached, eventually lighting up the Citroën's interior and reflecting off the rearview mirror on the windshield, all but blinding him.

A pickup truck, he concluded by the height of the lights from the road, blue-white halogen bulbs set on high. The lights remained on even as the truck came to a stop in line directly behind Cal. Turning the rearview mirror away to keep this light from straining his eyes, he looked forward, watching as the two vehicles on board the ferry disembarked.

A shiny black Town Car with New York state taxi plates and an E-type Jaguar with New Jersey plates. Once past the two waiting vehicles, the Jaguar accelerated suddenly, pulling out of its lane and rocketing past the Town Car. Gunning up the dark incline, the sound of its screaming exhaust was quickly swallowed up by the night.

The ferrymen—two of them, in their early twenties, dressed for the damp cold in hooded sweatshirts and down jackets—waved Cal aboard, guiding him with minimal, almost lazy hand gestures to a spot on what would be, upon the trip back to the island, the bow of the ferry. The pickup pulled in beside Cal, its lights finally darkening.

Looking over, he saw that were three people in its cab—a girl behind the wheel and two guys beside her, all of them in their late teens at the most. The guy closest to the passenger window studied the Citroën before looking at its driver, then was nudged by the one beside him. He turned away, accepted what looked to Cal to be a joint, then took a long drag from it, its tip a speck of glowing red in the dark cab.

One of the ferrymen stepped to the Citroën. Cal lowered the window, held up a ten-dollar bill, and asked for a two-way ticket. Just as the guy in the truck had, the ferryman studied the Citroën from nose to tail and only then looked at its driver.

"Where's your costume?"

Cal shrugged, thought for a moment, then said, "Don't have one."

"You're going to that party, right?"

"Yeah."

"Every fancy car we take over, the people inside are all dressed up in costumes."

"A lot of cars tonight?"

"Yeah. Busiest night I've ever seen."

The ferryman handed Cal the two-way ticket and change. His gloves were wool, the tips of the thumbs and index fingers cut off so he could better handle cash. Cal could tell by the ferryman's accent that he was a native East Ender, just like Cal was, a descendant of the fishermen who had worked this island for generations long before it had become the playground of the rich.

Cal pocketed the change and ticket. "Thanks, man."

"Saw inside one car," the ferryman said. "The guy was dressed up like the pope or something, and the woman next to him was naked. I'm talking not a fucking thing on. Next to *her* was this long mink coat. Just lying there on the seat. Fuck me. You think maybe you could get me and my brother into that party? We're off at two."

"Not staying all that long myself," Cal said. "Just picking someone up."

The ferryman nodded. "Bummer. Just so you know, the last ferry is at one forty-five. They start running again at five forty-five."

Cal nodded, said, "Thanks, man," and closed the window.

Something told him—an inherent instinct, perhaps, long dormant till tonight—that talking to this guy had maybe been a mistake.

He remembered Heather's warning to be careful, decided he should heed it.

The trip took less than five minutes. During the crossing Cal had listened to the shuddering drone of the ferry's engine and the steady sound of the waves splitting against its bow, watching through the windshield as the island grew larger and larger. The little the ferryman had told him about his destination only served to confuse Cal; not only was Amanda's presence out here, this far from the city, something he did not understand, but her being at a party like the one the ferryman had described made no sense at all. She'd always seemed to Cal to be a confident girl, to the point, even, of being stuck-up. A good head on her shoulders, selective about the men she dated, almost, well, prudish.

What was she doing here, with a crowd like this one?

Once the ferry docked, Cal let the pickup disembark first, then drove onto the island, pulling over and waiting till the pickup's taillights were out of sight before finally proceeding. The streets here were all unlit—the darkness back in the no-man's-land of Bridgehampton had nothing at all on this island—but a single left turn from Ferry Road, and another left turn less than a minute later, and Cal had arrived at the beachside parking lot on the southwestern rim of the island that was, according to Heather's directions, his destination.

Several dozen cars were parked in the lot, some of them black Town Cars, others a sample of every top-end vehicle imaginable. Most were brand-new, but Cal recognized some classics among them, out, no doubt, for their last joyrides before being locked away for the winter. Carver, were he here, would certainly be interested in seeking out the owners of those vehicles. Beyond this lot, to the west, was a strip of beach that ran north to south. Narrow, it led to water Cal could only barely see. He could hear it, though, the frequent and faint falling of tiny waves just yards away.

Looking along the length of the beach, he spotted in the distance a bonfire, saw that people were gathered around it, some standing, most sitting. A burst of orange sparks suddenly rose from the flames—someone must have tossed another log upon it. One more long look around the lot—at the cars for hire and the other vehicles—and then Cal stepped onto the sand. Wrapping the wool of the peacoat around himself against the gusts of cold—significantly different here in feel and smell from the gusts he had experienced out in the potato fields—he headed toward the fire.

He had only taken twenty or so steps in the soft sand when he spotted the house. It was off to his left, surrounded on three sides by a thick row of tall pine trees, the branches intertwining like thatch, which was why he hadn't been able to see the building from the parking lot. The only house in sight, most of its windows were lit up, but no outside lights were burning. Cal stopped to look at it, uncertain whether to continue toward the bonfire or head instead toward the house. As he was trying to decide he realized that two people were actually nearby, moving diagonally along the dark beach from the house. He didn't see them—couldn't see them—and then, suddenly, there they were. One was dressed in a long priest's cassock, the other as a Catholic nun—figures clad in black, moving through blackness. He could tell by the way they had trouble walking on the soft sand—laughing and clutching at each other—that both were, if not already drunk, well on their way.

Cal's eyes were getting used to the dark, and he could see that the couple was heading toward the bonfire. After a moment of watching them he felt certain that they had no idea he was even there. Looking back toward the house, he saw a figure standing at the property's edge. He wasn't sure if that figure had just arrived in that spot or if he had only now noticed it, but it seemed that this figure was looking straight at him. Staring, even.

Then the figure raised one arm high over its head, waving in a wide back-and-forth motion. Whoever this was wasn't just looking at him, was in fact beckoning him over.

Cal waited a moment more, then altered his course and began to make his way toward the house.

A three-story structure built from gray stone. Tall, narrow windows facing the beach. A monastery once, probably, by the look of the place, the *starkness* of it, but obviously a private residence now.

The figure that had waved Cal over was waiting on a narrow strip of grassy sand separating the beach from the driveway that ran the length of the house. Cal could tell soon enough that the figure was a man, but as he got closer he saw that this man was dressed in the brown robes of a Franciscan monk, a thick white rope tied like a sash around his waist. Cal could see, too, that this was a young man, not much older than he was.

"You're Heather's friend?" the mock-monk said.

"Yeah."

"She called back, said she was sending you. Is she okay?"

"She's fine."

Even with the seaside wind rushing past him, Cal could smell the alcohol on Angstrom's breath. Around the guy's neck, on a strip of worn leather, hung a rabbit's foot, dyed jet black, the same color as his shoulder-length hair. A good-looking guy, he had a narrow face and strong jaw, intelligent eyes and a Roman nose, didn't look at all the way Cal had expected him to. There was something almost scholarly about him. Healthy, too, and despite the fact that he'd been drinking, Angstrom seemed alert, in control. For some reason Cal had thought he would be none of these things.

"Where's Amanda?"

"I'll take you to her. We need to hurry, though. It's about to start."

Angstrom led Cal onto the driveway. Rounded white stones here, as noisy as gravel. Straight ahead of them was the door to the kitchen, its windows, and those on either side of it, brightly lit. Inside, chefs and waiters scurried, and outside, not far away, two white catering vans were parked.

Instead of heading toward that door, Angstrom was leading Cal in the direction of another, this one at the far end of the building, off to their right. Made of heavy wood—ornate, with wrought-iron fittings and an arched top. A row of windows was alongside it. Unlit, they reflected the dark, clouded sky. At the very end of the driveway, in the shadows of the giant barrier of pine trees, stood a silver Lexus. It and the two vans were the only vehicles here.

"I saw you pull in," Angstrom said. "Cool car. What kind is it?"

"Don't know," Cal lied. Again, instinct here, and the sudden urge to obey it. "I borrowed it from a friend."

"So it's not yours."

"No."

"Some friend, to let you drive around in that. It must be worth a lot."

Cal said nothing. These were probably just friendly questions, casual conversation meant to pass the time it took for them to reach the door. Still, the least said, the better, right?

Once they arrived at this side door, Cal noted that the row of windows just past it were the only darkened ones in the entire place—what he could see of it, anyway. So far, all he'd glimpsed was the side facing the water.

"I put her in here," Angstrom said. He opened the door, stepping into the dark room. Cal followed, stopping just beyond the threshold and waiting as Angstrom made his way further inside, looking, Cal figured, for a light. Angstrom hit something solid with his toe, whispered, "Shit." Then, finally, a light came on, a dim reading lamp standing beside an easy chair.

This room was a study, windows along three of its walls, the fourth wall a floor-to-ceiling bookcase filled to capacity with leather-bound editions. At the center of the bookcase was a door leading to the rest of the house. There were throughout this room a half dozen easy chairs, a desk the size of a king bed, and two long sofas—a bit crammed together, and yet each spot a private place. On the sofa nearest to the door, under an overcoat, lay an unconscious girl. Cal's eyes went to her immediately, found her face. He recognized her at once.

Amanda.

He walked to the couch to get a better look at her. "Is she okay?" It was more of a demand than a question. Something about Angstrom's bookish appearance brought out a toughness in Cal.

Angstrom went to the door around which the bookcase had been built. Opening it slightly, he made a thorough survey of the hallway beyond, then carefully closed it again.

"She was pretty much out of it when I found her," he said. His voice was a half-whisper. "By the time I got her down here, though, she was passed out."

Cal knelt and gently pried her right eye open; he knew what to look for, more or less, having watched Aaron take care of his on-again-off-again girlfriend for years. At the time, Aaron's troubled girl at home and Heather at work were the only women in Cal's daily life.

Unlike her half sister, Amanda was blond, and while Heather was tall and thin, Amanda was petite, with full breasts and hips. There were blackish half-circles under her eyes now, and her skin was pale. She looked nothing at all like the girl who had worked with them that long-ago summer. Radiant back then—a man-trap, Aaron used to call her. Now, too thin, worn out, ragged.

Her pupil responded sluggishly to the dim light, but that was to be expected. The fact that it had responded at all, Cal knew, was what mattered. He felt her wrist for a pulse. What moved beneath his fingertip was slow but steady.

She could be moved, he knew this much.

"We don't have a lot of time," Angstrom said. "He'll figure out in a little bit that she's missing."

"Who will?"

"The guy throwing the party."

"What's his name?"

"I don't know."

"What do you mean?"

"I don't understand."

"How did you end up at his party if you don't know him?"

Angstrom hesitated. "We're . . . business associates."

That answered the question, more or less, of how Angstrom, a drug dealer, got to be here. A party like this certainly offered a wide variety of refreshments. But what about Amanda?

Before Cal could address this, though, Angstrom said, "Listen, it's about to start. We need to get her out of here while we still can."

"What's about to start?"

"The show."

"What show?"

"I'm trying to do the right thing here, man. Seriously, it's now or never."

"What show?"

"Every woman here is a prostitute, call girl, whatever. When I saw her here and found out what she was here to do, I called her sister."

"What do you mean, 'what she was here to do'?"

"Everyone gets to fuck her. Or everyone gets to watch her get fucked. It's something like that. I didn't ask a lot of questions. She's a freaking mess, she can't possibly know what she's doing. C'mon, man, we've got to go. Now."

Cal saw no choice at this moment except to take Angstrom at his word, in every way.

On the floor beside the sofa was a large leather purse, packed to capacity and partially open. Inside it was a change of clothes, a mesh toiletry kit, and a portable hair dryer.

"That hers?" Cal said.

"Yeah. It's all she came with."

"Grab it."

Angstrom crossed to the sofa and picked up the purse. Cal stood, removing the overcoat covering Amanda and tossing it to Angstrom. He saw then that she, too, was dressed for the occasion.

A French maid's outfit—frilled lace, silk bows, flimsy and, for all its old-fashioned qualities, absurdly short. Black fishnet stockings, torn in places, and painful-looking shoes completed the costume.

"Jesus," Cal muttered.

Angstrom placed the overcoat on top of the large purse to conceal it, tucking the bundle under one arm. "We really should go, man."

Cal bent down and slid his arms under Amanda, lifting her as carefully as he could. He was scrawny but powerful, had, like his brother, a wrestler's strength. Equal parts muscular strength and tendon strength—the only strength, when it came down to it, that counted.

Angstrom held the ornate door open as Cal made his way through. Once outside, Cal looked at the beach. He didn't relish the idea of carrying Amanda over that soft sand—and out in the open.

Closing the door quietly, Angstrom whispered, "This way."

He led them away from the house, toward the line of trees that were, here, only several yards from the study door. As he reached the trees, Angstrom made a kind of zigzag motion, all but disappearing between two them.

Cal paused briefly, looked back at the house behind him, then followed. Carrying Amanda meant he had to turn sideways, and once he was through those two trees, he realized that he was standing on a well-worn path.

A shortcut to the parking lot.

Angstrom was holding a flashlight in his free hand. He felt around the shaft for the switch, then turned it on.

"Where'd you get that?" Cal whispered.

Angstrom ignored the question. "We need to keep moving."

He headed down the path, and Cal followed, noting as they went that their feet barely made any sound at all. The floor, hard-packed dirt, was clear of any debris. No pine needles, no twigs. The path was like a maze, full of sharp and sudden turns, but within thirty seconds they were through it and standing at the edge of the parking lot.

Angstrom reached the Citroën first and opened the passenger door. Cal placed Amanda inside and fastened the seat belt around her. Then, taking the overcoat and purse from Angstrom, Cal quickly covered Amanda with the coat and laid the purse on the floor beside her feet.

As simple as that.

Stepping back, Cal reached into his pocket for the money. Angstrom was looking back at that path, checking to make certain, Cal assumed, that they hadn't been followed.

"Here." Cal held up the wad of bills.

Angstrom looked at it, said, "Keep it."

"You and Heather had a deal."

He nodded toward Amanda. "Just get her out of here, okay?"

Cal had questions, a lot of them, but this wasn't the time. There was one question, though, that he had to ask.

"You going to be all right sticking around here?"

"I don't think anyone saw us. Anyway, I might not be staying all that long. I probably wouldn't have come out here if I knew what kind of party this was. A bit too . . . grown-up for me. I'm in a little over my head, you know what I mean?"

Cal understood that. He'd heard of such parties for years, had seen no reason to doubt their existence. After all, decadence and wealth had a tendency to go hand in hand. Human history was full of examples of that. Imagining such a thing, however, was different from standing so near it. In that former monastery, at this moment, women were pleasuring men for profit. As titillating a fantasy as that might be, it was, in reality, disturbing. Sexual greed feeding on desperation—what would Cal do had he found himself in a place like that, among men like that? He'd only been with a handful of women in his life so far; one-night stands, mostly, drunken encounters that had been stumbled upon on his nights out with Lebell—prior, of course, to Heather's arrival. Certainly he, too, would feel compelled to run from a place like that. Certainly fear—fear of doing wrong, yes, but also fear of his inexperience showing—would cause him to quietly remove himself and return straightaway to the safety of his narrow and empty bed.

Still, despite understanding Angstrom's unease, Cal thought of another question that he had to ask.

"You've never been to one of these before?"

"No."

"So you've never seen this place before tonight?"

"No." Angstrom was looking around the parking lot now, studying the cars. His eyes stopped on something. Cal followed his line of vision, spotted what had caught his attention.

In one of the Town Cars, behind the wheel, the vague features of a man's face lit the colors of a sunset.

One of the hired drivers, smoking a cigarette.

"You should get going," Angstrom urged.

Cal decided to opt for the cautious thing to do, which was to get out of there, get distance between him and Amanda and this place. He nodded his thanks and climbed into the Citroën. Heading toward the exit, he looked in the rearview mirror and saw that Angstrom was watching the car as it pulled away. The mock-monk didn't move, not in the slightest, was, in fact, standing exactly where Cal had left him, visible in the bright red glow of the taillights, when Cal made the turn from the parking lot back onto that long, dark road.

It wasn't long before Cal pulled over.

He parked on the shoulder, under a tree with low, angular branches, killed the lights and looked again in his rearview mirror, this time at an empty blackness.

He'd only driven a few hundred feet. Not nearly enough distance between them and that place, but it would have to do. After a moment he exited the car, stood by the open door, and looked toward the parking lot's entrance. The mirror had showed him a lot of nothing, but this direct view wasn't much better. He checked on Amanda—unconscious still, buckled in and covered up by her overcoat. He didn't want to leave her like this, in case she woke up, but he would need to if he was going to do the careful thing, go back and try to make sense of something Angstrom had said that didn't make sense at all.

Removing the key from the ignition, he closed and locked the driver's door, then stepped to the rear of the vehicle, pausing there.

Finally, Cal backtracked on foot to that unlit parking lot, crossed it quickly, and reentered the winding path that cut through the thick line of pine trees.

To see what he could see, satisfy somehow the nagging feeling that something else—something more—was going on here.

Knowing this time that the house was nearby, and with nearly all its windows lit up, didn't matter much; Cal still couldn't see it through the complex thatch of branches. Nor could he see much at all; without Angstrom's flashlight, the darkness within that tight cluster was as complete as any Cal had ever known.

He made his way through slowly, by feel, mostly. It wasn't till he was nearing the path's end that some of the light spilling from the windows along the back face of the house and reflecting off the white stones of the rear driveway began to seep in.

Clear of it finally, standing at its hidden opening—if hidden, and if Angstrom had never been to this house before, then how exactly did he know it was there? And why did he just happen to have a flashlight?— Cal paused and looked toward the row of windows straight ahead.

The dim reading lamp Angstrom had switched on was lit still, and standing near it were two figures. Face-to-face, talking—calmly, it seemed to Cal. One of the figures was obviously Angstrom—the monk's robes and the long hair were recognizable even from this distance—but it was the other figure that Cal was interested in now.

A tall man, from what he could see, broad-shouldered, wearing robes as well, but not a monk's robes, instead the dark, tattered robes of none other than the Grim Reaper.

He was listening to Angstrom intently, nodding occasionally. Cal watched them, waiting. When they finally moved in the direction of the door leading out to the driveway, he made his move as well.

Bent at the waist, ducking like a man under fire, he hurried from the path's opening toward the house. Reaching the side that faced the line of trees, he inched his way to the corner, stopping just as the ornate door was closed. He listened to the footsteps on the stones—two sets that covered a short distance and stopped—and then he heard a man's voice, deep and, even over the sound of the waves and wind, clear.

"Thanks for your help," the man said.

Cal got down into a crouch, peeked around the corner, had to see.

The two men were standing face-to-face again, Angstrom with his back to the beach, the Grim Reaper with his back to the house. The Reaper held out his hand, and Angstrom took it. They shook once, then released grips.

"Glad to do it," Angstrom said.

"You're sure he bought it."

"He seemed scared, got out of here quickly enough."

The Reaper nodded, then said, "What did he look like?"

"He was a kid. Dark hair, unkempt. Skinny."

"How old?"

"Twenty, maybe. Boyish. Do you know him?"

"That narrows it down. I'll have my man run the license plates, see what that turns up." He paused. "Did he say anything? About her? About them being together?"

"No. Nothing at all."

Another pause, then, "Thanks again."

"No problem."

"You're welcome to stay the weekend. In fact, I prefer that you do. I might need you to identify the kid when I bring them back later. Make sure he's the one."

"Whatever you need."

"There's a room for you upstairs. We gave you a water view. And, of course, whatever woman you want, she's yours till Monday."

"Thanks."

"I reward loyalty. Enjoy yourself. All I ask is that you keep your cell phone on. We don't go around knocking on doors here, for obvious reasons."

"No problem."

Angstrom thanked the man again—*so much for his not staying*—then turned and crossed the stones to the small grassy divide. Stepping over it, he headed down the beach, for the bonfire and the people gathered around it.

Cal, though, kept his eyes on the Reaper, was ready to lean back and hide again around the cornerstone the moment the man turned to head back inside.

He felt a compulsion to see this man's face. All that had been visible so far was part of the man's profile—not enough of it to identify him.

It sure as hell looked like him, though. Same build, same height, same arrogance in his voice . . .

After a moment the Reaper turned, and Cal ducked back behind the cornerstone, listening as the man returned to the study. The heavy door closed with a solid, metallic click, and Cal, still in his crouch, took a few breaths, then began to stand up, moving slowly.

He ceased his rise just below the bottom of the window above, his knees bent. He was preparing himself to rise the rest of the way and take this chance—maybe his last—at seeing all of this man's face.

Facing the wall, his hands on the cold stone to brace himself, he was just one electrical impulse away from peering over the sill when, from the pocket of his jeans, came the ringing of a cell phone.

He flinched—it might as well have been a gunshot, fired at close range, given the effect he had on him. He scrambled to reach into the pocket of his jeans to silence it, managed to do so just as the second ring began. Muffled by the fabric slightly, it was nonetheless loud enough to have announced his presence.

He froze, pressed against the stone. Looking up at the window, he was unable to see anything but the face of it. The light inside the study went out, and a second later Cal heard the sound of footsteps on wood. It didn't take long for the Reaper to reach the window. Cal didn't see him there, didn't dare look, but he knew the man was certainly standing at the glass and looking through it.

Cal pressed himself against the stone even more, holding his breath. A long few seconds passed, and then he heard the footsteps moving away. Seeing his chance, he bolted for the path, more concerned now with speed than stealth, and reached the hidden entrance in a matter of seconds. Ducking inside, he took a few strides, then stopped, crouched, and turned. Hiding beside the trunk of a tree, he looked back at the house. Even with the path floor clear of debris, finding his way through it would have meant making noise, enough for him to be detected. And anyway, there would be no hurrying through without a light.

His only hope, then, was to keep as still and silent as possible, stay out of sight no matter what.

He watched as the study door opened and the Reaper emerged. Moving to the corner of the house, he stood where Cal had been when the phone rang. When he turned the corner and saw no one, the Reaper stopped and looked around, first at his immediate surroundings and then toward the beach. Finally, seeing nothing, hearing nothing, he looked toward the opening to the path.

Cal didn't move, didn't breathe. Watching the Reaper, he waited for some indication that he had been spotted. By the way the man's head turned slowly, though, Cal knew he was scanning the area around the path's opening. If he was scanning, he hadn't found anything. After a moment, the Reaper started toward the path, stopped again when he reached its opening. He was now just feet away from Cal, and the light reflecting from the driveway running behind the house—just the edge of it reached him, a faint wash at best—made a black silhouette of the man.

No chance of seeing his face.

Neither moved, and finally a sound came from the Reaper, the rustling of fabric. He was reaching under his frayed robes for something. Cal couldn't see what it was at first, but then the Reaper moved, taking a step onto the path and turning in a way that allowed the light that had been behind him to fall upon his right hand.

A flash of illuminated chrome, a dim blur but unmistakable.

The Reaper had reached for a gun.

Another step, and then another, the Reaper moving cautiously. His shoes were so close at this point that Cal could have reached out and touched them. He could, too, hear the man's breathing, didn't dare breathe himself. Just a few more steps and the Reaper would stumble over him.

Then what?

Cal focused on the man's knees, or at least on the spot, based on the noise the Reaper was making as he moved, where his knees should be. He would need to hit his target just right—no room for error here. He braced himself for what seemed inevitable, saw it in his mind: a double-leg takedown, scooping the Reaper's legs out from under him; the Reaper hitting the packed ground hard; and once Cal was on top of him, had him pinned, the fight to possess the weapon, a blind and mad grab for it, everything coming down to Cal's prying it away or, at least, controlling it.

His heart pounded, and the sounds of the water and the wind had long since fallen away. His muscles flexed, hard, but he told himself to relax, stay loose, conserve energy. He'd had a hundred matches as a high school wrestler but no fights—certainly none that were a matter of life and death. He listened as the Reaper began to take another step, sensed the man's shift in balance, knew if he was going to strike, this was the time to do it.

Before it came to that, though, a voice called from the back driveway.

"Sir? Sir?"

It was a male's voice, but not Angstrom's, Cal could tell that much right away. Older, deeper—professional sounding. Faint, thanks to the waves and wind Cal could suddenly hear again.

The Reaper turned toward it. "Here."

A figure appeared at the driveway's end and stood there, searching the line of trees.

"Mr. Pamona, you all right?"

Cal's heart dropped into his gut at the sound of the man's name.

Heather's husband, just inches away.

Pamona retracted his pending step. He paused, perhaps less than willing to give up on the game he'd been hunting. Not that it was certain anyone was actually there.

He turned finally and stepped to the path's opening. "Yes, I'm fine." There was impatience in his voice.

The man took a few more steps in Pamona's direction. Cal could see him through the trees now. Backlit, but he didn't need more than that to see that this man was dressed in a business suit, not a costume. He was a big man, and yet, by the way he spoke to Pamona, subservient.

"There's something I need you to see."

Pamona walked to the driveway. The man moved in close, spoke in a subdued voice.

"The equipment is working fine," he said. "It seems, though, that the car has stopped a few hundred feet down the road. It might have broken down. Or the driver might be making a call."

Pamona looked back at the line of trees. "Take one of the Town Cars and drive past," he ordered. "See what's going on, then report back to me."

"Yes, sir."

The man in the suit headed back toward the house. Pamona continued to study the path's opening. Cal still couldn't see his face—the man was, again, nothing more than a silhouette—but what did he need to see?

After a long moment—Cal counted half a dozen waves—Pamona returned to the house. Once the man was inside, Cal stood and made his way through the path, moving as quickly as he could till he was clear of it.

Then he bolted with all he had across the parking lot and ran down that dark road.

The ferry was docked when he arrived, and right away he was waved aboard by the ferrymen. He handed his round-trip ticket to the same guy he'd purchased it from. Looking at the unconscious girl in the passenger seat, the ferryman said nothing, though he did glance at the part of Amanda's legs—in black fishnet—that her overcoat didn't cover.

When the ferryman was gone, Cal watched the rearview mirror for any sign of headlights—a Town Car's headlight, specifically—but saw nothing. Even as the ferry pulled away he kept an eye on the landing, but he saw no activity at all there in the minutes it took to cross to the mainland.

Yet, as he disembarked, leaving that island behind for good, he felt no sense of relief, wouldn't, he knew, till he took care of one more thing.

He chose to leave North Haven by a different route, taking the back roads through the woods of Noyac instead of retracing his tracks south through Sag Harbor and then west through the potato fields of Bridgehampton. It was on an empty stretch of Noyac Road, a good ten minutes from the ferry landing, that he pulled over once more.

Removing the cell phone, he saw that the call that had come in was, just as he suspected, from the garage. Who else would it be? He located and hit REDIAL, keeping an eye on the rearview mirror as he waited for Heather to answer.

A little over a half hour later he pulled into the parking lot of Helenbach's, her old restaurant. It had stood dormant all summer—that way since the disappearance last spring of the man to whom Heather's husband had sold it. Blades of wild grass, some a foot tall and bent, grew in clusters through cracks in the pavement. The building was, of course, dark, its windows boarded over.

The BMW X3 was waiting behind the building, out of sight. As the Citroën approached it, Heather, dressed in the same dark slacks and black silk blouse she had been wearing when she arrived two months ago, climbed out from behind the wheel. She had on Cal's motorcycle jacket, which she wore unzipped to allow for her stomach. It was an old Schott café racer jacket, the black steerhide worn but still stiff. Like the Triumph, it had belonged to his brother. Short-waisted and tight on Cal, it was on Heather a surprising near-fit.

Hurrying around to the passenger side, she opened the door and immediately got down onto one knee. She took hold of her kid sister's face with her good hand, gently turning it so she could see it better. "Has she woken up at all?"

"No."

Heather was clearly pained by what she saw. She took a breath, shook her head a little, then let the breath out and said, "We don't have much time."

"Just tell me what to do," Cal said.

"Come around here."

He got out and hurried around to the right side of the Citroën.

Heather grabbed the purse from the floor in front of the passenger seat, tossed it to Cal, then pulled the overcoat off her sister and tossed that to Cal as well. "Check these."

"What am I looking for exactly?"

"It's probably a small cylinder, maybe the size of a triple-A battery. It can't be smaller than that, or it wouldn't have enough range."

Heather leaned in through the passenger door and undid the seat belt. Laying her sister across the seat, she rolled her onto her back. There was nothing gentle at all about the way she handled her now. Removing the stiletto shoes one at time, she threw them into the woods behind the parking lot without even looking at them.

Cal placed the purse on the hood of the Citroën and began to remove its contents. Glancing through the windshield, he saw that Heather had unzipped the maid's costume and was beginning to peel it down her sister's torso. He looked away quickly.

Unfolding a pair of jeans, he felt the pockets, then stole another glance through the windshield, couldn't help himself. Heather had stripped the costume from her sister and discarded it just as she had done with the shoes. Amanda was now dressed in only the fishnet stockings and a black see-through bra. Under the stockings she was wearing nothing at all.

"If it's not in the pockets, check the waistline or hem," Heather said. "It could be sewn in."

He widened his search of the jeans to those places but found nothing. Setting the jeans aside, he went through the remaining clothing—underwear, a few T-shirts, and a hooded sweatshirt. He found, again, nothing. Next was the hair dryer, but the moment he removed it from the purse, Heather said, "Ditch it. He could have opened it up, planted it inside."

Cal tossed the dryer into the woods.

"She has a toiletry kit," he said.

"Get rid of it, too."

He did. There was only one other item left in the main compartment of the purse.

"What about her wallet?" He glanced through the windshield again and saw that Heather was removing her sister's bra.

"Empty it, then toss it."

Searching through it, Cal found less than twenty dollars, a driver's license, and some photographs, one of Amanda and a much older man, the others of people Cal did not recognize. He placed these things on the hood beside the clothes, then threw the wallet into the woods.

There were, he noticed then, outer pockets on one side of the purse. He noticed, too, from the corner of his eye, that Amanda was, with the exception of the torn fishnet stockings, entirely naked.

Searching the outer pockets he found an iPod with earphones wrapped around it, and a ziplock bag containing a glass vial capped with an eyedropper. He shook it, determined that it was full, then held it up for Heather to see.

"What about this?"

She took a quick look at it, said decisively, "Keep it." She leaned out and stood up straight, holding her sister's black bra, feeling along its underwire.

"My money says it's here," she said.

"Why?"

She didn't answer, focused on her search. Suddenly she stopped, nodded. She tried to tear what she had found free of the thick fabric, finally had to bite it with her back teeth to rip the stitching holding it in place.

Dropping the bra to the ground, she held up exactly what she'd said they had been looking for.

A small cylinder, no bigger than a keychain penlight.

"We need to go, Cal. Now."

"What do we with that?"

"We use it," she said.

She opened the driver's door of the X3 and tossed the tracking device onto the passenger seat. Moving around to the rear of the vehicle, opening the hatch, she removed a blanket. Back at the Citroën, she covered Amanda from neck to thigh with the blanket, then pulled the girl up to a seated position. She refastened the seat belt, then emerged from the car again and said, "Follow me."

"Where are we going?"

"You'll see."

She climbed into the X3 and started its engine.

"What about her stuff?"

"Grab the clothes and things. Toss the purse and coat, just to be safe."

He did what he was told, then hurried around to the Citroën's driver's door and climbed in.

Fifteen minutes later they were at the East Hampton train station.

Heather parked the BMW by the small station house, climbed out, and tossed the keys as far up the tracks as she could. She walked around to the Citroën's passenger door, leaned in again, undid the seat belt and slid her sister over, then climbed in beside her. Putting her arm around the girl, Heather eased her over gently till she was leaning against her shoulder.

"Maybe he'll think I got her and left town," Heather said. "If not, at least he'll know I'm onto him. At least the fucker will know he's not as smart as he thinks."

Leaving East Hampton Village, they took Montauk Highway back toward Bridgehampton, riding together in silence. For the first few miles Heather kept looking back to see if they were being followed, but then she seemed satisfied that they weren't and gave up, focusing on her sister beside her.

Cal, though, kept his eyes on the rearview mirror the entire way. He didn't allow himself to feel any relief at all till the Citroën was parked in that middle work bay and the door was closed and locked and the alarm system was set.

Five

He sat on the edge of his bed and watched his hands shake. He couldn't help but wonder what would have happened had Heather's husband not been prevented from taking those last few steps. Aaron wasn't afraid of the man, had always made that clear, but Cal was. No doubt that he could have taken Pamona down to the ground, if he landed the leg dive right, which, of course, he would have. Big guys were easy to take down when you got their knees together and turned them into an upside-down pyramid. But what *then*? He had grown up in a house where there were guns. His father's guns, but Aaron knew where they were kept. When Aaron was old enough to drive, they'd even taken one to the pine barrens beyond Westhampton and had taken turns shooting off a few rounds. Cal still remembered the feel of the gun in his hand, the weight of it, the menace. And he remembered the sound of the shots being fired, too—so loud, like a clap against both ears. Would he really have been able to wrestle Pamona in the dark for control of his gun? If he did get control of it, again, *then what*?

He wondered, watching his hands, what exactly he was capable of.

He was nowhere near an answer when, from his open doorway, Heather whispered, "You okay?"

He snapped from his thoughts and looked at her. "Yeah," he said. "How is she?"

Heather was still wearing his motorcycle jacket. "The same." In her hand was the vial of liquid Cal had found in Amanda's purse.

"Any idea what that is?"

"It's morphine," Heather said.

"Are you sure?"

She nodded.

"Do you think she's addicted?"

"It's oral morphine. I checked, and she doesn't have any track marks or anything. I don't know what to think, exactly. If she is addicted, then the next few days aren't going to be much fun."

"Taking her to the hospital is out, right?"

"Yeah. Not much they could do for her there anyway. My guess is the morphine was the bait to get her out there. It was Ronnie's recreational drug of choice."

"Is that why she's out of it tonight?"

"No. Someone must have given her a heavy tranquilizer." Heather paused, looked at Cal for a moment, then removed his jacket. Stepping into the small room, she handed it to him. "Thanks."

"No problem." He laid the jacket on the foot of his bed.

She was standing over him, looking down at him. "If you hadn't gone back like you did . . ." She didn't finish the thought, didn't have to.

"I figured something was going on. It didn't add up, you know."

"He wanted you scared, so you'd come running back here. That's why Angstrom said what he said."

Cal nodded. "I guess, yeah, but there were some weird things going on there. Everyone dressed up like religious figures, plus what the ferry guy told me."

Heather didn't say anything at first, then, "There's a side of Ronnie no one knows about."

She left it at that. Cal didn't press the matter. Besides, there were more important things they needed to talk about.

"When I was pulling out of that parking lot, Angstrom was watching us drive away. Later on your husband said something to him about running plates."

Heather understood what Cal was getting at. "Who does that car belong to?"

"A guy in Southampton."

"His address is on the registration."

"Yeah."

"Ronnie could get it from the DMV."

"And he could find out from the owner where his car was tonight."

Heather nodded, said nothing.

"I know that the owner's out of town for a while," Cal offered. "We're storing it till he gets back."

"How long?"

"Till the middle of next week."

"So much for having three months to figure things out."

"Who's to say the owner of the Citroën is going to just tell your husband where his car was."

"Ronnie has a way of getting what he wants. Plus, he might already know the guy."

"So what do we do?"

"I don't know." She thought for a moment. "You said the party was supposed to go all weekend, right?"

"That's what I heard."

"So we have one advantage he doesn't. We know where he is."

"What good does that do us?"

"Maybe none."

"We could tip off the cops, have them raid his party. I'm sure there were drugs there. And I know there were prostitutes."

Heather shook her head. "I'd have to swear out a statement before they could get a warrant. That would leave me exposed."

"Wouldn't they have to protect your identity?"

"I don't necessarily trust the cops."

"Why don't I do it? I mean, I'm the one who was there, saw and heard things. I don't even have to mention your name. I could go right now."

"It's too much of a risk. Besides, Angstrom got a good look at you, right? So did the ferryman. That's two people too many. I doubt Ronnie remembers you, but . . ." Again, she didn't finish her thought.

"This was close, wasn't it?" Cal said after a moment.

She nodded. "Yeah. Too close. I knew he wouldn't give up. He won't be discouraged by what happened tonight, either. If anything, he's *really* mad now, and he'll try even harder next time. I wouldn't mind seeing the look on his face, though. When he sees his tracking device sitting there on the front seat. I wouldn't mind seeing that."

Cal said nothing. He'd never loved anyone long enough to see that love get twisted into hate. He'd seen it enough to know that it was something that did happen; he just didn't know what it felt like.

"We need to be extra careful from now on," Heather said, "and we've only got, what, a few days to figure out what to do."

"Yeah."

"He's not getting his hands on my child, that I know for certain. He probably thinks that, whoever you are, you and I are together, which means all kinds of fantasies of killing you are running through his head right now. I'm telling you, if I had any luck at all, he'd get hit by a bus or something."

Again, Cal said nothing. For a moment he regretted not having tackled her husband when he'd had the chance, not having battled with him for the gun—but that was, he knew, foolishness.

Heather leaned down and laid the vial on top of his jacket.

"Keep this for me, okay? In case we need to give her some. Weaning her off it might be better than just stopping cold turkey. It depends how badly hooked she is."

Cal looked at the vial. He knew enough about morphine from having observed Aaron's on-again-off-again girlfriend to know both its pleasures and its dangers.

It was, in fact, according to the police, Aaron's attempt to obtain morphine for her—the drug buy somehow gone bad—that had gotten him killed.

Glancing past Heather, toward his bureau, Cal said, "Your phone's there."

"Get rid of it."

"You sure?"

"Ronnie has that number. I don't even want to touch it now. I'll go into town tomorrow, get a new one."

"I'll take you."

"I might need you to stay here and watch Amanda."

"Okay."

She reached down, took his hand, held it for a moment.

Her own hand was warm, her fingers, intertwined with his, strong.

It took all he had to hide the severity of his reaction to this touch.

"Thanks, Cal. Really. Things would be very different if you hadn't done what you did. Mr. Fix-it strikes again."

"Of course. You know the rule. Anything for Heatherlicious."

She smiled at that—a bit sincere, a bit forced, but he'd take it. She left his room and went back to hers to tend to her sister. Watching his hands for a moment more, Cal then checked his watch. It was almost eleven.

Time to work.

He made headway on the last stages of the engine rebuild. It was difficult to avoid flashing back now and then to certain moments from the hours before—Ronnie Pamona just inches away on that dark path; Amanda in fishnet stockings and nothing else on the front seat of the Citroën; Heather taking his hand and holding it for a moment. It was difficult, too, to avoid listening for sounds—a car in the distance, footsteps outside, any indications that someone might be approaching. Eventually, though, Cal was able to settle down and focus on his work. Several hours passed, and he was maybe a little over halfway through when the solemn silence of the garage was broken by a ringing phone.

The office phone, the garage's landline.

He hurried to the adjacent office—an extension was upstairs, in the living room, and Heather was, he hoped, sound asleep by now. Still, he paused to look at the caller ID and saw not a number but the words OUT OF AREA.

His first thought was that this could be Heather's husband, that somehow he had tracked them to here already. Was that even possible? Then he thought it might be Lebell calling to check up on him, from God knows where, drunk and looking maybe to make one last attempt to tempt Cal to come out. Or maybe he had come across some piece of information about Carver that Cal needed to know right away. He'd said he'd call if that happened.

In the end, Cal answered so that Heather wouldn't be disturbed. He picked up the receiver at the tail end of the fourth ring.

From the other end of the line came a female voice.

"Is Lebell there?"

He didn't recognize the voice, nor did he understand why a woman would be looking for Lebell here, and at this time of the night.

"No," Cal said. He felt—and sounded—a little guarded. "He's not."

"I need to talk to him." Her voice was quiet, emotionless. She had an accent that Cal couldn't place. Spanish, maybe, *but not exactly.*

"I'm sorry, he's not here. Who's calling?"

"It's important." Her tone didn't alter in the slightest.

Cold, calm.

"I can take a message," Cal offered. Something about the quality of the connection told him that whoever this woman was, she was calling from a cell phone. Something about her voice, too, told him that she was a young woman. *Well, not old.*

"Do you know where he might be?" she said.

"No, I don't." Cal paused. *Something wasn't right about this.* "Who is this?"

A long silence, and then, abruptly, the line went dead.

He lingered in the dark office after hanging up, wanted to be within quick reach of the phone in case she called back. She might have been drunk—maybe that was what hadn't sounded right to him—so he could imagine her trying again right away. When the phone didn't ring after a good minute, Cal thought of calling Lebell's cell phone but decided against it; chances were the guy was with a woman, and chances were the woman he was with was another man's wife. *His compulsion.*

Cal began to think that maybe the call just now was from an ex-lover of Lebell's. A late-night call, born from sleeplessness or longing, or both. There'd been many a night, alone in his narrow bed, that he had wished that he could just call *someone*. But he couldn't remember ever having met or even heard of a woman with such an accent. Though Lebell was secretive about his past, he was not at all discreet about the women he pursued in the here and now.

Whatever the case, whatever her story or problem, it wasn't any of Cal's business.

Back in the first bay, he resumed his work, managed eventually to get lost in it, the precision of the engine, the solemn silence broken only by the clanging of tools and the occasional grunt as he tightened down a bolt.

Just a few miles south, in her room in what was left of the Hotel St. James, Evangeline Amendora lay the prepaid cell phone on the table next to her bed. Still cold to the core, her hair still frozen and her solid body trembling uncontrollably, she stood by the small electric heater, absorbing what little warmth it gave off, and prepared herself for what she was going to do next.

She needed a plan. *I have failed, yes, but I am on top of things, will take care of this, please understand that.* She had to think this through, apply all that she had learned—all that he had taught her—and come up with a way to complete the job.

She knew that the number she had dialed could be used to obtain the location of the friend that Militich called most frequently, the man to whom she had just spoken. That was where she would start. If this particular friend—closest friend, certainly—didn't, as he had claimed, know where Militich was, then he might know where he might have gone.

It couldn't have been far, not in the condition he was in, not after the cuts she had made before he slammed the heavy glass against her cheek and bolted for the door.

Stepping away from the heater, Eve grabbed her tank mechanic's bag. There was plenty of room in it now that the dress and the wig and the padded bra were gone. At the bottom of the bag, along with the .357 and the other tools of the trade she'd brought with her, was a second cell phone that, from this place, was her only connection to the man for whom she had killed many times before.

For whom, she was determined, she would kill once again.

He would need to know that Militich—the man who was calling himself Lebell—was still alive. She would have to tell him that she had failed.

This phone was already powered up. The room had warmed a little, but she was trembling nonetheless as she entered his number and waited for him to answer.

PART TWO

October 31

HALLOWEEN

───◆◆◆───

Six

———◆———

Cal finished around dawn but needed to take the '62 Benz for a test ride before he'd be able to call the job done. Backing the vehicle out of the garage, then heading back inside to activate the security system and close and lock the door, he carefully studied his surroundings in all possible directions, saw, though, nothing out of the ordinary.

There were advantages, he realized, to being in the middle of nowhere: any car, either passing or parked along the edge of Scuttlehole Road, particularly at this hour, would stand out, have no chance of appearing as part of normal traffic or blending in with the vehicles that normally parked at the curb for the night, which would have been the case if he, like Lebell, lived in a village.

There was nothing to see or hear now, simply the morning's first vague shadows forming at the foot of the trees. It was calmer than it had been the night before, less gusty, but the briskness remained, an autumn chill that made it clear winter was coming.

Taking Scuttlehole north to its end, he turned around and headed back—just a ten-minute round-trip run was all he needed to know that his work was at last done. As he rode, though, looking in the rearview mirror every now and then, he couldn't shake the feeling of being on dangerous ground. If he were to cross paths with Pamona—or the man who worked for him, the man in the suit—there would be no one around to hear or to see, and no place, this time, to run to or hide.

He felt better when the garage came into view, felt better still when he was back inside with the doors closed. He knew that Heather and her sister—*what was it Aaron had called her, way back when? Demanda?*—would still be asleep, so he entered his apartment as quietly as he could, crossing the drafty living room to his bedroom.

Once his work boots and coveralls were removed, he stretched out on his bed in his jeans and T-shirt and told himself that this disruption in his routine was close to being behind him now. If he had gone out drinking with Lebell, it was likely he would be just getting home around now anyway—a few hours' sleep, as usual, to let the tequila clear from his blood, and then he'd be free to drift, to the degree he ever allowed himself to drift, till Monday. Since there was no tequila in his blood to process this morning, he would then sleep till noon, when the owner of the Benz was due to arrive, take care of that piece of business, and then be at last back on schedule. With the exception of Amanda's presence, there would be, he expected, no real difference between this Saturday and any other—any other since Heather had arrived, at least.

There was even a part of Cal that hoped Lebell had learned nothing from George the bartender regarding Carver's recent problems. Better yet, maybe Lebell had forgotten to even ask. Maybe some beautiful woman had come along early in the evening and distracted him from his promise to find out what he could.

The problem of Heather's husband—they had only days now, not months, to figure something out—was enough to worry about.

It took Cal a while to relax, but sleep didn't seem to want him. He was too wound up, too riled.

He realized after a while that part of the problem was that he was expecting the phone to ring—Lebell had said he would call in the morning and see if Cal needed help. He was always good about calling when he said he would, so Cal decided that the thing to do was to stretch out on the couch in the living room, be within quick reach of the phone should it actually ring.

He grabbed his blanket and his alarm clock and entered the living room. Settling down in the couch, the phone on the coffee table just a few feet away, he wound the clock and set it for a quarter to twelve.

He fell asleep, eventually, to the sound of the ticking clock and was awakened all too quickly by the sound of it ringing.

Silencing the alarm, he sat up and looked toward Heather's door. It was still closed, and he heard no motion or voices coming from behind it.

Moments later, his work boots on, Cal was downstairs in the office, waiting for the owner of the Benz to show up. By half past twelve there was no sign of the man, so he called Carver. Getting no answer, he left a message. A few minutes later he pulled the work order from the file cabinet, got the owner's number, and called him directly. A woman answered, but she wasn't much help, would say only that the man he was looking for was out. The best she could do was take a message. Cal left one, then waited another half hour for the man to call back.

Nothing.

Finally, he decided to call Lebell's cell—it was one o'clock, and Lebell should have called hours ago, like he'd promised. Not to do so wasn't like him. There was, though, no answer. Cal left a message, saying that it looked like he had busted his hump for nothing; the owner of the Benz was a no-show, and Carver wasn't answering his phone. He ended the message by asking Lebell to give him a call, let him know how last night went.

When he returned upstairs, the living room and kitchen were empty, and Heather's door was closed, her room quiet. There were dishes in the sink that hadn't been there when Cal had left at noon, so someone had, at one point, been up. He made himself something to eat, then waited in the living room for a little while, standing at a window and looking out at Scuttlehole Road in case the owner of the Benz pulled in. Several cars approached from the west, the direction of Southampton, in the ten or fifteen minutes he stood watch, but none came even close to slowing to make the turn into the driveway.

Eventually he picked up the phone and dialed Lebell's cell again, got, again, his voice mail. Leaving no message this time, Cal hung up and felt, suddenly, a little lost. He didn't know how to shake it till he decided to return to the kitchen and wash the dishes in the sink. He looked out that window as he did this, this time not for the owner of the Benz but for Lebell's Mustang. It had finally occurred to Cal that maybe Lebell wasn't answering because he was on his way here and needed, as he pushed his vehicle to its limits in the many bends in Scuttlehole Road, both hands on the steering wheel.

When the dishes were done, Cal went into his bedroom. The vial of morphine was on his bureau top, along with Heather's cell phone; his old Schott jacket was hanging on his doorknob. He grabbed the jacket, put the vial in one of the pockets, zipped it closed, then hung the jacket up in his closet, where it belonged. He realized, though, that the vial wasn't really safe there. Should Amanda go hunting for it, this would be one of the first places she'd look. He lifted up the floorboard at the bottom of his closet, placed the vial in the fire box with his stash of cash, and slipped the floorboard back into place. Heather's cell phone he placed in the pocket of his peacoat, making a mental note to toss the thing into some Dumpster, or into one of the sinkhole ponds on the edge of a nearby field, the next time he was out.

Once his room was straightened up, Cal had no choice but to face the fact that there was nothing at all for him to do now. Before Heather had come into his life, he would spend his free time riding his old Triumph from village to village, taking the back roads to avoid traffic and enjoy the scenery and twists and turns—and, too, to avoid the police, since the bike wasn't registered or insured. A stolen bike, from back in the day, when his brother would steal anything he could. The VIN numbers had long since been filed down, so Cal couldn't register it even if he wanted to. This was his one and only bit of lawlessness, the only thing in his otherwise careful life that connected him to the Rakowski tradition—nothing less than that, in his mind. Harmless, as far as lawlessness went, yes, not at all unlike his Friday nights out with Lebell, nights of drinking and, prior to Heather's arrival, pursuing women. But a lawlessness nonetheless.

There wasn't a day when Cal didn't know, in one primal way or another, that he was a Rakowski.

He had, he realized, grown dependent on Heather. Without her, his day seemed suddenly shapeless, unmanageable. There was nothing else with which to occupy himself, so he decided to grab some sleep— not unusual, a nap on a Saturday afternoon, so no real deviation from his routine here. He wanted to give Lebell another try, though, so he dialed his number one last time from the phone in the living room. As before, he got no answer and left no message. He returned the receiver to the cradle and was about to head to his room when he heard the sound of Heather's bedroom door opening.

He turned to see Amanda quietly closing the door. She was wearing her sister's kimono but hadn't tied it closed, had no idea, clearly, that Cal was there. Stepping toward the open bathroom door, she finally realized Cal was standing by the couch in the center of the living room. Stopping, she looked at him but made no effort at first to cover herself. She was still, he could see, in a stupor.

"Hey," she said.

Cal stared for a second, couldn't help himself, then quickly glanced away. It was then that Amanda realized the degree to which she was exposed. Reaching down, she casually pulled one side of the robe across her torso.

"How are you feeling?" Cal said.

"Shitty." Her voice was soft, young, but, at the same time, *worn out*. "Heather told me what you did," she said. "Thanks."

"No problem. Is she asleep?"

"Yeah. We've both been sleeping on and off all day. Do you need the bathroom?"

"No, I'm fine. Go ahead." He wanted to ask her about Heather's husband, hoping that she had some information that could help them, but it was obvious this wasn't the time to grill her.

"You going to be around tonight?" Amanda said.

"Probably, yeah. Why?"

She smiled as best she could. "I probably I owe you a blow job or something."

Though they were opposite in many ways, Amanda and her older half sister both derived pleasure from teasing Cal. Amanda was simply the more shocking of the two.

Stepping into the bathroom, she closed the door.

Cal, not really sure if he was coming or going, stood there for a moment before finally heading into his bedroom.

It didn't take long for his inability to get hold of Lebell to become a concern.

Was it possible, he began to wonder, that asking questions about Carver's business, if Lebell had actually done so, had gotten him into some kind of trouble? Could he have asked the wrong question of the wrong person?

Wild thoughts, maybe, but anything to keep his mind off the half-naked girl and the joking promise she'd made. Dwelling on such thoughts could only lead to trouble, and Cal wasn't interested in trouble, not even that kind.

He dozed off now and then, looking out his window when he was awake, at the gray day beyond. Because of the overcast he couldn't track the motion of the sun. It was never more than dusk, though, even in the middle of the afternoon. Always, shortly after waking, he'd fall back into a light sleep, dreaming brief, inconsequential dreams. It was when he awoke to find the false dusk giving way to a real one that he realized what was ahead of him.

A night he didn't care to repeat, one much like the night Aaron had disappeared.

He had no desire to sit around and wait for as long as it took for bad news to find him, so he sat up, put on his Sidi boots and grabbed his peacoat, then opened his bedroom door.

He heard voices from Heather's room, so he paused. Uncertain whether he should interrupt, he finally knocked on her door; he needed to tell her where he was going, didn't want to cause her any needless worry.

Heather called to him to come in. She was sitting on the edge of her bed, wearing her kimono now. Amanda, under the blankets, was curled up on her side, Heather's hand on her bare shoulder.

It was clear that Amanda had been crying, that he had interrupted a serious conversation.

"Hey," Heather said. She glanced at his coat. "Where are you off to?"

"I need to run an errand."

She nodded, gave her sister's shoulder a reassuring rub, then stood and walked to the door. Cal backed up to let her through.

"How is she?"

Heather closed the door softly, remained next to it, her hand on the knob, and spoke in a whisper. "A little roughed up."

Cal matched Heather's hushed tone. "Did she tell you anything?"

"Yeah. Apparently Angstrom was the one who invited her out to the party, promised her there'd be plenty of drugs and rich men. He said if she played her cards right, she might leave with a sugar daddy. She says the last thing she remembers was getting there and being given a drink."

"So she didn't know it was your husband's party."

"No. And she said she never once saw him there, that it was just Angstrom and a bunch of strangers. She had no idea about what was really going on till I told her."

"So the whole thing was just this elaborate scheme. The party, the house, her being there—all just to draw you out."

"Yeah. Like fucking Gatsby. When he couldn't find me, Ronnie must have tried to track down Amanda, the same way I did, through her friends. He must have offered to pay Angstrom if he helped get Amanda to his party."

"And Angstrom had your new number."

"Ronnie's lucky day, yeah."

"So the party was what? A diversion?"

Heather thought for a moment, uncertain whether to actually say what was on her mind now. Finally, she just came out with it.

"He used to have orgy fantasies," she said. Her voice was even more hushed now. "He used to like to imagine me with other men. Sometimes many men. Jealousy, I don't know, turned him on in a big way. He said he heard about these parties. People would rent places—isolated places—invite friends, hire women. Strippers or prostitutes or whatever. He used to try to get me to go to them with him."

Cal's gut tightened, hard, and he felt a lump in his throat. His mouth was suddenly dry. "Jesus."

"Like I've been telling you, Cal, he's a sick man. Anyway, the party was probably cover."

"What do you mean?"

"To get Amanda out there. I mean, if she arrived and there was nothing going on, would she have stayed? He's not a fool, he's not going to leave himself open for a kidnapping charge. Remember, though, his original plan was to lure me out there. Angstrom's call was to get me to pick her up. Either the tracking device was a fallback plan they came up with when I told them I was sending someone, or Ronnie wanted to track me to where I was staying, find out who I've been staying with."

"Kind of elaborate for a cover. I mean, it could have been a regular party, you know. Not an . . . orgy."

"Maybe Ronnie had hopes that I'd see him with all those women and get jealous and immediately want him back. He's a narcissist, Cal. He assumes everyone feels the same way he does. People who don't are inferior. He was never able to understand why jealousy didn't turn me on."

At first Cal said nothing. He didn't like to think of them together. In fact, though he'd never admit it, their sex life seemed a little over his head. Finally, he asked if Amanda was going to be okay. It was a quick change of subject, but who would blame him?

"She says she's been clean for a while, went to the party with the intention of starting up again. If she's telling the truth, we don't have to worry about withdrawal. But like I said, she's roughed up. It's been a bad year. She's been living on the street, doing whatever it took to survive."

"Can I get her anything while I'm out?"

"Where are you going?"

There was no reason not to tell her.

"I need to look for Lebell."

"What's going on?"

"I don't know. He was supposed to call me this morning, and I haven't heard from him. Plus, I got this weird call last night from some woman wanting to know if I knew where he was."

"Maybe an irate husband finally caught up with him."

"Maybe. Reason enough for me to go looking for him. But he was supposed to ask certain people some questions last night, and I'm wondering now if maybe that got him into trouble."

"What kind of questions?"

"About Carver. If he's doing drugs, if he's dealing drugs. If maybe I should be looking for another job and place to live."

"Jesus. When it rains around here it pours, huh?"

"I'd rather not sit around all night and wait for the phone to ring."

She understood, completely, and nodded once. "How long are you going to be?" she said.

"Not long. An hour, maybe."

"Where's his place?"

"He has an apartment in Southampton, on Meeting House Lane."

"How are you going to get there?"

"Take the train from Bridgehampton. The station's only a mile from here."

"I was hoping to get a new cell phone tonight."

"I forgot." He felt his pocket. "I have yours, by the way."

"You need to ditch that."

"I will while I'm out."

"The sooner, the better. I suppose I could call a cab."

"Do you think that's safe?"

"It's just a ride into Bridgehampton and back. Anyway, I need a phone; I feel naked without one. A friend of mine owns a cab company. I can get hold of him directly. I can ask him to send a cab and not keep a record of it."

"You trust him?"

She nodded. "Yeah."

"Are you going to take Amanda with you?"

"I don't think so. She'll probably want to stay here."

"Tell you what, I'll keep your phone with me, so you can reach me if you need to. When I'm on my way back here, I'll ditch it."

She nodded, then said, "I wonder if he tried to call it."

"He might've. It's off now. I can turn it on and check."

"No, that's okay. I don't want to know."

Cal nodded. He understood, of course.

"I'll be back soon," he said.

"Be careful."

"You, too."

He sealed up the garage as he left and studied his surroundings as he crossed Scuttlehole Road. There was, of course, nothing there to see.

Following Mitchell Lane south to the train station, he arrived at six fifteen. Only fifteen minutes to wait for the westbound train.

From the platform he watched the sunset, or what was left of it, just as he had the night before.

Another mile walk south, this time from the Southampton station, and not through dusk but full night, the streetlights that lined North Main Street glowing pale white.

There was something unusually bright about tonight, he noticed. He realized finally that it was Halloween, and all the front porches of the houses on both sides of this wide residential street were lit up for the trick-or-treaters who might still be around.

Cal looked for some—a cluster of small, restless children being guided by an adult, a group of boisterous teens, anything—but saw no one. Strange, then, to be walking down a street so inviting and yet so utterly empty.

He crossed into the village, which was just as bright and just as empty as North Main. All the many little shops were closed, but the restaurants were open. He passed 75 Main, glanced through its tall windows, saw a half-full bar and, for the most part, empty tables. Early still, though. He noticed that the staff—in danger of outnumbering the guests—were all dressed in costumes. Women as sexy kitty cats, geisha girls, Playboy bunnies; men as comic book superheroes, Hollywood monsters, cowboys. He recognized them all, knew most of them by name.

He continued on till he reached the end of Main Street, crossed there, and headed east along Meeting House Lane. A narrower street, houses crowded closer together, cars parked along its curbs. These porches, too, were lit, but again there were no trick-or-treaters to be seen.

It took him just a few minutes to reach Lebell's place—the only house within sight with absolutely no lights on at all. The windows of Lebell's second-floor apartment were dark, as were the windows of his neighbor's apartment below. Cal remembered that Lebell's neighbor worked nights. No need for a porch light to be left on, Cal supposed, not with the street as well lit and public as it was.

He studied the cars parked at the curbs, eventually spotting Lebell's Mustang GT a few spaces down from his place. That didn't necessarily mean anything, though; Lebell often left his vehicle at home and did his Southampton pub crawl on foot. One of the advantages of living in the village.

He stopped in front of Lebell's place. Maybe the guy had met a woman last night and gone with her to her home, was still there. Maybe that explained his not calling or coming by.

But maybe wasn't good enough.

Cal crossed the short walkway and stepped onto the small porch. He knew that Lebell left the downstairs door unlocked, so he wasn't surprised when the knob turned freely. Opening the door, he looked up the steep stairs. He felt around on the wall for the light switch, found it, and flipped it, but nothing happened. The bulb, out the last time Cal had visited, obviously hadn't been replaced. He found the railing and held on to it as he made his way up the narrow stairway. When he reached the top, he searched for the knob in the darkness but realized soon enough that the door was ajar.

He pushed it gently, moving it back an inch at the most. Through the crack he saw not darkness, as in the stairwell, but a muted light—from a streetlight, he knew, spilling in through the front windows, across the living room, and into the kitchen. He knocked on the wood with his middle knuckle, said, "Hello," but got no response. Pushing the door back even farther, he stepped inside and felt the wall for the light switch. This light, a lamp hanging from the ceiling above the small kitchen table, worked just fine.

But Cal wasn't at all prepared for what it showed him.

He saw the overturned kitchen table first, the scattered chairs, then the large stain of blood on the linoleum, a trail of drops leading away from it and into the living room.

He instantly felt a rush of fear. It was ice cold, a blast from within. He stiffened, as if against an actual wind, and it took all he had to finally make himself move again.

Stepping into the living room, he followed with his eyes the trail of dried drops to another large stain. This one, though, looked like a spatter. The coffee table had been overturned, the couch was on its side, and there was, in one of the walls, the kind of dent that could only be left by a person being slammed against it.

His first instinct—to flee—was difficult to resist. There was a chance, though, however slim, that Lebell might be somewhere else in the apartment. Maybe hurt, maybe worse. The only room Cal couldn't see into was the bedroom. He hurried to its doorway, adrenaline rushing into his limbs. Opening the door, he found the complete opposite of what he was expecting.

This room was undisturbed, no sign of blood anywhere.

He lingered in that doorway for a moment, both confused and relieved. Eventually, though, he stepped back into the kitchen and noticed that the blood trail also led to the doorway. The lamp above the overturned table cast enough light for him to see down the narrow stairwell beyond. The trail continued there.

Again, he fought the instinct to flee; knew, though, that he had to think through it. He was, after all, standing in a crime scene. A genuine shock, his suddenly being in the middle of one. *So this was what it was like.* His fingerprints, he realized, were everywhere—on the doorknob downstairs, the railing, as well as the door to the apartment and the light switches—God knows where else. Too many places for him to run around and wipe them away. Certainly his boots had brought in trace elements from the garage—oil, fibers, bits of stone from the gravel driveway. Not to mention that he must have at some point stepped in the dried blood.

No, fleeing—with so many traces of himself here—was out of the question. Anyway, where would go? Back home? To do what? Wait? That was what he had come here to avoid. Besides, all this blood—all the signs of violence—meant that in some way or another that Lebell was in trouble.

Realizing that there was only one thing he could do—the right thing to do, the expected thing to do, what, certainly, a *good boy would do*—Cal removed Heather's cell phone from the pocket of his peacoat and switched it on.

Once the phone had powered up and located a signal, he dialed 911.

Seven

————◆◆◆————

From the back of a patrol car, Cal watched the cops.

The first to arrive, moments after he'd made the call, was an officer named Clarke. She was in her late twenties, attractive and fit, brown hair, oval face, sharp eyes that never wavered from Cal's as he told her his story. It was her patrol car that he was in now, having been put there when the second cop to arrive, a sergeant named Spadaro, instructed her to do so. Spadaro had also instructed her to take Cal's driver's license and cell phone. In that backseat, stripped of his only piece of identification and with no way to open the doors or even lower the windows, he felt both trapped and shut off from the world.

Well, not the world, he didn't care about the world—but Heather. What if she needed him? What if she tried to call while the phone was in the possession of the police? He remembered what she had said about not trusting them. He could barely think of anything else. Did either of these cops know Heather's husband? Did both of them?

Of course, he hadn't forgotten about Lebell, or all the indications of violence up in his apartment. From the backseat of the patrol car Cal watched as the two cops set up a perimeter with yellow tape, hoping to see something in what they did that would mean something, tell him anything. Did they already know that Lebell was dead, and would it show in how they moved? Cal saw nothing, and it wasn't long after the perimeter was set that a third patrol car arrived. Through the closed window Cal overheard—from this third cop as he walked past Clarke's patrol car—that a detective was on the way. This third cop gave further instructions, but he had already stepped out of Cal's earshot.

Again, shut off from the world.

The three cops then studied the blood trail on the sidewalk, pointing down the street, away from the village, not toward it. It was in this direction that the trail went. Cal watched them discuss it. By now, drawn by the commotion and the flashing lights, the neighbors had begun to emerge from their homes. They gathered together, some on the sidewalk, some in the middle of the street. It was obvious by the way the three patrol cars were parked—not to mention the yellow tape strung across it, from one signpost to another—that the street was now closed.

Cal did see something in the behavior of these cops that was telling. Once the third cop had arrived, all communications, which had up to that point been via radios, switched suddenly to cell phones. Telling, maybe, but of what Cal didn't know.

Ten minutes passed before another vehicle, an unmarked sedan, arrived. Cal recognized its driver the moment he got out as the detective who had been assigned to Aaron's disappearance—and then murder—four years before. His name was Messing, and he was, from what Cal remembered, a decent enough guy, polite, straightforward; he had seemed genuinely sorry for Cal's loss, for this young man left now to fend for himself.

Messing talked to the three cops for a few moments, then stepped aside with the third one and talked to him privately. Finally, Messing headed inside Lebell's apartment, waving for Spadaro to join him, leaving Clarke and the third cop to remain outside.

As Cal waited he began to sweat under his peacoat. It took fifteen minutes for Messing and Spadaro to exit the building. As they spoke to Clarke and the third cop, the four of them standing on the narrow sidewalk, Messing looked toward Clarke's patrol car. Clarke was talking now, giving Messing her report, and he nodded as he listened, looking away from her patrol car—the solitary figure in its backseat, actually—only long enough to quick-check his watch, which he did several times.

Cal was feeling restless now. Just as Clarke finished giving Messing her report, the detective's cell phone rang. Cal could barely hear it through the glass. Messing answered, stepping away, talked as much as he listened, then ended the call and immediately gave orders to Clarke and Spadaro. The two cops began to clear the street of the neighbors, and Messing stepped aside again to speak privately to the third cop.

It seemed clear to Cal that they were now preparing for the arrival of another vehicle, and sure enough, not long after Clarke and Spadaro had gotten everyone back on the sidewalk, another unmarked sedan turned onto Meeting House Lane and came to a stop behind Messing's.

Its bright headlights filled the inside of Clarke's patrol car, then finally went out. A man emerged, dressed in a suit and an overcoat and shining black shoes. By the way Messing reacted to his arrival—he broke away from the third cop midsentence and walked quickly to meet this man—Cal knew that this was the person for whom Messing had been waiting, and that this person was someone important.

This man and Messing talked for a moment, alone, the two of them standing close together, as if in a two-man huddle. Now the man in the overcoat was looking toward Clarke's patrol car. He never once, though, unlike Messing, took his eyes off the kid in the backseat.

Messing did most of the talking—bringing the man up to speed, no doubt—and when Messing was done, the man in the overcoat said a few words. The detective handed him something, and then something else, but Cal couldn't see what.

Then the man in the overcoat nodded once, and he and Messing stepped off the sidewalk and headed toward Clarke's patrol car.

They crossed the narrow street with determined strides.

As Messing opened the driver's door, a gust of cold air came rushing into the interior, which had gradually grown chill in the half hour Cal had been waiting and watching. First flipping a switch on the door's console that unlocked the back door, Messing then climbed in behind the wheel. The man in the overcoat opened the back door and slid in beside Cal.

Someone's cologne quickly erased almost all trace of Cal's scent. The man beside him adjusted his overcoat and got comfortable, didn't look, though, at Cal. It was his cologne, Cal determined, that came in with all that cold air. Up front, Messing watched Cal via the rearview mirror mounted on the windshield.

"How are you tonight, Cal?" Messing said.

He was in his fifties—an older man, a larger and better-dressed man, certainly, but Cal, the scrawny kid in jeans and a thermal shirt and old peacoat, wasn't intimidated. Shy around cops his whole life, he nonetheless knew their ways, had learned all he needed to know about them from his father. Having done nothing wrong, he was determined not to let either of these men make him feel as though he had, which, his father used to say, was a favorite trick of theirs.

"It's Cal, right?" Messing said. "You prefer to be called Cal."

Nodding, Cal looked over at the man in the overcoat, could see now what it was Messing had handed to him before they had crossed the street.

Cal's driver's license and Heather's cell phone, in hands that were easily twice the size of Cal's.

The man in the overcoat was looking at the driver's license, holding it with fingers that were long and thick.

"Rakowski, Adam C.," the man read. "Cal, I take it, is your middle name."

The less said, the better, so Cal didn't answer. *In his head now, suddenly, his father's words, various warnings spoken over time so long ago.*

"Cal is short for what? Caleb? Religious parents, maybe?" The man paused, then said, "I'm curious why you don't go by your first name."

Cal shrugged. "I just don't."

"Messing here says your father was something of a career lowlife, and that his name was Adam. Apparently you've never once had a run-in with the law yourself, not even a traffic violation. So I was wondering if maybe there was significance in you not going by the same name as your old man."

He'd been Cal for as long as he could remember. His only real memories of his mother were of her saying his name. *A voice in the darkness, as she tucked him in—good night, Cal, good night.*

If there was any significance at all to his being called by his middle name instead of his first, it had never been shared with him.

"Actually," Messing said, "Cal here seems to have his head on pretty straight. So far, anyway. Which is pretty impressive, considering that the Rakowski clan was known to be something of a wild bunch. The only reason I know him at all, in fact, is because both his father and his brother got themselves killed. Years apart, but the circumstances weren't all that different. How long ago was it for your brother, Cal? Three years?"

"Four."

"Sorry to hear that," the man in the overcoat said. His voice, though, was flat, empty of feeling—empty even of the pretense of it. "How did he die?"

"He was shot," Messing said. "During a drug deal gone bad. A shame, actually; it looked like he'd finally gotten his act together. He'd been in lots of trouble when he was younger, but then he seemed to turn himself around, became an A student, was even an all-state wrestler. After graduation he even found a steady job and managed to keep it, which is pretty good for anyone out here. Then, one day, boom, out of nowhere, back to his old ways and shot dead."

Not exactly the whole story, Cal thought, but he didn't bother to correct the detective, didn't see the point in telling either of them that it wasn't a drug deal gone bad, at least not in the sense Messing meant. Only Cal—and the girl Aaron had been determined to help—knew this. Only they had cared.

If you are going to use, I want you to use here, not behind my back, Aaron had told her one night. It hadn't worked; she took off anyway, leaving not just Aaron but Cal, too. Several nights later, Aaron went out to buy her drug of choice, as a means, no doubt, of luring her back.

It was only then that Cal made the connection between what Aaron had done so long ago and what Ronnie Pamona had tried to do.

Two completely different things, he quickly told himself. *Two completely different men.*

The man in the overcoat, still reading the license, said, "There's that old saying. 'The apple eventually falls.' Just how far from the tree it lands, that's the question."

Cal looked at the reflection of Messing's eyes in the rearview mirror. His confusion—*who the fuck is this guy*—must have shown, because Messing promptly said, "Cal, this is Special Agent Tierno. He's with the FBI."

Tierno reached into his overcoat, removed his identification, flashed it for Cal, then returned it to the inside pocket. He did this, more or less, without taking his eyes off the license.

Was it really taking him this long to read the name and address? Was he taking note of every piece of information it contained? No eyewear restrictions, a motorcycle endorsement, the small icon of a heart to indicate that Cal was an organ donor. Maybe the man was looking to see if the license was a fake? Why would it be? Anyway, Messing knew who Cal was, and that he'd always been that.

The son of a thief who had been the son of a thief, and so on.

"I'm going to ask you some questions," Tierno said. He handed Cal the license, then turned his attention to the cell phone, flipping it open. "This is your phone, correct?"

"No."

Tierno seemed confused by Cal's response—and perturbed. He glanced forward at Messing's reflection. There was an element of hostility in the way he looked at the detective.

"You were carrying it, were you not?" Tierno said to Cal.

"Yeah, but it isn't mine. It belongs to a friend of mine. She let me borrow it."

Tierno nodded, looked back at the phone. "Not a lot of usage, I'm told. Two incoming calls tonight, nothing at all before that. No outgoing calls, either." He pressed buttons, scrolling through the various menus.

"Like I said, it's not mine."

Tierno closed the phone but held on to it. "Officer Clarke, is it?" His question was directed to the detective in the front seat.

Messing nodded. "Yes."

Finally, Tierno directed his attention to Cal. He was in his forties, Cal guessed, with short dark hair and a square, clean-shaven face. He wore a near-permanent look of skepticism: thick black eyebrows furrowed above squinted eyes, mouth held tightly closed, an expression that somehow conveyed both neutrality and mistrust. From this Cal had concluded that the FBI agent had already decided to doubt everything Cal told him—or at least make Cal think that.

Cal, though, wouldn't be so easily baited. *His father's words were like echoes now, faint but distinguishable, repeating again and again.*

He hadn't thought of his old man for a long time. Now, countless little memories Cal didn't know he retained.

"Officer Clarke," Tierno continued, "said that you arrived looking for your friend and that you found the door open. Is that correct?"

"Yeah."

"And you went inside because you saw the blood."

Cal corrected that. "No. I went in, then saw the blood."

"So you didn't see the trail on the stairs."

"The light was out."

"You left it off?"

"No. It doesn't work."

Of course, Tierno had to know all this—getting facts wrong in this way was just another part of the game authorities liked to play.

"I don't understand something," Tierno said. "Did you have plans with your friend tonight?"

"No."

"So you just happened to stop by?"

"I hadn't heard from him all day. I came by to see if anything was wrong."

"Is there any reason why something would be wrong?"

"Other than the fact that I hadn't heard from him, no," Cal said.

Tierno nodded, said nothing to that. Maybe he knew that was a lie, maybe he didn't. It was possible that this silence was meant to unnerve Cal, compel him to fill it, elaborate, confess something, *anything*. Cal didn't for even a moment think of taking this bait, either. He instead let the silence linger, leaving it for someone else to break.

"Your friend, his name is Lebell, right?" Tierno said finally.

"Yeah."

"How do you two know each other?"

Cal hesitated. Both he and Lebell were off-the-books employees. More than that, they worked in a garage that wasn't anywhere near up to code and would certainly, should the wrong people come to know about it, be shut down in a heartbeat. Good reasons, these, not to answer the question.

"You aren't in any trouble," Messing said. "We just need to know a few things so we can figure out exactly what happened here."

"Is he dead?" Cal said.

Maybe the detective was aware of the similarity between this night and the night Cal had been told that Aaron was dead. It had been, in fact, Messing himself who broke the news to Cal.

"We're hoping to find your friend alive," Messing assured him. "We need your help if we're going to do that."

"Frankly," Tierno said, "I am a little curious how you happened to become such good friends with a man like him."

"What do you mean, 'a man like him'?"

Tierno ignored the question. "I'm going to ask you again. How do you two know each other?

"We work together."

"Where?"

"An auto shop."

"You're a mechanic?"

"Yeah."

"What did your friend do there?"

"Body work. Part-time, when we need him."

Tierno nodded, thought for a moment. There was something in the way he did that that told Cal this detail was somehow significant.

Up front, Messing said nothing, continued to watch Cal through the rearview mirror. Cal suddenly felt a flash of anger. He no longer cared who these men were, what badges they possessed and the powers that came with such things. He was tired, had had enough of their games, was about to ask what the hell was going on, was about to demand that they cut the shit, when Tierno finally spoke.

"Listen, we don't have a lot of time here, Cal. We need to know everything you know, and we need to know it now. Do you understand?"

"Okay," Cal said. "Let's talk."

"Is there somewhere your friend might have gone?" Tierno said. "Someone he would go to if he were in trouble?"

"He knew a lot of people, but I don't really know where any of them live."

"What do you mean?"

Cal shrugged. "He had a lot of . . . lady friends, but I don't know their last names or where they live or anything. Anyway—" He stopped short.

"What?"

"Most of them were married. I can't imagine him showing up at their doors in the middle of the night, no matter what kind of trouble he was in."

"You'd be surprised what a man will do when his life is on the line," Tierno said. "That's all your friend is right now, a man desperate to save his own skin."

Cal said nothing to that.

"Maybe one of those husbands is out of town," Messing suggested. "It would have to be someone nearby, though. If all that blood was his, he couldn't have gotten far."

"It's his blood," Tierno said. His tone was decisive.

Before Cal could ask how Tierno was so sure all the blood was Lebell's, the agent continued.

"I'm curious, did your friend talk about what he did before he moved out here? Where he came from?"

"No, not really."

"You worked side by side with the guy, but he didn't once talk to you about his past."

"Pretty much, yeah."

"You didn't find that unusual?"

"No."

"Why not?"

"I got the sense early on that he liked to keep certain things private."

"He was secretive."

"No, just . . . private. Protective."

"Protective of what?"

"I don't know. The women he was seeing, I guess."

Tierno thought about that, then said, "Did he ever mention a friend of his named Pearson?"

Cal didn't remember ever hearing the name and said so.

"Are you certain?"

"Yes. Why?"

Tierno paused. He took a breath, then said, "Three weeks ago a guy named Pearson was murdered. Before he was killed, though, he was tortured. Several of his finger joints were crushed. It's a pretty old-fashioned method of persuasion, but effective. Pearson made a living providing false identities. Names, Social Security numbers, driver's licenses, everything anyone would need to start his or her life over. He and the man you know as Lebell grew up in the same neighborhood. They were old friends."

This bait Cal was unable to ignore. "What do you mean, the man I know as Lebell?"

"Your friend's name isn't Lebell," Tierno said. "His fingerprints in that apartment confirm this. His real name is Militich. Technically, it isn't even Militich, but don't worry, I'll get to all that."

Cal said nothing for a while, then, "Look, I really don't care about any of this. I've told you everything I know, so just let me out, okay?"

"You should know what kind of man your friend is," Tierno said. "The piece of filth you've been palling around with, the trouble that you're in now because of him."

"Seriously," Cal said. "I want to go. Now."

No one made a move to let him out.

"Ever hear the name Militich?" Tierno said.

"Just open the door."

"Ever hear the name Militich, Cal?"

"No."

"Are you sure?"

"Yes."

"Let me tell you a thing or two about your buddy, because my guess is you know where he is and you're trying to be a good friend by protecting him. Nothing wrong with being a friend, it tells me you're a decent guy, which makes me want to help you and gives me hope that maybe we can actually work together on this. But there's more going on here than you know, a lot more, and what you think is the act of a friend, my boss is going to see as a simple case of someone harboring a fugitive. So believe me, Cal, I'm trying to be your friend here. Do you understand what I'm saying?"

It took him a moment, but Cal eventually nodded. He glanced at Messing's reflection one last time. They looked at each other, but the detective said nothing.

"A few years ago," Tierno said, "your buddy, the guy you know as Lebell and I know as Militich, worked for a man named Donny Cleary. Ever hear that name?"

Cal said he hadn't.

"Cleary was a member of a gang called the Westies. They worked out of Hell's Kitchen in New York City, did enforcement work for the Gambino crime family. They murdered, we think, about a hundred people, many of whom were tortured first. Grisly shit, savage. The Westies began back in the sixties, were most influential in the eighties, and pretty much disappeared by the nineties. Some went to jail, some died or were killed, others pulled a Whereabouts Unknown. Cleary was one of the ones who went to jail, and when he got out eight years ago he partnered up with a Yugoslavian named Militovich. Militovich had a son who later on changed his name to Militich. This was your friend's first disappearing act. He's had a few."

Tierno paused to let this sink in, then continued.

"Cleary and Militovich worked as a killer-for-hire team, were responsible, we think, for at least twenty torture-murders over eight years. That's a lot. No one knows anything about Militich's mother; we doubt even he knows. He was raised by his father and Cleary, whom he knew as Uncle Donny. In fact, Militovich did two years in prison for assault, during which Militich lived with Cleary. He was thirteen, and Cleary put him to work in one of the other family business, a chop shop on the West Side. He cut up stolen cars, thousands of them over the years. When Militich was twenty, his father was murdered, and Uncle Donny promoted him from body-shop worker to body man. Do you know what a body man is?"

Cal shook his head.

"A body man is the person who disposes of corpses. Murder victims. He chops them up, gets rid of the pieces, some here, others there, and cleans up all the incriminating evidence. That's what your friend used to do. That's the kind of man he is."

Tierno again paused to let that sink in.

"A few years ago we got a break, arrested another Yugo thug who was eager to make a deal for himself. He confessed to killing Militovich, said he had been hired to do so by none other than Uncle Donny. We saw our chance, brought Militich in, told him what we had, and offered him a deal if he testified against Cleary. He of course agreed to—I mean, what son wouldn't want to avenge his father, right? He entered the Witness Protection Program, was given a new identity, a place to live, a job, everything. This was his second disappearing act. Shortly after he testified in court, though, he gave the U.S. marshals the slip, disappeared one more time. We've been searching for him ever since, and by the looks of his place tonight, it seems we aren't the only ones after him."

"Who other than you guys would be looking for him?" Cal said.

"That's what we need to find out. It isn't all that difficult to orchestrate a hit from prison, not for someone like Cleary. One man—Pearson—is already dead, and another—your pal—might already be. I didn't spend years putting Cleary behind bars so he could continue his work from his cell. To uncover what remains of his operation and shut it down, I need to know who came after your friend. His blood trail just ends, so maybe he only got so far before whoever came after him caught up with him again, pulled him into a car. If that's the case, then we lose, he's dead. If not—if he managed to get away and hasn't bled to death somewhere—then I need to find him. I need to know what he knows, and I need to know it now."

"I wish I could help," Cal said, "but I really don't have any idea where he is."

"You don't understand, Cal," Tierno said. "Whoever was sent to kill Militich didn't just show up last night and knock on his door. They watched him, closely, for a period of time, learned his routine and patterns, the places he went and the people he associated with. A lot of work to just let him slip away. If they can't find him, they'll do what we're doing, rely on the person closest to him. But they won't just ask questions. They'll wring from that person whatever information they can get. Just like they did with Pearson. They found that guy, tortured him till they got Militich's new identity, then killed him. With that information, they were able to track Militich to here somehow. I can assure you, Cal, you don't want to be the one they come after next. I'd feel for the person who had nothing at all to tell them. Nothing to make them stop the pain."

Tierno let the final image he had created linger for a moment. The silence was eventually broken by Messing.

"Is there anything you can tell us, Cal? Anything Lebell might have said, anything you might have seen over the past year?"

"No."

"Have you had any strange visitors recently, anything like that? Seen someone lurking about, hear any weird clicks on your phone, maybe?"

Cal looked at the detective.

"What?" Messing said.

"I got a call last night."

"From whom?" Tierno demanded.

"A woman."

"What did she want?"

"She kept asking for Lebell. She wanted to know if he was there."

"Where is there?"

"The garage."

"What time was this?"

"After one."

"What were you doing there so late?"

"I was working." No reason at this point to tell Tierno that he lived there. The address on his driver's license was a Southampton post office box.

"What did you tell her?"

"I told her he wasn't there."

"Then what?"

"She wanted to know if I knew where he was."

"She asked for Lebell, not Militich?" Again, Tierno was demanding more than asking.

"Yeah."

"You're sure about that?"

"Yes."

Tierno fell suddenly silent. Messing was watching him in the rearview mirror.

"They don't have him," the detective concluded. "He got away."

"At least they didn't have him last night," Tierno said. "But have they found him since?"

Tierno studied the cell phone in his hand, thought for a long moment. Finally, he said, "If the woman who called you last night is part of this, and it's pretty obvious to me that she is, then right now your life is in danger. They know who you are, that you're his friend. They'll be coming after you—maybe even have you under surveillance already. If you help us, we'll protect you."

"How can I help if I don't know where he is?"

"He's in trouble, so there's the chance he might try to contact you. That makes you our only chance of finding him."

"We can't leave him out in the open like a piece of bait," Messing objected.

"Then take him into protective custody," Tierno said.

"How will his friend get in touch with him?"

"You don't have a cell phone of your own, correct?" Tierno asked Cal.

"I don't, no."

"Does your friend have this number?" Tierno was holding up Heather's cell.

"No."

"You have a phone where you live, though, right?"

"Yeah."

"And he has that number?"

"Of course."

Tierno said to Messing, "Put him in a motel room, have all calls to his landline forwarded there and monitored."

Messing waited a moment, glanced briefly at Cal, then nodded. "Yeah, all right," he said.

"Look, I can take care of myself," Cal said. He was speaking to both men, to anyone who would listen.

"Maybe," Tierno said, "but this isn't just about you."

"What do you mean?"

The agent held up the cell phone again. "This belongs to a friend of yours, correct?"

"Yeah. So?"

"Close friend? Girlfriend, maybe?" Tierno asked.

Cal didn't answer.

"If they can't find you, they'll find the person closest to you. That's how it works. They'll either extract what they can from her or use her to lure you out into the open. Or, and this is actually the most likely scenario, they'll do both, just to cover all the bases. Do you really want that, kid? Do you want to get a call tonight from Ms. Heather Pamona, hear her screaming on the other end, in agony, pleading for you to help her? Because that's exactly what's going to happen if you don't let us help you."

Before Cal could ask the obvious question, Tierno, looking away again, provided the answer.

"You think we didn't run this number, find out to whom it's registered?" He paused, then said, "I'm offering to take you and your friend into protective custody, for as long as necessary. Who knows, maybe after sitting around in a motel room for a while you'll remember something that can help us. In the meantime, you and she will be safe. Like I said, one man is already dead."

"There isn't a lot of time to think about this, Cal," Messing said. "We're a day behind them as it is. It's now or never, son."

Tierno held up the phone, this time offering it to Cal. He said in a flat voice, "So what's it going to be?"

What other choice did he have?

"Heather's sister is staying with us," Cal said. "She has to come, too."

"No problem."

"Who else knows about her? Heather, I mean?"

"Just Messing and me. Why?"

"It's important that no one else knows she's with me." Cal's father wasn't the only one with a distrust of the police.

"No reason at this point for anyone else to know. Just tell us where they are, and Messing will send a patrol car right over."

It was only then that Cal remembered Heather's plan to go out and pick up a new cell phone. It hit him like a shock.

His heart suddenly pounding, he reached out and grabbed her old phone from Tierno's hand. Quickly entering the number of the garage's landline, he noticed the smell of his sweat again.

It had finally overpowered the cologne that, up till now, had masked it.

A flurry of activity, phone calls and radio calls, arrangements made, cops hurrying about. Throughout, Cal's heart pounding as though he were running for his life.

Amanda had answered, which meant Heather had already left. As Cal spoke to her, Tierno exited the patrol car, stepping away to make calls of his own. Messing, still in the front seat, gave instructions to Cal, who passed them on to Amanda.

Patrol car will pick her up, take her to a local motel, Cal will be there waiting for her. Pack for a few days, just to be on the safe side.

Amanda had nothing to pack, of course, and neither, for that matter, did Heather. Cal didn't bother to correct the detective. He did, though, have some instructions of his own.

The alarm had to be deactivated so the door could be opened, then reactivated when she left.

He made Amanda promise to remember to turn the system back on, had no choice but to give her the secret code—even Lebell didn't know it—while Messing listened.

Messing had remained to make certain only the one call was made. Once Cal was done, the detective got out of the patrol car, had Clarke take his place in the front seat and keep an eye on Cal. The detective stepped away and made calls of his own, but he was close enough for Cal to hear him through the glass. He dispatched a patrol car to the garage to retrieve Amanda and another to Bridgehampton Village—there was only one cell phone store in town, he assured Cal—to find Heather.

There was nothing for Cal to do after this but wait and watch—and be watched by the cop in the front seat. He thought of Heather out there alone, thought of her husband looking for her, determined to find her. Panic began to grow, and it took all he had to keep it from taking him over.

He wanted out of that car, saw himself hopping into Lebell's Mustang and going off to find Heather on his own. He didn't care if it meant being chased by every cop on duty tonight, didn't care about the consequences, *as long as she was safe.*

Foolish thoughts, but he knew himself well enough to know that there was nothing he could do about them. They would spin, and his heart would race, till he saw her again.

At one point, Messing and Tierno were off their cell phones long enough to stand face-to-face and talk. What they said to each other, Cal couldn't hear, but it looked to him like Tierno was giving orders.

Shortly after that, Tierno left the scene, and Messing waved Spadaro over and spoke to him. Passing on the orders, no doubt, Cal thought. When Messing was done, Spadaro stepped away, leaving the detective standing alone on the street.

Messing then approached the patrol car and tapped on the window of the back door with the knuckle of his middle finger.

Clarke turned the ignition halfway to draw power from the battery, then pressed a button on the door-mounted console. The window lowered and another burst of cold air immediately filled the interior.

It quickly erased the smell of cologne and sweat.

"Clarke here is going to take you to the motel," Messing said. "An officer just left the garage with Amanda. They still haven't found Heather yet. Once they do, they'll bring her to you."

Cal nodded, didn't know whether to thank the man or not.

"Everything's going to be okay, son. We'll take care of you and your friends. I give you my word." Messing reached into his pocket, removed a business card, handed it to Cal. "If you hear from your friend, or if you think of anything you want to tell me, give me a call, okay? Call my cell anytime, day or night, it doesn't matter."

Cal looked at the card, then slipped it into the pocket of his peacoat.

Stepping back, Messing tapped on the roof with the palm of his hand. Cal's window went up; Clarke started the engine and drove them from the scene.

Just a handful of turns and they were at a motel on the very eastern edge of Southampton Village. Clarke had watched Cal in the rearview mirror more or less the entire way. He had simply looked out the window, thought only of Heather.

He waited alone in a room that felt to him as though it hadn't been used for a long time.

Cold, dormant, foreign.

Off-season in Southampton, so maybe it hadn't been.

The motel, a single-story building with twelve units, was on Hampton Road. He occupied the last room, farthest from the street. Clarke's patrol car, the officer seated behind the wheel, was parked right outside the door. He was as safe here as in the garage, perhaps, but it was the wrong kind of safe.

He hadn't known till now that there even was such a thing.

His eyes on the bedside clock, Cal watched the minutes pass. He'd been there for maybe ten minutes—a long ten minutes—when he heard the sound of a car pulling into the gravel courtyard, slowly approaching the rear unit. Parting the drawn curtain, he looked out the window and saw that it was a patrol car. He watched as it parked beside Clarke's unit. Spadaro got out from behind the wheel, stepped to the rear door, and opened it. Amanda emerged, was immediately escorted by Spadaro to the room. Clarke met them there, unlocked the door with her key, and let the girl in. Cal felt a little like a prisoner getting a visitor. Amanda was dressed in the clothes Cal had removed from her purse last night and searched for a tracking device—a pair of jeans and a T-shirt and a hooded sweatshirt. They looked at each other for a moment. It took him a bit to get used to seeing her with clothes on. She asked about Heather, and Cal told her that she was on her way. Amanda nodded, said nothing more. The room had two beds, and, turning away, Amanda removed the bedspread from one and wrapped it around herself, then sat down on the edge of the mattress.

Cal walked to the other bed, sat on its edge. Amanda wasn't looking at him, seemed to be drifting off into her own world. Still hungover from whatever it was she had been slipped the night before.

After a moment, though, she spoke. "Is it him? Has he found us?"

Cal said, "No. This is something else."

"Are you sure?"

"Yeah."

She nodded but didn't ask what that something else was.

Moments later, deeply restless, he stood and stepped to the window again, parting the curtains and watching as Clarke and Spadaro, standing by Spadaro's car, talked. Five minutes went by, then five more. He thought of the night his brother had disappeared, thought of the long hours of waiting that turned eventually into two terrible days. A living hell that only ended when Detective Messing showed up to deliver the news.

Having tried to avoid that very same situation with Lebell, he had only re-created it with Heather.

Close to a half hour passed, and there was still no sign of Heather. A sick feeling made its home in his stomach. It grew till eventually it felt as if someone were tugging at his insides, each tug more violent, more urgent, than the one before it. Finally, though, a car turned from Hampton Road into the courtyard, its headlights swinging like a pair of searchlights.

A patrol car, heading toward the other two.

Cal held his breath, couldn't help it, waited, unwilling to exhale, as the unit parked and its driver got out from behind the wheel and opened the back door.

Heather emerged then, was led right away by Clarke—quickly, as though they were at risk of coming under fire—to the motel room door.

No routine to hide himself in, no ritual to ease his mind, Cal was adrift.

In the dark, he listened to breathing—Amanda's, Heather's, his own. Amanda was asleep, Heather he wasn't so sure about.

He had told her what was going on, had answered all her questions, the two of them speaking in hushed voices while Amanda, still wrapped in the bedspread, lay motionless on the other bed. It had been a short conversation; Cal only knew so much. Listening carefully, Heather seemed to him like someone formulating an opinion. This was confirmed when she, after running out of questions, said about Lebell, "I never did like him all that much."

"Why not, exactly?"

"He always seemed . . . up to something."

Cal had said nothing to that; she was right, Lebell had always been up to something, on his way to somewhere, coming back from somewhere. Motion to Cal's stillness, chaos to his order.

"Besides," she'd added, "he was a bad influence on you." She'd smiled knowingly. "All those women, those torrid one-night stands, before I came along."

Cal, feeling a blush begin, had smiled but said nothing.

Now they were trying to get some sleep. It wasn't late, not even nine, but with Amanda asleep, and nothing left to tell her, what else was there for them to do?

As tired as he was, though, Cal couldn't sleep. Every so often he'd glance at the beside clock, note the time. *9:30, 10:00, 10:30.* He made a point of not moving, not allowing himself to toss or turn. Even though Heather was on the other bed, in a room as small and as silent as this one, she would no doubt hear the noise. If she had found sleep, he didn't want it to slip away from her because of him.

It was at a quarter to eleven that this silence was broken by the sound of a phone ringing.

Not the room's phone but a cell phone.

Heather rose from the other bed quickly and crossed to the desk, where her new cell lay. She'd needed to charge the battery, and the only available outlet was there. The ringing was muffled and continued even after Heather had reached the desk.

Then, out of the darkness, came her voice.

"It's not my phone," she whispered.

Cal realized then that the ringing was coming from the pocket of his peacoat.

It was Heather's old phone, its sound muffled by the thick wool.

He scrambled for it, reached deep into the pocket, and took hold of the phone. It was vibrating wildly, like a frantic animal.

It wasn't an incoming call but rather a text message. Cal told Heather this.

"What's it say?"

They were both speaking in hushed voices. "'Need to see you,'" he read. "'Can you meet friend of mine tonight? Please reply. Lebell.'"

"Jesus," Heather said.

Cal heard her searching for the desktop lamp. She found it finally. The room was lit up suddenly with the pale white glow of a fluorescent reading lamp.

The number the text had been sent from Cal didn't recognize.

"What should I do?" he said.

"Nothing."

"He says he needs my help."

"First of all, how did he get that number?"

The question slowed Cal, but only slightly. "I don't know."

"It's Ronnie, trying to trick you," she concluded. "Angstrom was the only other person besides you that I gave this number to. And you didn't give it to Lebell, did you?"

Cal couldn't remember doing so. Maybe drunk one night, he thought. Possible, but not likely.

"No," he said.

"So then it has to be Ronnie. We need to get rid of that thing. Right now."

Cal wasn't giving up so easily, though.

"But how would he know Lebell's name?"

"He has his ways."

"Yeah, but *how*?"

"I don't know."

Cal studied the phone. If it was Pamona, it was unnerving to be connected to him, even in such an intangible way. *He out there on Shelter Island, they hiding in a motel on the edge of Southampton Village.*

If it wasn't Pamona, if it really was Lebell, and Cal had done nothing . . .

"I'm going to respond," he said.

"Don't. Please."

"I can't just sit here, Heather."

"Even after everything you've just learned about him."

"I should at least hear his side, don't you think?"

She said nothing to that.

"We're safe," Cal reminded her. "You guys will be safe. There's a cop outside the door, the police station is only, what, three minutes away."

"A lot could happen in three minutes."

"It's Lebell, Heather. I know it is."

She thought for a moment, watching him, then finally nodded. "Do what you have to do," she said.

Cal looked at the phone, then back at her. "I'm not sure how to text."

"Give it to me."

She walked to him; he handed her the phone.

"What do you want to say?"

Cal paused, then said, "How do I know this is really you?"

Heather entered the text, pressing the keys with one thumb, then sent it. Fifteen seconds later the phone rang again.

"'62 Benz,'" she read.

"That's the car I stayed home to work on last night," Cal said. "It's him."

The phone rang again. Heather read this text.

"'Angelica, at Long Wharf, Sag Harbor.'"

"Tell him I'll be there."

"How are you going to get there?"

"I'll figure out a way. Tell him I need an hour."

Heather nodded, composed the text, sent it off. They waited, saying nothing till a reply came back. As before, it did so quickly.

"'Thanks,'" Heather read. She handed the phone back to Cal. "So now what?"

Cal wasn't all that sure. He returned to the front window and looked out. Clarke was behind the wheel, talking on her cell phone. He stepped away, looked toward the bathroom at the back of the room.

Its small window was his only other way out.

He grabbed his peacoat, put it on. "I won't be long."

"He's not your brother," Heather said. "You know that, right? He's not Aaron. He's nowhere near it."

"I know that. I just think I should see what he wants."

"Why?"

It wasn't only the people who had tried to kill Lebell—or Pamona and his men, for that matter—that Cal needed to be careful of now. There was Carver and his recent suspicious activities, details of which Lebell had promised to attempt to uncover last night. If there was a chance Lebell had in fact learned something, Cal couldn't really just sit there.

Anyway, it occurred to him that it might be best, knowing what he now knew, if he determined the manner by which Lebell had come to possess Heather's number.

Cal didn't say any of this. He answered her question with a simple "I just think I should."

"I really don't feel good about this," Heather said. "Not one bit."

"It'll be okay, I promise. Trust me, I wouldn't go if I didn't believe you were safe. Messing's an okay guy, for a cop. He gave me his word he'd take care of us."

Heather waited a moment, watching him closely, then said, "Hang on." Back at the desk she tore off a piece of paper from a notepad, wrote something down, then handed the paper to him. "This is my new number."

Cal looked at the paper, then folded it and slipped it into his pocket with Messing's business card.

"I want you to call me in two hours," she said, "no matter what. If I don't hear from you by then, I'm going out there and telling that cop that you left. And where you went."

"Fair enough."

"Please be careful."

"When am I not?"

Heather stood at the front window, serving as lookout, while Cal opened the narrow window in the bathroom. He began to climb through, and it was easy enough to get into, but there was nothing on the other side for him to hold on to or climb down on. Losing his balance, he fell to the cold ground, but it didn't matter, he was out.

Getting to his feet, he looked around, made certain no one was watching, then closed the window and hurried away.

Moving blindly at first, he realized finally that he was actually heading north, the direction in which he needed to be going. He cut through a few backyards, then was standing on Elm Street.

At its far end, three blocks away, stood the Southampton train station.

Too late for trick-or-treaters now, so most of the porch lights were unlit. No eastbound train was due till much later, but there was a pay phone on the platform, and from it Cal called for a cab.

It arrived in less than five minutes, and in the warmth of its backseat, watching the dark scenery flash past, Cal felt a little relieved to be in motion, heading somewhere with something specific to do. Nothing routine about this, and yet, right now, he didn't really give a damn about that.

He had the cabbie drop him off at the Bridgehampton train station, just a stop away from the East Hampton station, where Heather had abandoned her SUV. As he waited for the cab to roll away he wondered if Heather's husband had found her vehicle yet. He imagined the man flying into a rage, but there was no reason to waste time on that now.

Once the cab was out of sight, Cal began retracing his steps back to Scuttlehole Road. He looked around as he approached the garage, just as he had done when he left it hours ago. Carefully, methodically. He didn't see a single car parked anywhere along that dark back road, was as certain as he could be as he crossed the pavement that it was, maybe even for miles, just him and this dilapidated building and the night.

Unlocking the office door, he entered and saw right away that the alarm was inactive. Amanda, despite her promise, had forgotten to turn it on before leaving. Cal passed through the office, into the first and then the second work bay. His old Triumph motorcycle was parked at the end of the third bay. He removed the canvas cover, pushed the bike to the third bay door, switched the ignition on and off to quick-check the battery, then pushed on the tires with his thumb to make certain each had the proper air pressure.

Hurrying upstairs, he took off his peacoat, laid it on his bed, then grabbed his steerhide jacket and helmet from his closet, pulled a scarf from a hook on the back of the closet door, and tossed them all onto the peacoat.

In his bathroom, he quickly washed his face, more from a need to brace himself than to clean himself up. His hands once again were shaking. When he was done, as he dried his face and then his hands, looking at himself in the mirror, he heard a noise, or thought he'd heard one. Stepping into the doorway, pausing there, towel still in hand, he looked into his large living room, saw, though, nothing but the usual shadows.

He waited for the noise to repeat but heard nothing more. *The wind, then, pushing against the rotting wood.*

A moment later, back in his bedroom, he put on the steerhide jacket, then the peacoat over that, wound the scarf around his neck. Grabbing the helmet and removing the heavy leather gloves from inside it, he hurried back down the plank stairs.

He opened the third bay door, rolled the bike out into the night, and switched the ignition again, this time starting the engine. It caught right away. Leaving the bike to warm up, he reentered the garage, closed and locked the bay door, and inserted its pins.

He exited through the office, making sure this door was locked, then reactivated the security system from the outside keypad. He put on his gloves and helmet as he crossed gravel, then mounted the saddle, pulled in the clutch, and stepped down on the shifter lever with his toe, dropping the transmission into first gear.

It was chilly, forty-five degrees, tops. A year-round rider, Cal was used to this. On a motorcycle, at forty-five degrees, doing forty-five miles per hour, the wind chill brought the temperature for the rider down to thirty, at least. The higher the speed, the greater the drop. Thirty wouldn't be unbearable; he'd ridden in worse, and anyway what other choice did he have? He had pressed his luck with the Citroën already, didn't dare try that again.

He pulled out of the garage, leaving it behind in the night. Less than a half mile down Scuttlehole Road, Cal pulled up behind a Ford sedan that was traveling just below the speed limit. He didn't dare pass it, though, not on this winding road, and not at night, so he remained behind it till Scuttlehole's end.

There the sedan turned right, heading south toward Bridgehampton, and Cal turned left. Opening up the throttle, he moved up through the gears quickly, reaching sixty-five in a matter of seconds and maintaining that speed till, a half minute later, he realized that he was being reckless and eased back sharply on the throttle till the needle on the speedometer dropped down to forty-five.

Tucking himself into a racer's crouch, more to limit the effects of the steady blast of night air rushing past him than anything else, Cal kept an eye on the horizon ahead, saw it grow gradually lighter with each mile nearer to Sag Harbor he got.

It was just shy of midnight when he reached the edge of the village. Crossing its border, he eased back on the throttle even more, downshifting to second gear and following that narrow, well-lit Main Street till the empty pier that marked its end was finally within his sight.

Long Wharf.

Eight

In her room at the end of the hall, Evangeline Amendora waited for Janssen to arrive. He was to be there at eight, was always prompt, but it was only half past six now. An hour and a half more, then. Her only window faced south, so she didn't have to watch the actual sunset, but that was a small consolation at best; around her darkness grew gradually till she was, sitting on the edge of a bed that was still strange to her after so many nights, surrounded by complete blackness.

It was difficult in these particular moments for her to remember that she had grown tall and powerful, possessed legs and arms that were roped with lean muscle, a stomach that was tight and trim, and a back that was strong yet still sleek, still feminine. The heart and body of an Olympian, that was what she was now, nothing short of that, all the skills that she could possibly need burned deep into her muscle memory. No one could do to her what had been done to that slum child long ago. No one but *he* would ever get to touch her, and ever expect her to touch him in return.

Too much time to sit around and think. She was beginning to *deteriorate,* could feel it. The scuffle with Militich, those few but significant blows he had managed to land before bolting—this carried more than the loss of pride at having been bested, more, too, than just the sting of failure. It had stirred something deep inside her, touched a nerve she had thought would never be touched again, that she had buried beneath an armor of musculature, that was guarded by an array of techniques.

She'd been taught how to break joints, gouge eyes, choke, cut with a knife. Hours devoted to this every day, over years and years. All for Janssen, yes, to become what he needed her to be.

Every skill she absorbed, every pound of lean muscle she gained, also served to calm that frightened and brutalized girl inside her.

Militich had only fought for his life with her, she knew this. He hadn't fought to dominate her, to wear her down so he could touch her in any vile way he wanted. He hadn't smiled at her, hadn't said things to her, hadn't made her say things to him.

Nonetheless, the effect was the same. The girl she had worked hard to put to rest was awake again. Seated on the edge of a strange bed in a postsunset darkness, waiting, she vowed that he would pay for this, and soon.

Men were the prey now, and she was the one with the power.

A little before eight she received a text, assumed it was Janssen informing her that he wasn't far away and that she should come down and wait for him outside. What it contained, instead, was a set of directions, brief and to the point.

A change in plan.

She tried not to read anything into to this—it *was* curt, there was no doubt about that—and quickly memorized these new instructions, then returned the phone to her pocket.

She slung the mechanic's bag over her shoulder, grabbed the Maglite flashlight, and followed its circle of white down the long hallway to ornate stairs, making her way to the ground floor and through the kitchen. Once outside, she switched off the light and paused in the shadow of the building to have a look around.

Without her overcoat—it was buried, along with her disguise, on the edge of that backyard—she was cold, but certainly he would bring her a replacement. Anyway, living the way she had lived these past several days, she was becoming used to such discomforts.

Sensing nothing unusual from her surroundings, she walked to the sedan. In it she rode west, back toward Southampton. Less than twenty-four hours ago, her dress torn and bloodied, she had fled that same town. Of course, the woman who had done that wasn't Evangeline Amendora—dark-haired, tall, sleek—but instead another woman, one who didn't resemble her at all: red hair, blue eyes, fuller through the torso, taller still, thanks to high heels. There was for her no reason to fear returning to these streets, no reason to travel them with anything other than confidence.

There were, if anything, things to look forward to.

Whenever he traveled, Janssen stayed only in the best of places, ate only at the finest restaurants—in a town such as this, there had to be plenty for him to choose from. She looked forward to the comforts she had long since grown accustomed to—plush beds, crisp sheets, silky soaps, hot baths. There was work to do, yes, but it wasn't unreasonable, she believed, to expect they'd share a warm meal first, maybe even go off for a little time alone together. She craved his touch, the way he looked at her, the smell of him. There was no doubt he craved her, too. He required nightly lovemaking, sometimes hours of it.

A vital man with complex desires. This was the longest they had gone without each other since the night he had saved her from São Paulo life.

Her destination was a municipal parking lot on the edge of a small park in the heart of that village. Not far at all from the apartment on Meeting House Lane. She wondered if Militich, bleeding and drugged and panicked, had run through here as he made his escape.

Arriving, she saw the black Town Car right away. She steered the sedan to a far corner, where the lot was darkest. Carrying the small duffle with her, she headed toward the waiting vehicle. As she did, the driver, Karl, emerged. He opened the back door for her, and when she saw that the rear seat was empty, she knew something was wrong.

She slowed, then stopped altogether. Karl was a giant of a man. He was wearing a dark, well-tailored suit, had narrow slits for eyes.

"He's waiting," he said.

She didn't bother to ask what was going on. Karl had been with Janssen long before she'd come along. It was Karl, in fact, who had found her, fed her the first real meal she'd had in a long time, then cleaned her up himself and brought her to Janssen. A filthy girl of sixteen back then, malnourished and, in all ways, *wild.*

It was Karl who had gotten her out of Brazil, whisked her across borders, guarded her as if she were his own as they traveled by car and train and ship. *Her first of many long journeys.* It was Karl, too, who had taught her so much of what she knew about hunting and killing men.

No point, then, in asking him any questions. She was Janssen's lover, his prized possession, most valuable asset, but Karl—brutal, ugly Karl, devoted and stoic and merciless—was Janssen's right arm.

"Come along," he said. His accent was Russian, his English, though, perfect. "We shouldn't keep him waiting."

Reaching the Town Car, she threw her bag onto the floor and climbed in after it.

Once Karl was behind the wheel—he all but filled the driver's seat—he looked back at her in the rearview mirror, studying the marks on her face. "Do you need medical attention?" he said.

"No."

He nodded, said nothing more as he drove from the lot.

A five-minute ride down a wide boulevard, beyond her window grand mansions standing behind tall hedges. Three long blocks of this, and then, suddenly, at this street's end, the Atlantic Ocean.

Karl turned into the empty parking lot—more than empty, *desolate*—and made a wide arc so that when he came to a stop, Eve's side was facing the water.

She looked at his eyes in the narrow frame of the rearview mirror. He said nothing, simply nodded off to the right, in the direction of the beach, indicating that she should look there.

She saw nothing at first, and then, down by the surf line, she spotted the figure of a lone man.

Despite the distance and the darkness, she recognized him at once.

Exiting the Town Car, she crossed from the pavement onto the soft sand. The noise of the crashing waves got louder as she got nearer to him. When she was halfway he looked over his shoulder and saw her approaching, turned to face her.

He was wearing a long overcoat and scarf, both dark, a black suit and shoes. The finest of materials, of course—wool, silk, cotton, leather. *Nothing less than that for him—nothing less than that for them.*

He was tall, elegant, regal; he exuded power—more, even, than the giant Russian who came with him everywhere he went. It was a physical power, yes, a promise of remorselessness and malice that showed in the way he stood and the way he looked at you when he spoke—and didn't speak—but it was also the kind of power that comes with wealth, that belongs to men who always come out on top, would have been dead long ago if they didn't. Cunning men, men cutting for themselves a trail marked with the broken and the dead.

His hands were deep in the pockets of his overcoat, and he was holding the garment tightly around himself. She knew by this not to expect a lover's greeting. She knew, too, in an instant, that there would be no invitation back to his expensive hotel room, no warm meal or hot bath, no brief but tender dose of him.

This was *business*.

As always, once she read his mood, she deferred to it.

"Hello, Evie," he said. His deep voice easily broke through the sound of the waves crashing behind him.

"Hello."

He looked her over, taking note of the scratch on her face and the bruise under her eye. *The evidence of her failure.* She just stood there, let him see her, see *through* her.

"Things have gotten . . . tricky all of a sudden," he said finally.

She waited, saying nothing.

"The best of plans can fall apart, I realize that," he said, "but last night's error has required me to get directly involved. The more directly involved I am, the more I risk exposure. Do you understand this?"

"Yes."

"I need you to make this right."

"I will. I promise."

"My sources tell me that Militich's friend has been taken into protective custody. The kid claims to have no idea where Militich has gone. Of course, I need to know whether that's true or not." He paused, glanced up and down the beach, studying their surroundings carefully, then looked at her again and said, "How badly do you think you hurt Militich?"

"I didn't hit any arteries. There would have been more blood, and he would have bled out in a minute or so. They would have found him out on the street. The closest I came was a cut to his inner thigh. The deepest cut, I think, was across his stomach."

"Enough to open his gut?"

"No."

Janssen thought about that for a moment.

"No one with any kind of knife wound has been admitted to the hospital in the past twenty-four hours," he said. "None of the taxi companies or train personnel have reported seeing a bleeding man. So he has to be somewhere nearby. Very nearby. Someone would've had to patch him up. If we're lucky, he's still with that someone, too hurt to move." Janssen paused again, then said, "Are you sure you heard him right?"

"Yes. He said things would go badly for you if he were killed."

"The bluff of a desperate man?"

"He seemed to believe what he was saying, but it's possible he was bluffing."

Janssen thought about that, too. Then he said, "Unless you hear otherwise, the objective is to kill him. The only hope we have right now of finding him is that kid. I want you to go to his place, do a complete search. I want every number on his caller ID, his last outgoing phone call. I want photographs, address books, matchbooks, everything. Are we clear?"

She nodded. "Yes."

"If worse comes to worse, we go in and grab him. They only have one cop watching him. I'd rather it didn't come to that, of course. I'd rather not start killing cops. We're supposed to be tying up loose ends here, not creating new ones."

"I understand."

"And I'm going to need you to stay at that place till this is over. I need this for two reasons. First, I want you to know what we stand to lose if we don't find Militich. Second, this just might have to end there, so I want you to set up the basement. Okay?"

Eve nodded again.

"Karl has some things for you. Food, clean clothes, some additional equipment. And he has photographs of the kid." He looked Eve up and down one last time. "You know your value to me," he said, "but you cannot fail again. Is that clear?"

"Very."

Janssen stepped toward her and removed his left hand from his coat pocket. He handed her a piece of paper. "These are directions to where the kid lives. His place has an alarm system, but my contact provided the code. It's written below the address. The police are on their way there right now. Apparently this Rakowski kid has two women staying with him. You'll have to give the cops time to clear out. With the kid in custody, you won't be disturbed, so take your time, be as thorough as you can."

Eve placed the paper in her pocket. Janssen stepped closer still. Even with the gusts of seaside wind rushing past them, she could smell him now.

Her stomach tightened.

"You have till morning to make this right," he said.

In the warmth of the Town Car again, the two of them in the dark backseat, together briefly, Karl driving, not once looking back at them in the rearview mirror. Privacy now, so she dared to reach across the seat and take his hand. He accepted the gesture, intertwined his fingers with hers—his hand thick, the brutish hand of a butcher, her fingers long and slender and strong. He kept his eyes forward, but she looked at him, studied his profile.

When they reached the village parking lot, Karl, without looking back, handed over the seat a package wrapped in festive birthday paper. She exited the Town Car, her mechanic's bag over her shoulder, the box under one arm. Not an unusual sight then, a beautiful woman, bearing a gift, exiting such a car. As the Town Car drove away, she walked to the sedan, got in and drove back to the abandoned hotel, then made her way to her room at the end of the upper hall.

It was there that she removed the wrapping and opened the box.

Inside was a black leather jacket, short-waisted, with a quilted flannel lining; black leather gloves; a few more days' worth of food, toiletries, and clothing; a lock-picking kit; and a hard plastic box, similar to a handgun case but slightly larger.

She knew what the case contained but opened it anyway, saw the tracking device and small notebook computer and micro satellite dish, checked to make sure everything was there and in working order. She let this task take time because she had time to kill, and because there was no room for failure.

Closing the case, she placed it in her mechanic's bag, along with the lock-picking kit, then grabbed the jacket and put it on—a perfect fit, of course. Placing the gloves in the pockets, she checked the directions and saw that the place where Militich's friend lived was actually only a few miles away—not far, in fact, from the train station at which she had arrived all those long nights ago.

She memorized the directions, then tore the paper to pieces and picked up the photographs of the kid, studying them. Surveillance photos, taken by the team that had observed Militich prior to her arrival. On the back of one were notes written in Janssen's hand.

Rakowski, Adam C. Goes by name Cal. Twenty-two, five-foot-nine, one hundred and fifty pounds. Shorter than she, and only ten pounds heavier. A pup, a pretty boy—no match for her.

When she was done with the photos she tore them up, too, flushed their pieces, along with the pieces of paper that had been the directions, down the toilet. Nothing left then but to let the time pass—an hour, and then another, just to be safe. It took all she had, though, to keep herself still and quiet her mind. Finally, at eleven, she was done with all her waiting. More than that, she felt the return of the one thing that would save her, the only thing that put real distance between herself and that slum child running wild: a purpose, and everything depending on her fulfilling it.

A slow drive past the garage—as sorry-looking as the hotel, easily. It was dark, not a sign of anyone inside or out. She maintained her speed as she passed, didn't once touch the brake pedal. *If you can't learn to see what you need with a quick look,* Karl had once told her, *then go back to selling your body for money.* A few hundred yards and several turns in the road later, she pulled over and parked, killing the lights and engine. She needed to leave distance between this vehicle and her destination, but not a distance that she couldn't quickly cross. A trade-off, but that was what this job was, a series of calculated risks, as reasonable a balance as was possible between precautions heeded and precautions ignored.

Carrying her bag, the leather gloves on, she backtracked on foot, walking along the edge of the dark road, careful not to stray from the pavement. Once she reached the building, she paused briefly, sizing it up, determining several routes of escape. Crossing the gravel driveway to the door, she entered the code into the keypad, deactivating the alarm. Using the picklock, she had the door open in less than half a minute.

With her small flashlight she quick-searched the office, conscious always of the fact that not far away was a large window that looked out onto the driveway and the road beyond. There wasn't much to this room—just a desk and chair, no filing cabinet or safe. Looking through the desk drawers, she found only work orders, names and addresses and phone numbers, makes and years of cars and lists of parts and total hours of labor. She placed the papers in her bag—one of these names and addresses might prove useful—then left the office, moving slowly through three work bays. In each was an old vehicle. Along the wall to her right was a workbench, on top of it several tool chests of varying size. A clean workspace—this kid, like her, took care of his tools. A tidy workshop, maybe, but the place smelled of oil and grease and gasoline, an odor that was both pungent and stale.

In the third bay was a shelf and what looked to her like a motorcycle covered with a canvas tarp. It was there that she saw what she was looking for: a set of plank steps leading up.

Climbing them, she felt soft, rotting wood beneath her feet. *Just like back at the hotel.* At the top was a door that wasn't any better. She walked through it, into a makeshift kitchen, and from there into a large living room.

On the other side of that living room were two bedrooms divided by a bathroom. She entered the bedroom to the left, began to search through it, smelled instantly a hint of roses; saw, though, none. It was a small room, just big enough for a single bed and bureau. She opened each of the bureau drawers, found that all but one were empty, and in that one only a handful of things. A woman's things. On the bureau top was a small vial of jasmine rose oil. This explained the smell. So, not this kid's room, his woman's room.

She then moved to the other bedroom, found that it, like the first one, was furnished only with a single bed and bureau. Unlike the other room, there was no smell of roses here. She opened the bureau drawers; all but one were empty. What that one contained wasn't anything that would help her. This room, she realized, had a closet. Opening it, she saw a leather jacket and motorcycle helmet, both hanging on hooks within easy reach. Further in the closet, on a long bar, hung clothes. Above the bar, shelves, upon which were small cardboard boxes. She stepped inside the closet, intending to examine these boxes, felt suddenly one of the planks beneath her feet give slightly.

She paused, shined her light down at it, then knelt.

A loose floorboard.

She was feeling around its edges, looking to pry it up, when she heard a noise coming up from the garage below.

The sound of a door being closed.

She stood, listened again, heard even more noise. *Someone was here.* She left the closet, then the bedroom, moving as carefully as she could. Finding a window, she looked down at the gravel driveway below, saw, though, no sign of a vehicle. A minute passed, and she heard even more noise coming up from downstairs.

Then, finally, the sound of someone coming up the plank steps, moving with purpose.

There was no time for her to make her way back into either of the bedrooms, so she hurried to the darkest corner of the living room, at the threshold between the living room and the kitchen. She backed into it and, once she was there, removed one of her Spyderco knives. As she opened it, the blade clicking into place, the apartment door opened.

She listened as whoever had entered moved through the kitchen and into the living room—moving right past her and heading straight for the bedroom to the right.

She got only a glimpse of him, saw enough, though, to recognize the kid.

Had the cops let him go? she wondered. Had he somehow sneaked out on his own? If so, why? The moment the kid entered the bedroom, she stepped from the dark corner and slipped into the kitchen and took cover in there, on the other side of an old refrigerator.

She waited only a few seconds, then leaned out a bit so she could see around it. She watched as this kid, visible through the open bedroom door, took off his peacoat and tossed it onto the bed. Then he disappeared, returning into her line of sight a moment later with the leather jacket and helmet in his hands. He was obviously going somewhere, and in a hurry. Maybe he would lead her to Militich?

To make her move to the door would mean leaving the cover of the refrigerator and risking being seen, so she held steady, waiting for the right time. After a moment the kid left the bedroom and stepped into the bathroom. He was out of sight, but she heard water running and knew that now would be her best bet; the sound of the water would cover whatever sounds she could not avoid making.

She hurried across the kitchen to the door, opened it and moved through, closing it as quietly as she could. She crept down the rotting plank steps, using her flashlight to find her way. Once she reached the bottom, she saw that the motorcycle had been uncovered and moved to the bay door.

It was exactly what she had been hoping for.

She stepped to the bike, dropped to her knees, and removed the hard plastic case from her mechanic's bag. She opened it, grabbed the tracking device, searched the motorcycle for a good place to attach it. The underside of the primary cover on the left side of the engine, she decided. A good hunk of metal here for the heavy magnet to cling to.

Once done, she packed up and hurried for the exit. The security system was still unarmed, so she opened the door and stepped through, was in the process of closing it as carefully as she could when a sudden wind hit it, pulling the knob from her gloved hand.

The door closed with a slam, but there was no time to worry about that. She took off down the dark road, in an all-out run, the sound of the wind filling her ears.

Her powerful legs pumped beneath her, her strong lungs held. She could run like this for miles if she had to.

Inside the sedan, she laid the gear on the seat beside her: the small notebook computer, satellite antenna, power adapter. Plugging the adapter into the cigarette lighter, she started the engine but kept the lights off, then powered up the computer and attached the antenna. Within two minutes she had the program running and was looking at the signal from the tracking device, set within a detailed map of the area.

She waited, and it was only a matter of minutes before the signal began to move, heading in her direction. She switched on the head-lights and pulled out onto the road, just as the motorcycle appeared in the rearview mirror. She didn't speed, there was no reason for that, simply followed the road to its end. The bike stayed behind her the en-tire way.

She had a fifty-fifty choice—turn right or left. She chose right, saw as she headed south the motorcycle turn left, heading north. She waited till it was out of sight—the kid had opened up the throttle, was over the crest of the long rising road in seconds—and then turned around.

Driving slowly, she monitored the signal, making a point of staying a good half mile behind it.

It was only a matter of minutes before the signal, after making a series of turns, came to a stop.

The map indicated a town called Sag Harbor was ahead. She could see it now, a nest of lights emerging out of the darkness.

Nine

———◆◆◆———

Cal reached the end of Main Street, paused at the stop sign long enough to satisfy any cop that might have been watching and to determine that the pier directly ahead was empty. Then he turned right, and right again, heading up a narrow and dark backstreet that ran behind Main.

He traveled a few hundred feet, then pulled into the parking lot of a deli, which was closed, along with almost everything else on this street. The only exception was Murph's Backstreet Tavern, a run-down watering hole directly across from the deli.

Switching off the motor, Cal swung the kickstand down with the heel of his boot and dismounted. His helmet hid his face, and he found suddenly that he was just a little reluctant to give up this mask. Still, he couldn't walk around like this—or could he? It was, after all, Halloween. As he removed his gloves, he focused on the tavern, watched as a couple exited—arm in arm, clearly drunk and happy, the man dressed in a top hat, white tie, and tails, the woman in a leopard print dancer's leotard, fluffy cat ears, and thigh-high leather boots with four-inch stiletto heels. As they approached their vehicle, the couple suddenly stopped and embraced, kissing passionately. The woman reached up under the tails of the man's tail coat and aggressively grabbed his buttocks with both hands, pulling him closer. The man removed his top hat and placed it on her head, where it stayed for a moment before falling off. Laughter interrupted their kiss, and their embrace was broken as the woman bent down to pick up the hat. She began to lose her balance, but the man caught her just in time. As she stood up straight, she placed the hat back on her head, then playfully grabbed the man's crotch and, laughing loudly, pulled him by it as if he were a dog on a leash. He happily let himself be led.

This couple only had eyes for each other, so they didn't see Cal, didn't even look up and down the dark backstreet as they crossed it. Cal nonetheless waited in the deli's parking lot till they had gotten into their vehicle and driven away.

The street quiet again—virtually lifeless, it seemed to him, like an unused movie set—he unfastened the chin strap and removed his helmet, stuffed his gloves inside it, then hung it on the right-side foot peg and began to backtrack down the half block toward the water.

He reached the marina first, which was to the right of the pier. There were only a few sailboats moored at its docks tonight, all of them covered with tarps and bobbing out of sync with one another in the steady chop. Beyond them, a little over a mile away, Shelter Island loomed. Cal looked at it briefly before turning and making his way over to the foot of the pier.

It jetted out one hundred yards into the harbor. No one was waiting upon it—no one was *anywhere*—so he headed toward its end. Upon reaching it, he found he had nothing left to do but wait alone in that rushing wind, only the short span of dark and turbulent water between himself and Shelter Island.

Were they still there? he wondered. Heather's husband; the man who worked for him; Angstrom; those guests; the women brought there to serve them? Or had Heather's husband, enraged at having been beaten by Heather, beaten at his own game, called the party off and sent everyone away?

Eventually he turned and studied the brightly lit Main Street ahead. The woman he was to meet would, of course, come from this direction. He saw no one on foot, though, and no vehicles in motion. It wasn't long before he heard from somewhere the sound of a car door close. It echoed, then was gone. He couldn't pinpoint where it had come from, but soon enough a figure emerged from a dark side street just a little ways up Main and began walking in his direction.

It moved with steady gait, on an unwavering path, and reached the pier in a little under a minute. By then Cal could see that it was, in fact, a woman.

She was wearing a dark wool coat, with an old leather belt around the waist and a paisley scarf around her neck. Holding her hands deep within the pockets of the coat, she carried no purse. The heels of her boots clicked on the pavement, a sound, due to the wind, that Cal only heard after she had crossed onto the second half of the pier.

When she reached him he saw that she was an older woman, maybe forty, maybe fifty. *Twice his age, at least.* She had long dark hair, stray strands of which blew across her face, getting caught in the corners of her mouth. She removed her right hand from her coat pocket and pulled the hairs free, first from one corner, then the other. There was enough light at Long Wharf for Cal to see that she was fair-skinned and had dark brown eyes—a beautiful woman, but there was no surprise here, Lebell had always attracted those. It would not have surprised Cal at

DANIEL JUDSON ✦ 162

all if he were to see, should she at some point remove her left hand from her pocket, a band of gold around her ring finger.

Composed, almost serene, she showed no hint of apprehension about being on the end of that pier, on the edge of a desolate town, with someone she didn't know—and, clearly, she was in no hurry. She smiled warmly, making Cal feel they were old friends who hadn't seen each other in a long time. Or, he thought suddenly, maybe that was for the benefit of anyone who might be watching. When she spoke, her voice was clear and steady and surprisingly deep.

"I'm guessing you're Cal. I'm Angelica."

Cal nodded, tried to offer a smile that matched hers. "Hi," he said.

"We're supposed to wait a few minutes and make sure you weren't followed," she explained. "Mickey gave me a long list of things we should and shouldn't do."

"Mickey?"

"Sorry. Lebell. I still can't get used to his new name." She looked over her shoulder toward Main Street, studied it for a moment, then faced Cal again. "I didn't realize you were so young," she said. "He said you were, but I didn't know you were this young."

Cal wasn't really sure how to respond to that. His first instinct was to tell her that he was twenty-two, but he couldn't think of a way to say that without sounding defensive and, therefore, young. In the end he simply asked how Lebell was.

"He needs a doctor, but he refuses to go to the hospital. Maybe you can help me with that. Maybe you can talk some sense into him."

"Do you know what happened?"

"He'll tell you." She nodded toward Main Street. "My car is around the corner. We'll go in a minute."

"I have my bike."

"You rode here on a bike?"

"A motorcycle."

"Oh. You're probably going to need to leave that here."

"Why?"

"He told me specifically to drive you to him in my car."

"The thing is, I didn't bring a cover or lock. If I leave it, it might get stolen. If I'd known, I would have found another way to get here. I don't own a car."

Angelica thought about that, glanced once more toward Main Street. "I guess you'll follow me, then," she said. "I guess that'll have to be okay."

"Where exactly are we going?"

"Don't worry, it isn't far. Just stay behind me."

Moments later they were crossing over the bridge to North Haven, just as Cal had done the night before on his way to the Shelter Island ferry. Angelica's vehicle was a brand-new silver Lexus with tinted windows. Perhaps, Cal thought, this was the reason Lebell had wanted him to ride with her—dark windows would mean no one could see who was inside.

Angelica paused at the end of North Haven Road. A right-hand turn would have taken them down the long incline to the ferry landing, so Cal was relieved when her vehicle turned left. She led him through the back roads of Noyac and North Sea, keeping at all times to the posted speed limit. She had suggested that Cal keep an eye on his rearview mirrors as they went, be on the lookout for any sign that they were being followed. He did so, saw, though, not one indication of a single soul in the darkness behind them the entire way to Southampton.

They took the long way through the village, a circuitous, precautionary route that ended at the entrance to a property guarded by tall hedges and a wrought-iron gate on Ox Pasture Road.

So, walking distance, more or less, from Lebell's apartment, just like Tierno and Messing had said.

The electronic gate, triggered by Angelica inside the Lexus, swung open. The Lexus proceeded through, and Cal followed, moving from the smooth pavement to a driveway of loose white stones that shifted beneath his tires. To the right of this driveway stood an old house—a classic Long Island mansion, four-story Nautical. Angelica, however, didn't head for that; instead, she made an immediate left turn and came to a stop beside a small cottage located just beyond the gate.

No, less than a cottage, Cal noted. A gatehouse. A square, single-story structure, its walls fieldstone, its roof dark overlaying shingles. Like the mansion—like most of the homes on Ox Pasture—it was easily close to a century old.

Cal parked beside the luxury car, dismounted, and removed his helmet and gloves. None of the property's many outside lights were on, and none of the windows of the main house were lit. The only source of light, aside from what strayed onto the grounds from a distant streetlamp beyond the tall hedgerow, was the flickering glow inside the gatehouse.

Like candlelight, Cal thought, but brighter, and with an orange tint. A fire, maybe.

Angelica emerged from behind the wheel, smiled her warm smile again, and waved for him to follow her. She led him inside the gatehouse, through a small living room, and into an even smaller kitchen. The place was warm and cozy; it smelled of burning wood. Cal immediately located the source of that smell, and of the dancing light he had seen from outside: an old stone hearth in the center of the kitchen, two halves of a log burning within it, a pile of glowing embers beneath.

Beside the hearth was an array of tools—black iron tongs, various pokers, a small ash shovel, even an old brass bed warmer. Antiques, every one of them, just like everything else around them.

Beyond the kitchen was a bedroom, the only possible remaining room in this tiny place. Before taking him to it, though, Angelica stopped. Facing him, she stood a foot or so away. He could see now the fine lines around her eyes and the corners of her mouth, could smell her perfume and shampoo. Her presence, her closeness to him, held him for a second like a spell. She undid the old leather belt and removed her overcoat, was wearing a black knit turtleneck sweater and jeans. A slender woman, he could see now, with a swimmer's build. Or maybe the build of someone who practiced yoga regularly. That would explain the poise, he thought.

"He's in pretty bad shape," she whispered. "You should prepare yourself, okay?"

He nodded, and Angelica led him to the doorway of that final room, which was lit only by the glow of a digital clock. It was, though, more than enough.

On a bed with a high brass headboard lay an unconscious Lebell. He was shirtless, his muscular torso a patchwork of bloodstained bandages—across his stomach, his chest, his left shoulder and right forearm. A white sheet and comforter covered him to his waist.

Angelica stepped to the side of the bed, reached down gently to wake him. Cal glimpsed both of her hands then, saw long fingers with manicured nails, prominent tendons and veins, and soft, slightly freckled skin.

Not a single ring, however.

Lebell stirred, opened his eyes, looked up. He seemed confused for a moment, almost recoiled, then, gathering his wits, recognized the woman leaning over him.

Like a man pulled from a nightmare.

"We're back," she whispered.

Lebell nodded once, searched for Cal in the dimly lit room, spotted him in the doorway. He smiled as best he could. "Thanks for coming, bro," he said.

The edges of his eyelids were red and swollen, like skin that had been freshly peeled. This, plus the bloodshot eyes themselves, set within a face that was gravelly pale, was more than enough to tell Cal that his friend was in constant pain.

Cal smiled back the best he could. He needed, though, a moment to adjust to the shock. He had never seen anyone so badly injured, and the thought that all this damage—so many cuts, so many *slices*—had been inflicted upon one person by the hand of another simply stunned him.

There wasn't time to dwell on that, he told himself.

"Cal and I need to talk for a little bit," Lebell said to Angelica.

"Of course." She stood up, turned to Cal. He was still lingering in the doorway. "Do you need anything?" she asked. "Coffee? A drink, maybe? You look like you could use something."

"No. I'm good, thanks."

She stepped to the doorway, then stopped, waiting with a patient smile for Cal to realize that he was blocking her way. When he finally did, he immediately moved into the small room. He had taken, though, only a single, tentative step.

Angelica touched his shoulder. "It's okay. Talk to him."

He looked at her. As dimly lit as the bedroom was, this was the brightest light they had so far shared. He could see more clearly the lines around her eyes and mouth, make out, too, a pattern of freckles across the bridge of her nose. *Delicate features, a pristine beauty.* She was— whoever she was—a well-tended woman, in that way wealthy women can be. Fit, polished, centered. For some reason it wasn't till this moment that he'd realized she was not only old enough to be his mother but Lebell's as well.

. "I'm going run up to the main house," she said. "There's an inter-com in the kitchen here. If you need anything, just press the talk but-ton."

Cal nodded.

"Try to talk some sense into him, if you can. I'll be back in a few minutes."

She glanced at Lebell, then left. Cal watched as she moved through the kitchen and living room. Once she was out the door, he and Lebell— the man he had known for this past year as Lebell—were alone.

Lebell had removed a cigarette from a pack and placed it between his lips, was lighting it with a slim silver lighter.

"Could you hand me that ashtray?" he said. His voice was both a gasp and a grunt.

Cal spotted an ashtray on the beside table, stepped to it. He picked it up—it was a heavy, ornate thing, made of thick, amber-colored glass— and placed it on the bed next to Lebell, angling it so his friend could get to it with a minimum of effort. It was obvious that even the smallest movement caused Lebell tremendous pain.

"Thanks, man," Lebell said.

He took a long drag, let the smoke out. It lingered between them briefly, then trailed upward in ghostly, shifting ribbons.

"Since when do you smoke?" Cal asked.

"It's been a while. Cigarettes make good aspirin. I read that in a book once."

Cal thought of the morphine under the floorboard in his closet, considered offering to get it but held off.

"So," Lebell said, "I'm curious. How exactly did you get out of pro-tective custody?"

Cal was taken aback a little. "How do you know about that?"

"Angel knows the chief of police. When I was able to, I asked her to have him send a cop to watch the garage. He said he'd arrange it, and then he called back and said you were already under guard. You and two women."

Cal nodded. "Heather and her sister," he offered.

Lebell smiled. "Building yourself quite the harem there, Cal. Sheikh Rakowski. It has a nice ring to it."

"Why did you try to send a cop to watch the garage?"

"Just in case in the person who came after me decided to come after you. Which she has, it looks like."

"She?"

"Yeah. Women, you know. Can't live with them."

Cal glanced at the bloodied bandages again. "How did you know she's after me?"

"She called the garage, didn't she?"

"You know about that?"

"Like I said, Angel knows the chief. She's done a lot of charity work for them over the years."

"This is her place?"

"Yeah."

"She lives here all alone?"

"Her husband died a few years ago."

"And how do you know her?"

"She's not one of mine," Lebell said, "if that's what you're asking. She used to . . . go around with my father. After my mother died."

"What do you mean, 'go around'?"

"Let's just say she's come a long way from the West Side. She was a kid, she was poor, there were only one or two ways for someone like her to make money. Do the math."

Cal immediately understood. If he hadn't gone to Shelter Island the night before, hadn't seen what he'd seen and heard what he'd heard, it might have taken him a bit longer.

"Everyone's got a past, Cal. That's hers. She's done well for herself since, and that's what matters, don't you think?"

Before Cal could say anything to that, or even think about it, Lebell said, "Listen, I need to ask you some things, okay? Things we couldn't ask the chief."

It was then that Cal remembered his reason for having come here. "I need you to tell me something first," he said.

Lebell nodded. "Okay."

"I need you to tell me how you got Heather's phone number. Because I don't remember giving it to you, and it was supposed to be secret."

By Lebell's reaction it was obvious this wasn't at all what he had been expecting to be asked. He seemed relieved, even smiled briefly. "I found it in your wallet one night, on a slip of paper," he said.

"What were you doing in my wallet?"

"It was a Friday night. We were out, and it was your turn to buy a round. You were off talking to some woman, so I called over to you, told you to pony up. Your jacket was on the stool next to me, and your wallet was inside. You told me to grab the money out of it."

Cal actually remembered that night. It was a week, maybe two, after Heather's arrival. He remembered the lack of interest he'd felt for the girl he was talking to. Sitting with her, half-listening to her, he couldn't stop thinking of Heather back at his place, alone.

A small amount of anger pulled him from that memory.

"And you just happened to memorize her number?" he said.

"A moment of weakness." Lebell waited, then said, simply, "She's hot."

"She's pregnant."

"She won't always be." He shrugged. "Like I said, it was a moment of weakness. I'm sorry, bro."

Cal said nothing. The trace of anger—foolish anger, a blind reaction of the male ego—was leaving him.

"Anyway," Lebell said, "it was a good thing I did since you weren't at the garage. Even if you were, that line wasn't safe anymore, according to the chief."

Call nodded. *If he had gotten rid of that phone like Heather had told him to . . .*

"What do you need to know?" he asked.

"The chief said an FBI agent named Tierno talked to you. What did he tell you?"

"That your name used to be Militich, and that before that it was Militovich. That you used to dispose of dead bodies for a man named Cleary, who you testified against and sent to prison for hiring someone to kill your father."

"What else?"

"That you ditched the Witness Protection Program and came out here." Cal paused. "Is that true?"

"Yeah. Well, most of it is, anyway."

"Which part isn't?"

"Cleary didn't hire anyone to kill my father."

Cal needed a moment. "I don't understand. Tierno said someone confessed to it."

Because of the cut along his stomach, Lebell could only breathe shallowly. Talking had left him winded, and he paused to catch his breath.

"I only ever disposed of bodies," he said finally. "I want you to know that. I didn't have anything to do with killing. I drew the line there, and I got out before it became time for me to cross it."

It seemed to matter to Lebell that Cal understood this. It didn't, however, ease Cal's confusion.

"I'm not sure I'm following. If Cleary didn't kill your father, then why'd you say he did?"

"Because that's what I was told to say."

"By who?"

"A man named Janssen." Lebell watched Cal's reaction. "Did Tierno by any chance mention that name?"

"No."

"I didn't think he would."

"I'm still not following," Cal said. He heard impatience in his voice.

"Maybe you should sit down, Cal."

There was a chair in the corner—an antique, like everything else in this place. Cal pulled it close to the bed. Sitting down, he leaned close and waited.

Lebell's cigarette was done. He removed and lit another.

"Do you know what a fixer is?" he said.

Cal shook his head.

"He brings people together. People who need certain things done but can't get their hands dirty, and people who don't mind getting their hands dirty as long as the money is right. He's a buffer for both parties."

"This Janssen guy's a fixer?"

"He's *the* fixer. He does work for everyone from big corporations to organized crime to government officials. With officials it's usually in exchange for some kind of favor or special treatment. As far as everyone else goes, as long as they can afford him, he'll take care of what they need. He started out as an international lawyer but realized soon enough that he could make a killing *by* killing, if that's what the job required. The person who tried to kill me works for him."

"How do you know that?"

"I made it a point once to find out everything I could about him. Word was he had this woman that he found somewhere. No one's sure where. He took her in, spent years building her up, training her. Now she's his own private assassin. No one has ever seen her—well, no one who lived to talk about it."

"Except for you."

"Yeah." He nodded, took another drag from his cigarette. "It turns out she was all done up in this disguise. A wig and all that. I was too drunk to notice when I sat down next to her. Or maybe I did but just didn't care."

"So why is this Janssen guy after you?"

"A few years ago he convinced me to testify against Cleary."

"Wait you just said Cleary didn't kill your father."

"He didn't. Cleary and my father were like brothers. Cleary was like an uncle to me. But Janssen was . . . very convincing."

"What do you mean?"

"You have to understand, I wanted out. Out of that life, the city, that whole . . . family thing. It was . . . rotten, but it was all I ever knew—my father and my uncle and men just like them, these were the people I grow up around. Janssen said that if I testified, I'd get a new life, not to mention immunity for everything I'd done. A fresh start, you know."

"How could Janssen offer you immunity?"

"He couldn't—but the man who had hired him could."

It took Cal a moment.

"Tierno?"

Lebell nodded. "There was a guy who was in prison already, for life. He had agreed to confess that he had been hired by Cleary. If he didn't, his family would have been killed. That's how Janssen works. He finds your weakest spot and fucks with it. All I had to do was testify that I saw this guy murder my father and I'd be free. It didn't really matter to me that the man I had called Uncle Donny my whole life went to prison for something he had nothing to do with. He had killed so many people—not just killed but tortured. I mean, sick shit. Anyway, he had made it clear after my father died that he wanted me to do start doing more. 'Gonna have to start pulling your weight', he kept saying. He wanted to promote me to killer. There was no way I was going to do that. No way."

"But why would Tierno hire a guy like Janssen? I mean, he's the fucking FBI. It doesn't get more powerful than that, right? My father used to live in fear of them."

"Tierno had made a career out of rounding up the Westies, was determined to get the last of them. He'd become obsessed with my uncle, got close to nailing him a few times, but the guy always slipped away—and slipped him the finger as he did. It became a whole thing between the two of them." He paused, caught his breath, then said, "Listen, Cal, I've known a lot of corrupt men in my life. Half of them, at least, carried some kind of badge or another."

"Why did you ditch on the Witness Protection Program?"

"I started to feel like a sitting duck. I kept catching myself looking over my shoulder everywhere I went, jumping at shadows. At my *own* shadow. It's no way to live, man, let me tell you. I started going nuts—I mean crazy, you know, Howard Hughes crazy."

"You were protected, though. What were you afraid of?"

"A man like Janssen—a man with resources and list of powerful clients—has a long reach."

"But you testified the way he wanted they you to. Why would he come after you?"

"My father told me something a long time ago," Lebell said. "'Don't enter into any deal without first knowing a way out of it.'"

Cal waited for him to elaborate.

"I had two face-to-face meetings with Janssen. I managed to record one of them, the second one, where he's coaching me to commit perjury."

"How?"

"My buddy Pearson wasn't only good at making false IDs. He was a whiz at surveillance, at the tech stuff. He was one of those natural mechanical geniuses, kind of like you."

Cal hesitated, then said, "Did the chief tell you? About what happened to him?"

Lebell nodded. "Yeah. It's hard to think about, the things they probably did to him to get him to talk. It's hard to think of my friend being put through that because of me. That's why I had Angel call the chief."

"Is that why Janssen's trying to kill you? Because you made recordings?"

"No. He doesn't even know about them. Neither does Tierno. I tried to tell that fucking bitch of his, but she wouldn't listen."

"If he doesn't know, then why did he come after you?"

"Janssen is retiring. The word was he was going around tying up certain . . . loose ends. People who know too much, people who have crossed him. I didn't know if I was on his hit list or not, but I didn't really want to sit around and find out the hard way, you know. The funny thing is, it might actually have been my ditching that put me on his list, made him think of me as a threat. But like I said, I couldn't just sit there, jumping at my own shadow."

Cal thought about that, nodding. Lebell took a few more drags on his cigarette.

"So what do we do now?" Cal said eventually.

"The chief said Tierno and a detective named Messing interviewed you."

"Yeah."

"Do you know him at all? The detective, I mean."

"Kind of."

"What do you mean?"

"He had been assigned to my brother's case."

Lebell, of course, knew the story. As much as he guarded his own past, he was still interested in Cal's.

"Do you think maybe he'll help us?" Lebell said.

"How?"

"If I can prove to him that Tierno is in on this, maybe he'll agree to do something for us."

"How are you going to do that? The tapes?"

"No, they only incriminate Janssen. My guess is Janssen got my new identification from Pearson and then passed it on to Tierno. The chief said Messing reported that Tierno was at my apartment within about a half hour."

"So?"

"Tierno lives and works in the city, Cal. His unit is in Manhattan. He just happened to be out here, a half hour from my apartment, the night after Janssen tried to kill me."

Cal said nothing.

"According to the chief, he got a call from Tierno two weeks ago— the day, in fact, after Pearson was killed. Tierno asked the chief if he would mind keeping an eye out for a fugitive. He gave the chief all my names, which is why they ran my prints so fast. When the name Militich was kicked out, Messing called Tierno."

"How did Tierno know you were out here?"

"I told Pearson where I was going. I didn't tell him why, thank God."

"What do you mean?"

"I came out here because Angel was out here. She helped me find my apartment, tipped me off to Carver, that his garage might be a good place for me to find off-the-books work. If I had told Pearson that, Janssen would have found me a whole lot sooner."

Cal thought about that. It reminded him, of course, of the woman he needed to protect—not that he needed to be reminded of her.

"What could Messing do to help?"

"Assuming he's not in on it, it would be safe to meet with him. He could get a message back to Janssen through Tierno, let Janssen know that I have evidence and that it'll be made public if anything were to happen to me."

"What will that do?"

"Give Janssen a reason to back off, for the time being, anyway. Long enough, I hope, for me to get on my feet again and get the hell out of here. I can't really travel far the way I am."

"Where will you go?"

"It doesn't matter. What matters is that the people I leave behind are safe. Do you understand?"

Cal nodded.

"If your detective friend tells Janssen that I'm leaving town and that no one knows where I went or how to get in touch with me, he'll have no reason to come after Angel or you or Heather or anyone. He'll have every reason, in fact, to just let me live. As long as I'm alive, he has nothing to worry about."

"Do you think Messing will do that?"

"Like I said, if he isn't in on it, and if I can get him to believe me, yeah. If he is in on it, he'll still pass the message along. Either way, it should buy me the time I need."

Cal considered all that. He looked again at Lebell's wounds.

"So what exactly do we do?"

"Do you know how to get in touch with Messing?"

"Yeah." Cal reached into his pocket and pulled out the detective's business card.

"I need you to set up a meeting with him."

"For when?"

"As soon as possible. Will you do that?"

"Yeah. Okay."

"We're going to have to take some precautions first."

"What kind of precautions?"

Lebell took a final drag on his cigarette. He had smoked it down to the filter. Stubbing it out in the ornate ashtray, he said, "You need to know that Janssen is a monster, Cal. He's the fucking Antichrist. I need to know you understand that going in."

Cal nodded. "I do."

"So you'll help me."

"Yeah. Of course."

"Good. Because I don't want what I have to tell you next to be mistaken for me manipulating you. I'm not saying it to scare you into helping, I'm just stating it because it's a fact you need to know and it'll help you understand everything that's at stake here."

"Okay. Yeah. What is it?"

"One local cop sitting outside of a motel room won't stop Janssen. It won't stop that bitch who works for him, either. Not for long, anyway. We need to make our move, and we need to make it now. Do you understand what I'm saying?"

Cal quickly entered Heather's new number into her old phone. He had stepped outside the gatehouse, was standing on the white stone driveway; Angelica had come back, and the fewer specifics she knew, Lebell had told them, the better for her.

Not a lot of time, Cal said to Heather, *so please listen.* He needed her and Amanda to get out of there, to go somewhere else, and he couldn't know where. *Certain precautions, I'll explain later.* They'd have to go out the bathroom window, just like he had, and because of Heather's condition—pregnant, wrist in a cast—Amanda should go through first and then help her sister down. After that, they should get to the train station and call a cab from the pay phone there—that cabbie friend of hers, and make sure the driver doesn't keep a record of where he takes them. *Jesus, Cal.* He ignored that, told her once she got to the train station to text him so he knew she made it that far, and then call him once she got to the safe place. If he didn't answer, she shouldn't leave a message; he'd call back as soon as he could. Wait for his call, don't call him again.

Just do what I say, please, everything is going to be okay, don't worry.

He ended the call quickly, then placed the next one. It didn't matter that Messing would see the number from which he was calling. Soon enough Cal would be getting rid of that phone, like he had promised Heather he would.

Standing in the driveway, the property unlit, the tall wall of hedges blocking out the streetlights along Ox Pasture Road, Cal could barely see his hands in front of his face.

He was certain, though, that they were shaking once again.

Back in the gatehouse, he announced, "We're all set. Messing will meet us in a half hour."

Lebell was upright, sitting on the edge of the bed, the white comforter around his waist. He was obviously, Cal noticed, naked beneath.

"Good," he said. "And Heather?"

"She should be on her way."

Angelica had retrieved a roll of silver duct tape from the main house and had wrapped Lebell's torso with it. Its stiffness was what was keeping Lebell upright. Tearing off a long piece of tape, she laid it on top of the bandage covering the wound on Lebell's shoulder, to help hold the bandage in place. In addition to the tape wound tight around his torso, from waist to upper ribs, there was tape around his forearm, covering it from wrist to elbow like a gauntlet.

Cal had never seen a man so battered.

"You know, I could go for you," Angelica said. She spoke softly, focused on her task. "Just tell me what to say, I'll say it word for word."

"No, I have to do it," Lebell said. "They need to know that I'm still alive. I need them to think they didn't hurt me, that he sent his best and I'm still walking around."

She pressed down on the tape as carefully as she could, needed to make it stick if it was going help keep the deep cuts from reopening. Despite her care, Lebell winced.

"That's if you don't bleed to death in the car on the way there," Angelica said.

"I'll be fine."

When she was done, it was time for them to get him dressed. Laid out on the bed was a change of clothes. Black pants and a sweater, shoes and a leather jacket. *Expensive.* These things, too, she had retrieved from the main house. It took Angelica and Cal working together to get Lebell into these clothes. It took them both to help him to his feet and, one on each side of him, guide him through the narrow rooms of the gate house.

Nearly every step caused Lebell to draw in air through gritted teeth. Once outside, they walked him through the chill to the Lexus.

When he was settled into the passenger seat, as Cal hurried around to the driver's side, Lebell said to Angelica, "We won't be long. Be ready to go when we get back."

She nodded. "Be careful." Looking over the roof of the vehicle, she said to Cal, "Both of you."

The meeting place was Road D, a narrow beachside parking lot on the far end of Dune Road. Secluded, it was impossible to approach by vehicle from either direction without being seen, and impractical to reach on foot via the beach—at least not by anyone pressed for time.

Pulling into the lot, Cal parked close to the beach. He looked around first. The lot was empty.

"You better help me before he gets here," Lebell said.

Cal hurried around to the passenger door, helped Lebell out and to his feet, then walked him to the back of the Lexus and leaned him against its trunk. Walking back to the lot's entrance then, he stood watch, facing east.

There was, of course, no traffic at this time of night; the homes that lined Dune Road were lavish summer houses, and it was long past summer. So, who else but Messing, coming to meet them, would be on this road now?

A minute or so passed, and then Cal finally spotted a pair of head-lights approaching. It wasn't till the vehicle was almost upon them that he recognized it as an unmarked sedan. Cal felt Heather's cell phone buzz in his pocket just as the car turned into the lot.

He grabbed the phone, read the incoming text.

Getting into cab.

He slipped the phone back into his pocket as the unmarked sedan parked beside him. Its headlights went dark, its engine silent. Messing emerged, looking first at Cal, then across the lot at Lebell.

Finally, he looked back at Cal and said, "What are you doing involved in this, son? I thought you were the one with his head on straight."

"I'm just trying to help out a friend."

"That's often how it starts. Harboring a known fugitive, that's some serious stuff."

"Just listen to what he has to say."

Messing glanced once more at Lebell. "Funny, that's the same ad-vice the chief gave me."

He waited a moment more, then walked the Lexus. Cal was too far away to hear what they said. He watched them, though, when he wasn't looking down the empty road for signs of headlights.

On the ride back, silence, two men deep in thought.

Lebell was laboring to breathe through the pain but also against the constraints of the duct tape wound tight around his ribs. What-ever strength had allowed him to hide his condition from Messing for the five minutes they'd stood face-to-face was all used up now.

Cal looked at the rearview mirror as he drove, saw no signs of any-one behind them. *Did that mean no one was there?* he wondered. *Or was someone lingering just beyond his sight, holding back, waiting to pounce?*

He thought of his father then, the man's obsession with every strange car parked on their street, his habit of hiding a cocked gun within reach every time he went to answer the door.

"I think one of my cuts has reopened," Lebell said. "I think I'm bleeding again."

"I should take you to the hospital, man."

"No, I just need to keep still. I can feel every fucking turn pulling on me, you know? Tugging, tearing me open."

"Do you want me to pull over?"

"No. Listen, we need to change plans. I don't think I can make it back to the garage tonight."

"What should we do instead?"

"You and Angel should go there still."

"We should stick together, don't you think?"

Lebell shook his head. "Now that they know I'm alive and well, they'll be after me. The reason I stood at the back of the car the way I did was so Messing couldn't read the license plate. If he isn't on the level, he would have used it to trace me to Angel. He still might be able to. He could run a search, find every silver Lexus registered in Southampton, which I'm sure is more than a few. It'd take time, but he'd eventually work his way to her. Anyway, once he gets the message to Janssen, they should back off, and I'll be able to slip out of town when I'm ready."

"When do you think that will be?"

"As soon as I can move without starting to bleed again. Tomorrow, maybe. I don't know." He took another stilted breath. "You're going to need to stay sharp, Cal. This could still go very wrong. Don't let them get their hands on the girls, whatever it takes. Promise me that, okay?"

"I promise."

Lebell closed his eyes, nodded briefly. After a moment he said, "From what I've heard, Janssen has this big Russian dude working for him. He's his driver and bodyguard, a scary fucker. And the woman he sent after me is tall and very beautiful, has dark, curly hair, so she'll be hard to miss. If you see either of these two fucks coming—for that matter, if you see anyone you don't know—you run, okay? You get yourself and the girls out of there, go far away and don't look back. Got that?"

"Yeah," he said. He thought not of the morphine hidden under the floorboard in his closet but the cash.

"Angel knows where the tapes are. She knows to get them and give them to a lawyer I've retained if I were to suddenly turn up dead. Janssen and Tierno can never know this, okay? They can never know that she knows where the tapes are. If they found out, they'd find her and fuck her up. So you can't let me down here, man. Do you understand?"

"Yeah."

"She's the closest thing to family I have left. I'm telling you now, I'd kill myself before I'd let them get their fucking hands on her."

Cal looked over at his friend, said nothing.

"Once I'm out of town I'll call you at the garage. I'll call from a pay phone, so you won't recognize the number. That'll probably be the last you hear of me. Maybe, if I think it's safe at some point, I'll contact Angel and have her get in touch with you, but that won't be for a while."

Cal nodded, said, again, nothing.

At least this time he'd know in advance when they would speak their last words.

"Make sure you wipe down this car, okay? Everything we touched. From this point on you're going to need to think that way. Like criminals. You're going to have to be very careful and cover your tracks as you go. Tierno's FBI, man. It took everything I knew about disappearing to run from him—and I know a lot about disappearing."

Cal turned onto Ox Pasture Road. They were approaching the gate when he thought of his other reason for coming here.

"You didn't happen to learn anything about Carver, did you?"

"No, man. I never even got to talk to George."

Cal thought of telling Lebell what else had happened last night—his having to make a run to Shelter Island in the Citroën, his run-in with Heather's husband, the possibility that Heather's husband might soon track them to the garage through the Citroën's owner, which mean that Cal's days at the garage were probably over.

He thought then that maybe they could all run off together—Lebell and himself, Heather and Amanda, the four of them finding some safe place and settling down there, getting jobs, helping Heather raise her son. It would be useful to have someone as smart and as experienced as Lebell to tell them what to do and not to do, the ins and outs of disappearing.

Cal didn't say anything about that, though, or about the events of the night before. Lebell looked like hell, and anyway they had already reached the gate.

Angelica was outside the gatehouse, waiting in the darkness, a small leather suitcase and a large plastic garbage bag stuffed full at her feet. *Ready to go, just as Lebell had instructed.* Cal knew that garbage bag contained the bloody clothes Lebell had arrived in, as well as the sheets and towels and comforter and used bandages stained with his blood. Every and any trace of his presence, he'd told her, needed to be accounted for and removed.

Cal got out and told Angelica about the change in plans, that Lebell needed to stay behind and rest. She took one look at Lebell's pale face and asked Cal to help her get him inside. Easing him down on the couch just inside the front door—Lebell simply couldn't make it any farther than that—Angelica told Cal to get the first aid kit from the bathroom.

He went to retrieve it, quickly glancing into the bedroom as he passed its open door. The bed was made, covered now with an old afghan. With the first aid kit in hand, he grabbed the afghan off the bed and a roll of paper towels from the kitchen counter as he returned to the living room.

He watched as Angelica worked, standing ready with the paper towels; there wasn't much else for him to do. She opened the leather jacket and shirt, cut the tape that bound Lebell's torso with rounded scissors, then peeled it back as carefully as she could.

It wasn't just one cut that had opened up but two—the large one across Lebell's stomach and a smaller one across one side of his chest. She held wads of towel against the wounds, applying pressure and soaking up the blood till the flow slowed enough so she could reapply fresh butterfly bandages. It was obvious to Cal that Lebell needed stitches, but there was no point, he knew, in expressing that.

When the butterflies were applied, Angelica placed clean gauze over both wounds, then reapplied the duct tape. As she laid the afghan over Lebell, she asked Cal if he would get a glass of water.

In the kitchen, Cal found a glass and the ornate ashtray in the dish drainer. He filled the glass from the tap, then returned to the living room with both items. He placed the glass on the coffee table and the ashtray on Lebell's lap.

"Thanks, man," Lebell said. "You should wipe off your prints."

Cal did with a paper towel. Angelica put two pills into Lebell's palm. He popped them into his mouth. She handed him the glass; he took a sip, then gave the glass back to her. A prescription bottle was on the coffee table. Painkillers, Cal assumed. Angelica slipped the bottle into the pocket of Lebell's jacket. Then, reaching into her overcoat, she removed the pack of cigarettes and silver lighter, placing them in the clean ashtray on his lap.

There was nothing more that she could do, Lebell told her. It was time for them to go.

"Are you sure?"

"It's better if we aren't together for the next few hours. Cal will take care of you. Maybe he doesn't look it, but, trust me, he's a tough son of a bitch. Hard as coffin nails."

Lebell glanced across the room at something then, did so suddenly, as if something surprising had caught his eye. Then, just as quickly, his attention shifted back to Angelica.

Cal turned and tracked Lebell's line of sight to the living room window. He saw nothing there.

When he looked back at the couch, Angelica was leaning down, adjusting the blanket covering Lebell. She kissed his forehead.

Like a mother would a son, Cal thought.

There was no time for more than this. It was clear that Lebell wanted them to go, and now. Cal walked Angelica to the door, held it open for her as she moved through. He looked at Lebell, nodded once. Lebell nodded back.

"Your harem just keeps growing and growing," Lebell said.

It was, of course, meant to be ironic—a harem took care of the man, not the other way around.

Outside the gatehouse, Cal geared up—jacket zipped tight, helmet and gloves on—then, on his old Triumph, led Angelica, in the Lexus, through the automatic gate and onto Ox Pasture Road.

It was three thirty, and much colder now, but his gear would keep him warm enough during the twenty minutes it would take them to reach Bridgehampton.

There was no room for the Lexus in any of the work bays, so Cal had Angelica park behind the building, between it and the bordering trees, where Heather had, till last night, kept the BMW.

Out of sight, in the shadows. The best they could do.

As Angelica watched, Cal quickly wiped the steering wheel and door handles down with the cuff of his steerhide jacket, then brushed the headrests for stray hairs. *We have to think like this,* Lebell had told him, *like criminals.* Doing so, growing up the way he had, came all too easy to Cal.

Deactivating the security system from the outside keypad, he led Angelica through the office and three work bays. She waited at the bottom of the stairs as he removed the pins and lifted the third door. Backing the bike inside, he closed and locked the door again, reinserted the pins, and ran into the office to reactivate the security system.

Sealed in tight, the two of them safe, he led her upstairs.

Her reaction to his rooms was one he'd seen before, from the few women he'd brought back here over the years. *You live here?* But it didn't matter what Angelica thought of it, did it? This was different. He showed her to Heather's room, asked if she needed anything. She said she didn't. Despite the late hour, despite all that had happened, and could still happen, Angelica had that same calm about her, that same composure. She was sitting on the narrow bed and looking around the bare room when Cal left her.

In his own room he removed his peacoat and steerhide jacket but kept his boots on. *Just in case.* Glancing at his clock, he saw that it was almost four. How long since he'd slept? *Long enough*. He was tired now, but he knew he shouldn't sleep—he wouldn't have been able to even if he wanted to. *Stay sharp*. With those two words in his head, how could he even close his eyes?

He sat on the edge of his bed, holding Heather's cell phone, wondering where she was right now, if the call she still owed him was overdue or not. Hard to know, one way or another. Perhaps it was best, considering everything, to assume the worst. He wondered what he would he do if he didn't hear from her in the next few minutes. What *should* he do if he didn't hear from her in the next half hour? Shortly after he had begun thinking that, though, the phone, still in his hand, suddenly buzzed.

It both relieved and startled him.

On the display was her new number.

"You okay?" he said.

"Yeah. Where are you?"

"At the garage."

"Are you coming here?"

He had no idea where "here" was, thought to ask, then remembered that he couldn't know. "Not yet," he said.

"Why not?"

"I'm waiting for a call."

"From who?"

"Lebell."

"What the hell is going on, Cal?"

"It's a long story."

"I'm not going anywhere."

"Lebell is in trouble."

"What a surprise."

"It's not that. Someone from his past found him. They tried to kill him."

"Jesus."

"Everything's going to be okay, though. We might have to take off. I mean, like tomorrow."

"Does this have anything to do with your boss Carver?"

"No. Like I said, it's someone from Lebell's past."

"He always seemed . . . up to something to me."

"Everyone's got a past," Cal parroted.

Heather was silent for a moment. "When will you know for sure? You know me, the farther we can get from here, the better."

"Tomorrow," he said. "Sometime tomorrow. Lebell can't travel yet."

"Why not?"

"He's hurt pretty bad."

Another pause, then, "You okay?"

"Yeah. I'm just tired."

"Get some sleep, Mr. Fix-it."

He smiled at that. "You, too, Heatherlicious. I'll call you in a few hours."

"Please do."

So many directions from which violence could strike.

Cal thought about them all; there wasn't much else for him to do as he lay on his bed and studied the darkness beyond his only window.

His life had changed like this—suddenly and violently—three times before: first when his mother had died, and then when his father was killed during a robbery, and, finally, when Messing came to him four years ago to tell him that his brother was in fact not missing but dead.

There was a part of Cal that had believed—wanted to believe, needed to believe—that the life he had been lucky enough to find—Carver, an acquaintance of Aaron's, had sought Cal out in the days after Aaron's death, offered him this job—would last forever.

Yet there was another part of him that had always been on the lookout for the next sudden, inalterable change, anticipated it. Despite this, being, as he was now, on the verge of another drastic transformation, he nonetheless felt shocked, the kind of shock that comes with loss—loss of loved ones, loss of the familiar, loss of the bliss of youthful ignorance . . .

Each caregiver one by one had disappeared from his life till he was left alone. Now, four people relied on him for their very lives.

How quickly everything can change, he thought.

Every now and then he'd hear from the other room the sound of mattress springs squeaking. Angelica, sleepless, turning over in Heather's bed. It wasn't long, though, before his door opened and he heard her slip into his room.

Pausing inside the doorway she asked if he was there, then followed the sound of his voice through the darkness to his narrow bed and climbed in beside him, all without another word.

Both were fully dressed, she on her left side, her back to him, he stretched out flat and looking up at the ceiling. Not touching, but under the same blanket. *A presence in the dark beside him.* Once they'd taken their positions on the narrow mattress, their only movements were those associated with breathing.

At some point, out of the darkness, her voice:

"Good night, Cal."

"Good night," he replied.

It took a long time, but eventually her breathing sounded to Cal like that of someone who had finally found a way through to sleep.

He lay there, watching the window for the dawn and smelling her perfume.

Lilac, he thought, *with a touch of vanilla.*

Ten

The map displayed on the screen of the notebook computer indicated that a street called Ox Pasture Road was where the signal had come to its second stop of the night.

Evangeline Amendora waited a moment before making the turn onto that street, needing to be certain that the paused signal meant that the motorcycle, and the Lexus it was following, driven by the woman with dark hair, had in fact reached their destination.

Not doing so would risk being seen, and yet waiting too long might mean, once they'd left their vehicles, losing track of them altogether. It was obvious by the map that the Lexus had led the motorcycle here via a less than direct route—an indication that they were concerned someone might be tailing them. So the possibility that they might pull some kind of last-minute maneuver here was real.

But this was the job, weighing the risks, taking some, not taking others.

Patience.

When she felt she had given them enough time, she made the turn onto Ox Pasture, traveling at the speed limit. Halfway down the street she came upon the location of the signal, an estate set behind a wall of tall hedges and a wide wrought-iron gate. Glancing quickly through the gap in the wall created by the gate, she glimpsed only the shape of a four-story mansion rising upward from the rear of the dark property, and the white stone driveway leading to it from the gate.

There was no sign of any movement, no sign of anyone, not even the motorcycle or the Lexus. Just dark and more dark.

The equipment was reliable, though, so they had to be in there, somewhere.

She continued on, came to the last side street off Ox Pasture, and turned, parking the Ford sedan on the shoulder. Opening her bag, she removed the snub-nosed .357 and pliers, then put the handgun in the left inside pocket of her leather jacket and the pliers in the right outside pocket. A quick check of the left-hand pocket of her jeans told her that her trusted Spyderco Scorpius was clipped there. Closing the computer, she placed it inside the bag. There was no point in shutting it down; she might need quick access to it again. Exiting the vehicle, she walked back to Ox Pasture and, pausing, looked down the long street.

Lined on both sides with old trees whose branches reached toward each other and intertwined, making a kind of thatched roof, this street looked to her like the entrance to a dark tunnel. Gusts of wind caused the leaves above, some still alive, some dead, to rattle and hiss. Those that had already fallen onto the pavement stirred noisily, some scurrying away like tiny animals.

She observed all this, then, determined, headed into that long darkness ahead.

— ✦✦✦ —

She knew better than to approach the wrought-iron gate—not only would she be exposed there, but that area might be monitored by security cameras—so instead she searched the hedge-wall for a place to slip through. Well maintained and at least three feet thick, this wall was a significant barrier, but she found an opening just beyond the first corner, between two roots, where the branches had begun to rot and were brittle and bare. She had to crawl to make it through, but she was used to such discomforts.

Once she was through, she rose to a crouch and surveyed the grounds. The main house was still only a shape in the darkness, and the white-stone driveway appeared empty. Then she saw, just beyond the gate, a smaller house. The only light visible in the entire property burned there—a dancing, glowing light behind a large window. It took a moment for her eyes to adjust, and when they did, she saw, beside that house, in its shadow, both the motorcycle and the Lexus.

Keeping close to the hedge-wall, she followed it to the edge of the driveway, crouched down again, and waited. Nothing for a moment, but then a figure moved past the lighted window. Seconds later it exited the building and followed the stone driveway to the main house. A dark figure to Eve's eyes but, by the way it walked, by the sound of its boots on the stones, a woman.

Reaching the main house, this woman entered through a side door, and immediately a light came on, then another, and then more lights still, marking the path being taken. *Moving from room to room, then upward, floor to floor.* Looking back at the gate, Eve searched for signs of a surveillance camera—she knew every model on the market, how and where a camera would be mounted, both those that would be in clear sight, to discourage trespassers, and those that would be hidden. She saw none.

Studying the gatehouse now, she detected no further activity within.

Eventually the lights in the main house began to go out, one by one, and the woman reappeared, heading back down the driveway. She was carrying something in each hand—Eve could see this as she got closer, but she could not see what those things were. Once the woman had stepped back inside, Eve rose and moved across the driveway, hurrying toward the smaller house. Its stone foundation was surrounded by shrubs, its walls covered with criss-crossing ivy vines. Making her way between two shrubs, Eve pressed her back flat against the foundation, instantly felt the cold stones through her leather jacket.

Directly above her was the lighted window, and she could make out voices, two male and one female, each speaking calmly. Voices, but no words.

Finally, she rose high enough to peek inside. At first she could see no one, only a small living room leading to a kitchen with a large stone fireplace, the source of the dancing light. Then, beyond the kitchen, she saw a bed, and a man being seated upon its edge, helped there by the woman who had driven the Lexus. Eve could not see this man's face— the light in that room was dim, probably nothing more than the glow of a digital clock, and he was seated with only his side to her—but the bloodstained bandages across his naked torso told her it was Militich.

Her heart raced a little.

She'd found the bastard, was so close now.

Someone left the room, and she ducked down just as this person passed the window. *The Rakowski kid?* She heard the door open, was unable to see it from where she was, but this person began to walk across the driveway. It was the kid—that big old peacoat on a smallish guy. So, then, all were accounted for. The kid made a call on his cell phone, and she heard every word—instructions to a woman named Heather to escape, go somewhere safe. Mentions of a motel, a train station, her calling for a cab. Information that might prove useful later, should things go that way. The kid made a second call, this one a bit more interesting. A meeting with someone at a place called Road D, in a half hour. *Something you need to know,* the kid said.

Ending the call, he returned inside, and once he passed the window, she rose up again, saw Militich still on the edge of the bed, his torso bound in silver tape. The kid and the woman—an older woman, she noted now—began to dress him. The guy could barely move.

Closer still.

After a few minutes, the trio had made their way outside, were helping Militich into the Lexus. *We won't be long,* he said to the older woman. *Be ready when we get back.*

The vehicle passed through the gate. There was no need for her to risk following it if they were coming back.

Nothing for her to do now but wait for her chance.

Back inside the gatehouse, the older woman stripped the bed of its covers and sheets, stuffed them into a garbage bag, then made up the bed again. She moved quickly, was an attractive woman, Eve noted, in shape, but nothing compared to the condition she herself was in. When she was done with the bed the woman got out a broom and swept the wooden floors—not the entirety of any of the rooms but rather the pathways through them, the places where footprints would collect. When she was done with this, the woman exited the gatehouse with the garbage bag and left it on the edge of the driveway, then went back to the main house. Emerging fifteen minutes later with a suitcase, she walked down the driveway and stopped beside the garbage bag, setting her suitcase down.

She was directly across from where Eve was hidden within the shrubs, and every time the wind paused for a second or two, Eve could hear in the silence this woman's breathing.

Ten minutes later the Lexus returned. The kid and older woman helped Militich inside. Something was obviously wrong; he was leaning on them even more than he had when they'd first left. Eve moved to the side of the window, stood, looked through it. Militich—she could see his face now—was on a couch, and the woman was tending to him, the kid returning from the bathroom with a first aid kit and a roll of paper towels.

It was as they finished up with Militich that Eve received a text on her cell phone.

Set on vibrate, it danced in the pocket of her jeans. She reached for it, crouched down, cupped her gloved hand over the display to minimize its glow.

Then, a quick peek at the words.

Target now needed alive.

She replied immediately: *Target currently under observation.*

A thrill for her, informing Janssen of this. Nothing better than pleasing him—with the exception, perhaps, of being pleased by him.

Mere seconds later: *Karl on route to assist.*

She returned the phone to her pocket, knew there'd be no more communication. Her cell was equipped with a GPS locator, so they had already pinpointed her location. She would have preferred the original plan—wait for her chance to kill Militich, enter and put two bullets in his head, or, if no chance for a single kill presented itself, then two bullets in his head and two bullets in each of the heads of his friends. A last resort, of course, a bloodbath as such, but one she was easily capable of.

End this once and for all, silence his last enemy, then leave no trace as she slipped out of town.

If Janssen needed Militich alive, then she would take him alive. If he needed her to work on Militich, then she would do that, too. Crush his fingers, stick pins into his manhood, sever it and burn it before his eyes.

Whatever it took.

It wasn't long after she had received the change in plans that the kid and woman left the property, the motorcycle leading the Lexus this time.

Militich was alone now—and as badly wounded as he was, he would have been such easy prey.

Something happened that she didn't expect.

Militich, struggling, rose from the couch, walked past the window, and disappeared from her sight.

She waited a moment, then quickly crossed to the other side of the window, looking into the kitchen and what she could see of the bedroom beyond.

Maybe he went to lie down on the bed, needed something more comfortable than the couch, but there was no sign of him there. Could there be a back door to this place? But where, in his condition, did he think he was going? Was it possible that the extent of his pain had been an act? No, she knew wounds, and she knew pain; she had seen his injuries as the woman had tended to him, knew what she had done to him the night before. Anyway, why fake being in pain? To trick his friends? What, exactly, would that get him?

She listened and watched, heard and saw nothing. Every second he was out of her sight was a second too long. Losing him twice just wasn't an option.

She needed to secure the target.

Moving around to the side of the gatehouse, she paused outside the door, reached for her .357, and switched off the safety with her thumb. With her gloved hand she tried the doorknob, felt it turn freely. From inside now she suddenly heard music, some kind of up-tempo jazz. Loud. Had he really gotten up just to turn on music?

Opening the door she entered quickly, surveyed the room, the .357 held up, her elbows bent, the firearm close to her chest. She finally closed the door, softly, paused for a moment more, then crossed the living room, passing the window and entering the kitchen.

In the large fireplace two halves of a single log burned, their fires almost dead. Eve moved forward, slowly, stopping with each step to study what was ahead. She saw the bedroom, saw that there was no-where else to go in this tiny house—and no doorway, at least that she could see from where she was, that led out or even to a basement.

There was nowhere else for him to go, nowhere but that bedroom for him to be.

The room, she noted, was dark now, much darker than before—the source of dim light she had seen moments ago was gone. Ahead, then, nothing but dark shapes—a bed, a bureau, the outline of a curtained window—and deep shadows.

With the music as loud as it was, she wouldn't be able to hear any movement, so what else could it be, she realized, but cover?

Militich had seen her, she knew this now. He had lured her right to the bedroom door. She held the gun up, the weapon tucked in closer still, aimed into the dark bedroom, then took her first step backward, to nullify the trap he had set.

It was already too late.

One of the dark shapes in the bedroom moved suddenly, crouched down low and lunged at her, not two separate motions but one. Savage and fast, like an animal. *A wounded animal, lashing out from its cave.* She fired but knew the instant she had that her shot was too high. As the figure closed the distance between them—three feet, at the most— it screamed, in anger and pain, and swung something at her, striking her hand hard.

The pain was instant, felt like a jolt of electricity. It shuddered through her, and the heavy revolver was gone from her grip before she even realized what it was that had been used to hit her.

Then she saw it.

A fireplace poker. Antique wrought iron, like the gate outside.

Militich completed his charge, slamming into her and sending her backward. She didn't resist, just wound her right arm around his neck, put her feet together, and sat down on her heels. The momentum of his own tackle carried him forward, and she simply rolled with him, do- ing a reverse somersault till he had flipped himself over and she was seated on top of him like a schoolyard bully.

She went for a choke hold, but his head slipped free. Wasting no time, he placed his hands on her waist and lifted her off him, tossing her away. Every motion he made caused him to scream out, so he couldn't, she knew, keep this up for long. His cuts were certainly open- ing up again, gushing blood. He was bigger than she, stronger, but she was skilled at ground-fighting, could maintain, at least, a draw with any man and therefore wear him down, wait for the blood loss to catch up to him, for the pain to strip him of the last of his will to fight.

He wasn't, though, looking for a ground fight.

The moment he had flung her away, he rolled onto his stomach and began crawling for the revolver. She quickly scrambled after him, caught him just as he reached it. Before he could aim the weapon at her, she lay all her weight upon him, spreading herself out and grabbing his wrist, applying a joint lock. He resisted it with all his remaining strength—a stalemate, of sorts; he could not aim the gun at her, and she could not yet complete the lock and break his grip on it.

Again, he did something she did not at all expect.

He began pulling the trigger.

Blasting a hole in the kitchen cupboard, he pulled the trigger again, immediately. A third shot went off, and she realized what he was up to: emptying the gun. Four shots now in total had been fired, so two remained. She reached up with her other hand, but he managed to fire again. *Five shots.* Before he could pull the trigger and get off the final round, she managed to press her thumb against the hammer and prevent it from cocking back. Lifting herself off him, she brought her knees up and then quickly reapplied her weight again, pressing her knees onto his torso. The pain this caused him gave her the edge she needed to complete the wrist lock. His grip weakened, and she struck the gun with the heel of her palm, once, a second time, then a third. It flew free finally and slid across the floor, skidding from the kitchen out into the living room, well beyond the reach of either of them.

Several elbow strikes to his head to stun him, digging her knees into his torso to inflict even more pain, and then she was up on her feet again, bolting toward the gun. She dropped down, grabbed it, was standing up and turning when he tackled her again. Together they flew a few feet, and then they fell, crashing onto the coffee table and smashing it.

She sensed clumsiness in his power, knew by it that this charge was pretty much all he had left. Ignoring her own pain, she spun, then rolled, mounting him again. He was just a lummox now. She went to place the muzzle of the revolver against his forehead, figured this would put a stop to all this foolishness, but before she could she saw him grab at something and swing once again, this time at her head.

From the corner of her eye she saw it coming, but there just wasn't enough time to react.

The heavy ashtray struck her on the temple—she heard glass shattering and the dull, sickening crack of bone, saw in her mind's eye a black egg with a center as bright as the sun—and then suddenly everything went black, everything fell utterly silent.

When she came to again all she could hear was a ringing in her ears, like the steady peal of a tuning fork struck hard and held too close. An unending wave of nausea gripped her gut, and when she finally opened her eyes, she could only focus one of them. It took all she had to see with any hint of clarity.

There was confusion, pain deep within her head, and a feeling that she might need to vomit. She was seated on the floor, must have just dropped like a stunned boxer—too stunned, even, to do anything more than sit in a slump. Militich was across the room, propped up against the wall, himself seated in a slouch. He was holding the .357 in his hand, but the way the weapon rested in his lap, she knew he didn't have the strength to lift it. He was talking, but she, of course, could not hear over the tuning fork what he was saying. She reached for her left pocket, removed the Spyderco knife, opened the blade with her thumb. A well-practiced move, not discreet by any means, a gesture to tell him that she wasn't done yet, not by a long shot. He was tough but she was tougher, *don't you forget that*. She felt the jolt of the blade locking into place, and only then realized that he wasn't talking to her, he wasn't even looking at her at all, was rather talking to someone behind her. She didn't understand this at first; finally she glanced over her right shoulder—this slight movement of her head sent an even greater wave of nausea through her—and saw that Karl was standing in the doorway.

He had his hands up, not in surrender but as a call for calm and reason. She looked back at Militich, was still unable to hear anything or do anything more than sit there and hold her knife. She watched as he said something to Karl. He was smiling now, Militich was, a defiant smile, an angry smile. He said something else to Karl, then looked at her.

Lifting his left hand, he gave her the finger, his smile now a sneer of contempt, his eyes suddenly empty.

This man, it turned out, was full of surprises.

Next he lifted the revolver, placed its muzzle under his chin, and, without a second's hesitation, pulled the trigger.

The sound of the gunshot had broken through the ringing in her ears; she could hear now, heard Karl as he ran past her, his footsteps heavy on the wood floor. She watched as he crouched down and carefully peeled her gun from Militich's hand. There was no need to check for a pulse; the top of Militich's head was gone.

Moving behind her, Karl told her that they had to go, got her to her feet, wound her right arm around his neck and guided her through the door, out into the night. This motion made her sick, but she didn't dare show it, kept up with him as he ran. *Her trainer, her teacher.* Ahead, the wrought-iron gate was opened slightly. As they moved through it, she noticed that the lock had been pried open. The Russian led her to the Town Car, which was parked a good hundred feet from the gate. Approaching it, she saw that the rear license plate was one of the many dummy plates Janssen had in his collection.

Opening the passenger door, Karl got her in, buckled her up, then hurried around to the driver's side. He removed from inside his coat the crowbar he had used to open the gate, tossed it into the backseat. He started the engine, then took off, one hand on the steering wheel, the other across the seat, holding Eve's arm.

He was talking, but for some reason she couldn't hear him again. She watched him talk—whatever he was saying was clearly urgent— but all she could do was shake her head.

It went like that till she blacked out again.

She was being carried.

Cold air around her, the clouded night sky above. Suddenly she was indoors, moving through dark rooms, then rising up a set of stairs. Not cold here, but not warm either. Drafty. *The staircase of that abandoned hotel.* She saw Karl's face above her, saw that he was looking down at her, talking to her. She remembered the night he had found her, brought her to that luxury hotel room in São Paulo, got her out of her filthy clothes, cleaned her up before bringing her to Janssen.

Was this that night? Had the years since all been some fucked-up dream?

Finally, she was on a bed. *That bed in that room at the end of that hall. Strange before, it was familiar now.* Three men were present, she could tell this much—Karl, another man by the bed, and a third man watching from the doorway, his arms folded across his chest.

She heard Karl say, "Militich is dead."

"What happened?" This was Janssen's voice. *Angry.* He was, then, the other man by the bed. She looked for him in the darkness, found him, or at least the blurred shape of him.

"Shot himself," Karl answered. "There were two of us and only one bullet left. He said he wasn't going to let us take him alive."

Silence for a few seconds, then, "We need to find that friend of his.

We need to know what he knows about the tapes." More angry than before.

Even Karl—giant Karl, merciless Karl—seemed flustered by Janssen's rage.

The Russian immediately nodded. From the doorway, the third man, still unknown to Eve, said, "I'd bet good money he's back at the garage."

Janssen looked at him. "Why?" It was more of a command than a question.

"It's all he knows," the third man said. "Trust me, I know this kid, the family he comes from, the way he thinks. I can bring him to you."

There was a local contact working for them, Eve knew that much. This had to be him.

"No, Karl will do it. Give him the code to the system."

"No problem," the third man said.

"I want you to retrieve her vehicle. There's equipment inside we might need. Wake Tierno, tell him to help you. I'll confirm whether or not the kid's there."

"How?"

"Never mind," Janssen snapped. He turned to Karl. "If he is there, get him and bring him here. If he isn't, we'll use her equipment to track him again. I want this settled by tonight. No more fuckups."

Karl nodded and left, taking the man from the doorway with him. She heard their footsteps receding down the hallway, the bodyguard's heavy steps plus the sound of hard-soled boots.

Janssen was above Eve now, leaning over her. *Just the two of them.* She could barely make out his face, wanted to see more of it, to see it clearly. A kitchen pot filled with water was on the bedside table. Janssen began to wash her wound with a rag soaked with warm water. His touch, as always, was firm but loving, and the rag in his hand, she noticed, quickly became tinged with red.

It was only then that she realized she was bleeding.

Afterward, her wound cleaned and dressed, he loaded up a syringe. She watched him. Her arms were vascular, so he had no trouble finding the vein. As he injected her, he told her that she couldn't fall asleep, not for a while, that there was the chance she might have a concussion and if she went to sleep she might not wake up again. She didn't need to worry, he assured her; he'd stay with her, keep her company.

It didn't take long for the sensation of floating to overtake her. The familiar rush of morphine. *Like a terrible grip finally loosening.*

Sitting on the edge of the bed, Janssen stroked her dark hair, gently, tenderly, did what was necessary to keep her from crossing into unconsciousness.

Eleven

———◆———

At a little before six, the eastern sky only just beginning to soften, Cal, still awake, was startled by the sound of a ringing phone.

It wasn't Heather's cell on his bedside table but rather the garage's landline out in the living room.

He hurried to the extension. Reaching for the receiver, he looked down at the caller ID, saw a number he didn't recognize at first.

Then he did.

Messing's cell phone.

He pulled his hand back, was still trying to decide whether or not to answer when Angelica appeared in his bedroom door.

She watched him, and, in the silence between third and fourth rings, said finally, "Aren't you going to answer it?" She sounded groggy.

"It's the detective."

She folded her arms across her stomach, guarding herself against the chill of the drafty living room. She said, though, nothing.

This call wasn't part of Lebell's plan, but that wasn't all. Messing had once before—four years before—brought Cal bad news. Cal had no desire at all for a repeat of that.

The fourth ring had begun and ended. Finally, during the fifth ring, Cal answered.

Messing, his voice muffled by what sounded like a poor connection, didn't waste any time. "Your friend is dead," he said. "I'm sorry."

Only he didn't sound sorry at all.

Cal said nothing.

"A neighbor called in gunshots," the detective continued. "He was staying at some estate on Ox Pasture Road. A uniform responded, saw a broken gate and blood trail, found the body in the gatehouse." A pause, then, "It looks like he shot himself."

Cal was still unable to speak. He realized that his eyes were closed, so he opened them.

"That evidence of his, Cal. The tapes. Do you know where they are?"

"No."

"He told me that someone did. Do you know who that someone is?"

"No."

"I need you to tell me the truth, Cal."

"I am."

"I'm trying to help here. I'm trying to help *you*."

"And I'm telling you, I don't know."

"I need that evidence. It's very important that I get it right away. Do you understand me?"

"Whoever has it will make it public. You'll get it then."

"You're not listening to me. I *need* that evidence. If you don't have it, I need to know who does. I'm going to assume you know who that person is."

Cal said nothing. An urge, an instinct—*something* told him to just hang up, but he didn't.

"I'm sending someone to get you," the detective said. "I need you to stay put till he gets there. If you disappear on me again, I'll get a warrant for your arrest. Do you understand me? We're not playing, Cal. I'll put you in a jail cell if I have to. Is that what you want? I thought you were the one with his head on straight. I thought you weren't going to end up like your father—"

Cal hung up.

"What's going on?" Angelica said.

He couldn't look at her. "Lebell's dead. Militich, Mickey, whatever. He's dead."

"How?"

"We have to get out of here."

"How was he killed?"

"They must have cornered him or something. He told me he'd do this if he had to, but I didn't . . ."

"He told you he'd do what?"

He still couldn't look at her. "He told me he'd kill himself before he let them get their hands on you."

"Christ."

"We have to get out of here, Angel. Now." He was looking everywhere, knowing he must appear to her like a man unable to decide in which of the several different directions he should move, but he didn't care now how crazy he looked.

"What's going on, Cal?"

"Just please, get your things."

"What's going on?"

"Messing is sending someone to get us."

"What do you mean?"

"Someone is on his way to take us in."

"We haven't done anything wrong."

"It's not that."

"Then what is it?"

Cal said nothing. He decided which direction to go, turned, and walked past her, heading into his bedroom.

She followed him, stood in the doorway. "Cal, I've lived in this town for thirty years," she said. "I helped the goddamn mayor get elected. Mickey told me a little bit about you. You don't have to be afraid of the police. They've cracked down, cleaned up the department, it's not like it used to be back when your father—"

"It's not that."

"Then what is it?"

Cal had stepped to the only window, was looking down now at the dark street beyond. "Messing's working with them."

"How do you know that?"

"I just do."

"But how?"

"He must have followed us back to your place from the beach. How else could they have found Lebell so quickly? Or maybe he saw your license plate—whatever, he didn't sound right."

"How did he sound?"

Cal needed to think for a second to find the right word. There was only one he could come up with. "Threatening."

"Isn't that an old cop trick?"

"Listen, I know all their tricks. This was . . . different." He looked at her. "I promised Lebell I'd take care of you, and that's what I'm going to do. I'm going to protect you."

"Protect me from what?"

"Lebell told me that you're the only one who knows where his evidence is, and that if something happened to him, you'd know what to do with it."

Angelica hesitated, then said, "What does that have to do—"

"Lebell told Messing about the tapes so Messing would get the word back to Janssen. Lebell wanted to fix it so he could leave in a way that guaranteed they wouldn't bother him or us. Messing just said he needs to know where the tapes are, that he'll arrest me if he has to."

"He can't just arrest you, Cal. That's not how it works. Anyway, I know the chief, he's a friend—"

"They'll make us tell them what they want to know, Angel. You don't understand. Lebell told me the things these people do to get people to talk. I promised him I wouldn't let them get their hands on you."

"Let me just call the chief. He'll take care of this—"

"We can't trust the police. We can't trust anyone. We need to get out of here, we need to get somewhere safe. Please."

He heard the fear in his voice. If he had neighbors, they would have heard it, too. It had been his father's fear, one he'd heard the man express every day, in one form or another, for years. Clearly, though, it belonged to him now.

The kind of fear that can't be ignored, that is there to save your life.

Cal was out of breath—out of words, too.

A moment passed, and then Angelica nodded once and said softly, "Okay. So let's go. Later on I'll call Mickey's lawyer, and we'll figure out what to do."

She returned to Heather's room to get her belongings. Cal put on his steerhide jacket, then his peacoat over that. Wrapping his scarf around his neck, he placed Heather's old cell phone into his jeans pocket, felt as he did a piece of paper.

He pulled it out and unfolded it. It was the number to Heather's new cell phone. Knowing it was stored in her old phone, he tore the paper into little pieces and placed it in a glass of water on his bedside table to destroy it.

He remembered then that the directions to Shelter Island were in the pocket of his peacoat. He tore that paper up as well and put its pieces in the same glass.

We have to think like criminals, Lebell had said. *Leave no traces.*

Cal hurried to his closet; if they were going to run, they'd need money. He still had in his pocket the five hundred that had been meant for Angstrom, and that would do for a few days, but they'd eventually need more, so it was probably best to get it now.

He was removing the loose floorboard, wondering how much to grab and how much to leave for later—or should he just grab it all?—when he heard Angelica call his name.

Quickly replacing the board, he stood and ran out to the living room. She was standing by the window, had her overcoat and scarf on and was buckling the old leather belt.

"I think I just saw someone," she said.

"Where?"

"Down there?"

She nodded toward the southeast corner of the driveway, where the property met the road. Cal saw nothing but the faint shadows cast by the first somber hints of morning.

"What did you see?"

"I don't know."

"A cop?"

"I don't know. It was just a quick glimpse of someone moving."

Cal continued to look, saw, still, nothing.

"What do we do?" she said.

"We're safe in here," Cal told her. "If there is someone out there, he can't get in without the code."

"So we just wait and hope he goes away?"

Cal didn't have an answer for that. He thought for a moment, said finally, "Wait here," then headed toward the kitchen.

"Where are you going?"

"I'm going down to have a look."

"Won't he see you?"

"The windows are all covered up."

"I'm coming with you."

She followed him through the kitchen and down the plank steps. It was dark in the third work bay, the only light source right now the dim glow of a wall-mounted clock in the far corner, above Cal's tool chest. This had little influence, did nothing more, in fact, than cast a dozen long and deep shadows.

Cal walked to the second work bay and through that to the first. He could have done this in pitch black if he needed to; he knew this place that well. Angelica was right behind him, her hand on his back so she wouldn't lose him. Just outside the adjoining office, Cal stopped.

Its large storefront window wasn't covered, so he stood to the left side of the door, out of sight, keeping Angelica behind him. Leaning his head to the side, he looked through the door and toward the window.

He could see the keypad to the right of the main door, its indicator light red, and the window to the left. His line of sight was angled, so all he could see was part of the narrow driveway that ran past the window and a segment of the dark road beyond.

This wasn't enough.

He told Angelica to stay where she was, then stepped into the office, moving quickly to the wall beside the window. This exposure, as brief as it was, sent a jolt of adrenaline through him. He pressed his back flat against the wood, paused, then, turning his head and leaning again just a bit, looked through the glass.

Nothing, no one. Again, though, his line of sight was limited. There was little hope of seeing whoever might be out there, if there even was someone out there, unless that person actually strolled past the window—

—and, just as he thought that, this was exactly what happened.

Out of nowhere a figure appeared, moving swiftly and silently past the storefront window. The figure of a man, large, in a dark coat. There, and then gone. The direction from which he had come told Cal that this man had been at the western side of the building. What was he doing there? Cal looked back at Angelica, saw her peeking around the corner. He could just see her face. He raised his finger to his mouth. *Shhh.* She nodded. There was nothing for either of them to do but wait and listen.

Cal could hear footsteps now. The man had continued past the door, was walking down the length of the garage along the gravel driveway, moving away.

Walking the perimeter? Cal wondered. *Casing the joint? Taking note of all exits?*

Listening till the sound of the footsteps faded, and only then allowing himself to move, Cal hurried back to Angelica in the first bay. The look on her face was clear: *What do we do?*

Cal held up his finger once more, took a second to listen again, then whispered, "Take off your coat."

A whisper came back. "Why?"

He was removing his peacoat. "We'll make a break for it on the bike."

"What?"

"We'd never make it to your Lexus. Anyway, I can lose him on the bike, cut across fields if I have to. Trust me."

Angelica began unbuckling the leather belt. "Why do I need to take my coat off?"

"It's too long."

He handed her his peacoat, then hurried to the third work bay, where the Triumph was parked, nose to the door. His helmet was hanging on the right-hand grip, but his spare helmet was on the shelves under the stairs, so he quickly grabbed that. Angelica, still by the office door, her overcoat in a pile on the oil-stained floor, was putting on the peacoat.

Suddenly she looked into the office, then quickly ducked away from the door.

"Cal," she whispered.

Cal froze, but only for a second. Approaching the first work bay, he was careful to follow a path that would keep him out of sight of the office. Reaching the door, standing to the right of it, he looked across at Angelica. She tilted her head to the side, gesturing into the office. Cal took a breath, peeked around the corner, and immediately saw what it was that had startled her.

Standing outside the window, looking in, was the man in the dark coat.

Perfectly still, hands hanging at his side, almost casual in the way he was studying the office.

Unafraid, that much was certain.

Cal remembered Messing's words. *Sending someone to get you.* Here already, which meant Messing had sent him before making his call.

Cal also remembered Lebell's warning about Janssen's bodyguard.

Big guy. If you see him, fucking run.

This man was clearly a big man.

Shit.

Cal looked at Angelica, got her attention, and nodded toward the third work bay. *Get ready to go.* He peered around the corner again, checking the window. The man was no longer there. Cal crossed the doorway quickly, like a man expecting to come under fire, grabbed Angelica by the elbow, and was guiding her through the first work bay when he heard something that made him stop dead in his tracks.

A faint but steady beeping.

Someone was working the outside keypad.

He turned, could still see the interior keypad from where he was standing. He counted six beeps, each one slow and deliberate, and then—*what the fuck?*—the indicator light switched from green to red.

Disarmed.

The door, then, to his disbelief, began to open.

His heart was suddenly pounding.

Angelica crouched down, had to pull a stunned Cal with her. Together—it wasn't certain which one was leading the other—they took cover behind the rear fender of the Benz.

His mind reeled now; he was trying to make sense of this. He remembered that Messing had listened to him give the code to Amanda.

What more did he need? This, plus the fact that it wasn't a uniformed cop Messing had sent to get him, left no doubt in Cal's mind.

Messing was working with them.

He grabbed Angelica's elbow again, guided her to the front of the Benz, staying low as they moved. It was a better hiding place for them, and his toolbox, and all the makeshift weapons it contained, would be in easy reach.

The office door closed, carefully, almost silently, and then Cal heard the sound of footsteps, counted enough of them to know that the big man had arrived at the door to the first work bay.

There was a pause, and then the click of a flashlight coming on, its beam making a slow sweep of the garage.

Cal and Angelica kept still, neither daring to even breathe. Finally, the beam came to rest on the stairs in the far work bay.

The man started toward it, through the first work bay and the second, pausing in the third to aim his flashlight at the motorcycle parked by the door. Reaching the steps, he turned and made another sweep of the garage, then began to move upward, stepping as softly on the old planks as his great weight would allow.

At the top, the man opened the door. Cal kept track of his progress through the apartment by the creaking of the wood above. When he knew the man was well into the living room, had the two bedrooms and bathroom still to search, Cal made his move.

He stood, pulled open the bottom drawer of the tool chest, and grabbed his ball peen hammer, doing it all as quietly and as quickly as he could. Taking hold of Angelica's elbow once more, he guided her through the maze of vehicles and equipment and support beams till they reached the motorcycle.

Hurrying to the bay door, he removed the locking pins and slowly spun the center-mounted lever. All that was left was for him to raise the door, but that would make a racket, so he knew he had to wait till they were ready to go before doing that.

Back at the Triumph, he handed Angelica the spare helmet, then grabbed his own from the right-hand grip. Angelica, uncertain how to put the helmet on, stepped toward Cal. She wasn't paying attention to where she was going, though, focusing instead on figuring out how the helmet strap worked. She bumped into a wheeled cart as she walked, the cart that Lebell used to keep his tools handy while he worked.

The cart coasted for about a foot, silently at first, then collided with an old rusted oil drum they used as a trash can.

Above them, silence, and then the sound of footsteps moving from Cal's bedroom, hurrying toward the kitchen.

There was no chance now of them mounting the bike and getting out before the man could reach them, so Cal dropped his helmet, grabbed Angelica again, and pulled her to the middle work bay, yanking her down to a crouch in front of the Citroën.

From there he ran for the first work bay, to the far side of his tool chest, where the fuse box was located. The ball peen hammer in his left hand, he opened the fuse box with his right, flipped the four breaker switches, killing the only light source.

Reaching for the top drawer of his tool chest, he opened it and grabbed two large sockets, all that would fit in his hand. Ducking down again, he took cover by the front of the Benz, just as the door opened at the top of the stairs.

In total darkness now, Cal couldn't even see Angelica in the next bay, less than six feet away. He dared to whisper, though, said, "Stay there," then lifted his head and looked over the hood of the Benz.

He could see, of course, nothing. Then, through the windows of the Citroën, he glimpsed a light shining down the plank steps. He listened as the man began to move slowly down them. When he reached the bottom, the man first swept the garage with his flashlight one more time, then eventually began to search the nearby wall, looking, just as Cal had known he would, for a light switch.

Locating one, he stepped to it and flipped it. Nothing. He flipped it again. Still nothing. Searching the garage one last time with his flash-light, he finally aimed the beam on the motorcycle.

The helmet that had been hanging on the right grip was now on the floor.

The beam of light moved again, going to all three work bay doors, one right after the other. The man was, Cal knew, checking to see that they were locked. Seeing that the third one wasn't, the man stepped into that bay and shined the light down one side of the old MG parked there.

Moving past the rear bumper, he shined the light down the other side. He then moved to the second work bay, did the same there. In-stead of moving on to the first, though, he began to walk between the Citroën and the Benz, his flashlight now focused on the area around the nose of the former.

He must have seen something, or at least believed he had seen something, and was attempting to put himself between that some-thing and the office, which was the only quick way out.

Cal passed the ball peen hammer from his left hand to his right, readying himself. Step by step the man drew closer to where Angelica was hiding, and though the light had yet to shine upon her directly, Cal could see that the shadow that concealed her was beginning to diminish.

Just a few more steps and she would be exposed.

Was this man armed? He must be. Was he the Russian Lebell had warned Cal about? Whoever he was, he was seconds from getting his hands on Angelica.

Cal listened to the creaking of the soft wood beneath the man's feet. One more step, then another, his light trained on the Citroën's nose.

Cal knew he had to make his move, and do it soon. He knew, too, that once he did, there would be no turning back, no escaping the consequences.

He placed one of the sockets on the floor, held the other in his palm, then, as quietly as he could, he threw the socket across the dark garage. It landed in the third work bay, and Cal expected that the man would turn his flashlight toward the sound, giving Cal the opening he needed to rise up and come at the man from behind and strike the back of the man's head with the metal hammer.

Instead, the man aimed his flashlight at the Benz, at the spot from which the socket had been flung.

Had he heard Cal's movements, the sound of his steerhide jacket maybe? Whatever the case, the light caught Cal in the eyes, blinding him. The man moved quickly to the front of the Benz, was immediately standing over Cal, between him and Angelica. In a heavy Russian accent, his voice flat and full of menace, the man ordered, "Stand up. Now."

So this was the man Lebell had warned about. The one man from whom Cal should, no matter what, run.

Except there was nowhere to run now.

Cal stood, the blinding light remaining in his eyes as he rose.

"Drop the hammer. Step toward me."

Cal did what he was told. The Russian backed up, keeping the distance between them equal. He was standing by the nose of the Citroën, must have been just inches from Angelica.

"Who else is here?"

Squinting, Cal said, "No one."

"Move to the door."

Again, Cal did what he was told, stepping around to the side of the Benz and walking past its driver's door. The Russian followed, his flashlight on Cal, casting the kid's shadow ahead. Large and dancing, it stretched the length of the work bay. Cal had taken three, maybe four steps, was frantically trying to think of something to do, when he heard a commotion behind him.

The light suddenly swung away, his shadow disappearing with it. Turning, he heard a scream—a woman's scream, not a frightened scream but an angry one, a wild, guttural battle cry.

It was followed by the dull, sickening thud of the ball peen hammer's steel head connecting with fragile bone.

The Russian staggered, and Cal saw his chance.

He went low, executing a wrestler's leg dive, wrapping his arms around the Russian's knees and drawing them together, further compromising the man's already waning balance.

It didn't take much at all to bring the man down.

Scrambling on top him, Cal yanked the flashlight from his hand. He was ready to beat the man with it, do whatever it took, whatever needed to be done, his lean body surging with adrenaline.

But even in this crazed state he was able to recognize right away that his opponent was motionless. More than that, the man was lifeless.

Looking up, Cal saw Angelica standing over them. The flashlight showed the bloodied ball peen hammer in her clenched fist. He stood quickly, a cold chill rushing through him, his breathing fast and frantic, and aimed the light at the Russian's face.

Blood, shimmering in the harsh glare, was rapidly pooling around the man's head. His eyes were open but stared vacantly at nothing.

Cal looked at Angelica again. Her chest, too, was heaving, but the rest of her graceful body was rigid, frozen. All sense of her serenity and calm was long gone. Her eyes were fixed on the felled man, but unlike his, hers were anything but vacant. Dread, shock, fear, anguish—they showed all these.

After a moment, realizing she was still holding the hammer, Angelica dropped it, couldn't wait to get rid of it. She looked at Cal.

He didn't know what to say at first, then managed to utter the one thing that mattered. "We need to get out of here."

Reaching out, he gently touched Angelica's elbow. Her mind must have wandered, because this gesture startled her a little. She looked at Cal for a moment, seemed to want to speak but couldn't. There wasn't time for this, though, he knew that, so he guided her away from the man in a heap at their feet, mindful of the spreading blood, leading her quickly toward the unlocked door.

Outside, they headed around back, where the Lexus was parked. Before they even reached the vehicle, however, Cal stopped short.

"What?" Angelica demanded.

The flashlight illuminated the front end.

"The tires are flat," he said.

The Russian had obviously done that. They hurried back around to the front of the garage. Cal quickly searched the dark street as they moved, saw nothing there—*but*, he wondered, *would he*?

He told Angelica to meet him at the middle bay door, then entered the office, moving through it to the first work bay. He aimed the flashlight at the Russian as he approached him. The pool of blood around his head had grown even larger, and his eyes were still open, still staring.

Cal had never seen a corpse before—he'd seen the dead bodies of his father and brother, laid out in caskets, faces made up, dressed in suits, but never a corpse, never a *dead body*.

Certainly not the body of someone he had played a part in killing.

A chill shuddered through him. His knees suddenly went weak, but he remained standing, remained as cool as he could possibly be.

Though the immediate danger had passed, adrenaline was still surging through him. Chaos swirled like a storm within him, but he had to stand still, had to resist it.

He found then a degree of sense, grabbed a rag from the nearby work bench, then knelt down and picked up the hammer, wiping the handle, erasing Angelica's fingerprints. Dropping the hammer again, he stood and made his way to the second work bay, lifting the unlocked door.

Angelica was waiting for him just beyond it. He pushed the motorcycle through and started the motor, then hurried back inside, grabbing his helmet and searching for Angelica's. He quickly spotted it, picked it up, and, back outside, handed it to her. Pulling the door closed, he locked it out of habit.

He didn't bother to arm the security system from the outside keypad, though. What would that matter now? He felt that he was forgetting something but could not remember what and didn't think about it for too long. All that mattered now was getting out of here, putting this place—and the dead man inside it—far behind them.

He helped Angelica put her helmet on, then pulled the gloves from his and got them on. With his helmet on, he fastened the chin strap and mounted the bike, telling Angelica to get on behind him. She did. He unzipped the pockets of his steerhide jacket, told her to put her hands inside them. He had no gloves to offer her, but this would help keep her warm and, at the same time, allow her to hang on to him. He felt her lean close, laying her torso against his back, clinging to him.

Turning right onto Scuttlehole Road, he rode west, toward Southampton—it was an instinct; west was the way off the island.

Once they had Southampton behind them he'd pull over and call Heather, but that was as far ahead as he could think.

He took the back roads through Bridgehampton, to avoid the main streets for as long as possible. His steerhide jacket did little against the cold morning air, but he didn't care. The clouded sky behind them was beginning to lighten, and he wanted to get to wherever the hell they were going before morning light could surround them.

He drove aggressively, leaning into the many corners, slowing but not stopping for stop signs. He didn't care about obeying traffic laws now.

Turning from Seven Ponds Road onto David White's Lane, all that remained between them and Sunrise Highway, the main route west, was a straightaway—or, rather, a straightaway relative to the winding back roads he'd just maneuvered. He twisted the throttle, watched the speedometer spike as the bike quickly reached fifty miles per hour. It wasn't an unsafe speed but was still above the clearly posted limit. Halfway down that straightaway Cal could see the main road ahead of them. *Almost there.* Soon he could give thought to where they were going. Soon he'd be far enough away to think of something other than running.

It was just past the halfway point, with only a few hundred feet left to go, that he spotted something else ahead.

A patch in the road, starkly and strangely black, shimmering in the predawn light.

Wet pavement? How could that be? And why there and only there? It wasn't till it was too late, till the bike reached this section in the road and all hell suddenly broke lose, that Cal realized what in fact that odd patch of blackness was.

Oil.

The rear tire, losing its contact with the pavement, immediately began to spin wildly, creating a gyroscope effect that not only caused the back end to whip around suddenly but made the bike itself begin to lay over. Cal pulled in on the clutch to cut the power to the rear tire, but as the bike went down, leaning to the right, the left grip was ripped from his hand and he completely lost his hold on the lever.

The right-hand grip remained with him, but as the bike continued its spin-out, the rear tire taking the lead, he naturally clamped down on the throttle—it was the only thing he had to hang on to—causing the engine to redline and, with the clutch engaged, the rear tire to spin even faster.

In a quick second the bike was gone from beneath him, and he went down hard, Angelica still clinging to him, the two of them landing on the pavement. They began to slide on their sides, the bike spinning out ahead of them like a four-hundred-pound top.

Cal rolled onto his back, putting his elbows and heels down to help slow him. Angelica didn't know to do this, so she maintained full momentum, speeding past him, still on her right side. Within seconds they were beyond the oil patch, skidding across dry pavement. The bike crossed onto the road's shoulder and came to an abrupt stop against a bank of dirt. Cal watched as Angelica's body, still traveling close to fifty miles an hour, slammed into the underbelly of the motor-cycle.

One second in motion, a sudden and complete stop the next.

Crossing onto the shoulder as well, slowing but still moving, Cal came to the bank, rose up and over it like it was a ramp. He was suddenly airborne. His flight lasted only a second, maybe two, just long enough for his body to turn in midair. He landed hard, facedown, his right hand caught between his ribs and the solid ground.

He immediately felt several bones in his hand break. The pain was like long needles of fire piercing him. He slid a bit more, then came finally to a stop. Dazed, he wanted to stand, felt the need to do so, immediately, but he couldn't. He barely knew which way was up. He could smell the motor oil; his clothes and jacket were covered with it. He heard voices, sensed people rushing toward him. He lifted his head, struggling to remove his helmet and looking for these people. He saw instead Angelica, maybe twenty feet away, her body, motionless, all but tangled with the bike.

Someone was dragging him suddenly. Roughly. His helmet was off now. Had he taken it off or had someone else? Above him, the clouded sky was rushing. There were open patches now through which he could see fading stars.

Then he was being lifted and placed in the backseat of a car. He glimpsed a face above him, Tierno's face, heard Tierno speaking to someone else but couldn't see who.

"Angel," Cal muttered. "*Angel.*" No one responded to him. He craned his neck to see back to the field they had crashed into, but then a car door swung closed and cut off his view.

The next thing he knew the vehicle was in motion, making turns. Streetlights above, approaching, passing, then *gone*. Some time later he was being carried again, by two men now. Tierno and someone else—the same someone who had helped get Cal to the car after the crash. They brought him through a dark kitchen, down a set of narrow stairs, into a basement.

Cold, damp, dimly lit.

Placed in a chair—an office chair with a high back—he was stripped of his jacket, boots, and socks. His forearms were quickly secured to the arms of the chair with duct tape. The pockets of his jeans were emptied. His left hand was throbbing, the pain searing, unbearable.

Not far away, in another chair, secured in a similar manner, was someone else.

A man. Cal's view of him was blocked, but then, as people moved about, the way was finally cleared and he could see the man's face.

It was Messing. His head was hanging limp, the front of his shirt bibbed with blood. Cal looked at him for several long seconds before he was even able to focus on the bullet hole in the man's temple. Even then it took a bit for him to realize that this meant Messing was dead.

Cal squirmed suddenly, feeling the overwhelming, if not delayed, urge to get free, but the tape held. His strength quickly diminished, his will to run undermined by the pain surging through his hand.

Standing beside Messing was another man. Someone Cal had never seen before. Tall, well dressed, in his sixties.

"Where's Karl?" this man said.

He was in charge, that much was clear by the way he stood and the tone of his voice.

Janssen? It had to be.

"We don't know," Tierno answered. "We were able to track them, though, with the device. We managed to get ahead and spread the oil." He nodded toward the other man. "We were lucky he had some in his trunk."

Cal looked toward the man to whom Tierno had nodded. He was standing to the right of the chair, behind Cal, in a corner. Cal couldn't see him.

"Angel," he said again. He was able to do little more than mumble now. "Angel."

"What the hell is he talking about?" Janssen said.

"A woman was with him," Tierno answered.

"Who?"

"I don't know."

"Where is she now?"

"He crashed his bike when he hit the oil. She was killed."

Cal closed his eyes, lowered his head.

"Jesus Christ," Janssen said, suddenly angry. He told Tierno to go the garage, see if Karl was still there.

Tierno turned away, saying nothing, and climbed the stairs.

Janssen spoke to the man standing in the corner, behind Cal. "Help me put him out," he ordered.

The second man approached.

Cal's head was still hung low, so the first thing he saw of this man was snakeskin cowboy boots.

Looking up, Cal found the man's face, didn't want to believe what he was seeing.

"C'mon," Janssen said. He was getting impatient. "Hold his arm. He's going to squirm."

Eric Carver nodded, then placed both hands on Cal's right forearm, pinning it against the arm of the chair. Janssen found a vein, pierced it expertly with a syringe, and pressed the plunger forward with his thumb. *All so fast.* Cal, when he finally realized what was happening, struggled as best he could, but Carver held firm, kept his arm still.

"Now what?" Carver said to Janssen

"Leave him. He'll be out for a while. When she's ready, she'll go to work on him."

Carver let go of Cal's arm, straightened his back. He remained for a moment, looking down at the kid.

"Sorry, buddy," he said. "I tried to keep you out of this. I really did. Fucking Lebell, you know. He had to drag you into it."

"Let's go," Janssen ordered.

His heart still pounding, Cal's mind quickly began to spin and roll. The last thing he saw was the two men climbing the stairs.

Then the basement went dark and the door above was closed and locked.

So cold, and the whole of the world reduced to only pain and wild fear and the sound of his own breathing.

Then, suddenly, nothingness.

PART THREE

November 1

THE DAY OF
THE DEAD

◆◆◆

Twelve

In her room at the end of the hall, lying flat on the worn-out bed, Evangeline Amendora waited for the sunset.

The morphine Janssen had given her had put distance between her and her pain but hadn't knocked her out—it never did, not in all the times they had used it together, at first during her training and then, later, recreationally, to pass the occasional night. Unable to come and go freely, not till all the loose ends were tied up, they sought escape in other ways. One night a week, usually a Saturday, he would inject them both and they would lie down together, giving themselves to the effects. Instead of making her drowsy, morphine caused in her the side effect of excitability—her body would be perfectly still, her breathing deep and easy, as though she were sound asleep, but inside her chest, an ever-spilling euphoria, and in her mind, pleasant, calmly racing thoughts. The joy of morphine was that, ultimately, nothing could reach her—memories that would otherwise fill her with fear or rage suddenly had no power to do so, evoked in her no reaction whatsoever.

Medicinal, then, these nights with him. Precious escapes from old wounds.

Medicinal, too, now; the blow to her head, as Janssen had pointed out, meant she shouldn't fall asleep, which she hadn't done at all during the long day. Nor had she felt any pain, or fear, or rage. Nothing but hour after hour of a waking sleep, an alert but profound peace, and Janssen, through most of it, right there with her, solid anchor to her drifting balloon.

He was gone now, though, and she heard voices coming up from downstairs. *Business, unavoidable, otherwise he'd be here.* Good to hear, after so many days of silence. Night was approaching, and it had been a few hours prior to dawn when she was brought back here, so she was out of danger, or at least far enough out of it.

Lifting her hand, she touched the bandage covering her temple. Crisp, dry—her bleeding had stopped. She was still high, but at the tail end of it, pain beginning to emerge. Touching the wound wasn't the right thing to do; she felt a deep nausea when she did, and suddenly couldn't focus well with her left eye, so she stopped fussing with it, instead lay still and watched what could be seen of the sky through the window on the other side of the room.

This sunset would be, thanks to the morphine, the first sunset in a long time that didn't send her back to those days of humiliation and terror, those long-ago hours when she was a child in bed, waiting for the sound of footsteps in the hallway outside her door. Just a girl then, nothing about her even remotely womanly. He, though, was a fully developed man, hairy and smelling of sweat and booze, and so hard. Normally, these thoughts were enough to cause her to relive those nights as though they were happening in present time, or as though they were just about to happen. *The dread, the shame.* Now, though, she could look at these thoughts and feel nothing but joy that she was alive, that she would never again be that little girl lost to desperation and fear, nor that young woman selling her body in the slums of São Paulo.

So the sunset came, light autumn gray darkening into blackest night. Dark out here, the darkest place she'd ever known, easily. Downstairs, men were moving about; she heard the sounds of boots upon old floors. Several voices, doors closing.

It would be time, soon.

She made herself sit up. It wasn't the easiest thing to do. Janssen had stripped her at some point, but she had no memory of that. She remembered bleeding, though, so that was why. In panties and a half-shirt, she looked at her strong legs, and her stomach, lean and hard, then, finally, studied her long arms, muscular and crisscrossed with veins.

She was the strong one now, she held the power.

There were clothes nearby, on the chair Janssen had sat in all day. She stood, felt a wave of blinding nausea, but fought through it. Dressing herself—again, not the easiest thing—she then stood at the window, looking out at the vehicles parked in line in the rear driveway. Her Ford sedan, the Town Car, and two other vehicles, an unmarked police car and an old Corvette. *A full house, below.*

Eventually the nausea became too great, and she returned to the bed, sitting on the edge of the mattress. The sick feeling subsided, but in its wake was a headache, the sensation of pressure, like something was growing inside her head.

The drug was wearing off; she'd need more to continue. She had a high tolerance for pain—her training, at times, thanks to Karl, had bordered on brutal—but this was something else, a kind of pain she'd never known before.

Waiting on the edge of that bed now. Waiting to do what she had been trained to do, what she did so well.

Cal heard the sound of his name.

"*Cal. Cal.*"

A whispered voice, sounding distant at first, and then, suddenly, right there in front of him.

"*Cal. Cal.*" Spoken with an insistent tone.

It was Eric Carver's voice, that much had been clear almost from the start. Cal opened his eyes, followed the voice to its source. A dim light was on, and it stabbed his eyes. Nonetheless, he could see Carver, standing just a few feet ahead of him, dressed in the same clothes he had been wearing two nights ago. European jeans, designer black sweater, Belstaff leather jacket—and those cowboy boots. He offered Cal a bottle of water.

"You must be thirsty," he said softly.

Cal nodded, closing his eyes against the light. He felt the bottle touch his lips. Water poured into his mouth. He swallowed.

"More?" Carver said.

Another nod, more water in his mouth. Cal opened his eyes again. Carver waited a moment, then capped the bottle and placed it on the cement floor. He pulled up a chair and sat, just feet from Cal now, directly in front of him and eye to eye.

"I need you to listen to me," he said. "Are you listening?"

Cal didn't have another nod in him. He just looked at his boss, saying nothing.

"They're going to be coming down in a few minutes," Carver said, "and they're going to hurt you. Do you understand me? They're going to hurt you, bad. But that doesn't have to happen. They want to know where the tapes are. They want to know if the tapes even exist or if the whole thing was Lebell trying to bluff them. Just tell me the truth right now, and I'll go upstairs and tell them. I swear, they won't hurt you if you tell them what they want to know. Do you understand me?"

Cal shook his head once. It took all he had. He felt groggy and weak. He remembered being injected but had no idea how long he'd been out.

Carver leaned closer. "Cal, I need you to listen to me. Are you listening to me?" He paused, holding out for eye contact. Eventually Cal gave it to him. "They've got someone who's supposed to be very good at this, at hurting people. Do you hear me, Cal? She's going to come down here and fuck you up. And trust me, you'll tell them what they want to know. It's just a matter of how long it takes you to give in. Hell, Janssen got Messing to make that call to you in a matter of minutes. A couple punches to the face, a threat to his wife and kids, and he did what Janssen wanted him to do. That's how serious they are, Cal. They killed a fucking detective. They used him for their own ends, and when it became necessary, they tied him to a chair, made him talk, and then shot him in the head with his own fucking gun. These people, they do whatever it takes. I'm scared for you right now. They're going to get you to tell them, and it won't just be a few punches to the face. So tell me now and save yourself the torment."

Carver paused again to allow that to sink in. Then, in a softer tone, the tone of a friend, he said, "I tried to keep you out of this, you realize that, right? That's why I had you work on the Benz, so they'd be able to make their move without anybody in the way. I was looking out for you, Cal, like I always do."

"You gave them the code. It wasn't Messing, it was you."

"Messing was a Boy Scout. In fact, it sounded like he was trying to scare you into running with those threats of arresting you. He was supposed to get you to stay put till Karl got there, not take off. Janssen put a bullet in his head for that. He tried to save you, and it got him killed. These people, man, they don't leave anything to chance. They know what they're doing, they don't fool around. So let me help you, okay? Tell me what they want to know, and you won't have to go through what they're about to put you through. Do you hear me? Cal? Do you understand what I'm saying here?"

Cal shook his head again, then said, "I don't know where the tapes are." Despite the two sips of water, his throat was painfully dry, so dry that it pained him to speak.

"So they do exist?"

Cal said nothing.

"According to Messing, Lebell said that if something happened to him the tapes would become public. So someone has to know where he hid them. Who knows, Cal? Is it you? I fucking hope not."

"She did."

"She who?"

"You were the one who laid down the oil, right?" Cal said. "It was the oil I had given you the other day. That was you, right?"

"Cal, who knows? Do you know? Just tell me."

"You laid down that oil, right?"

"What does that have to do—"

"You laid down the oil?"

"Yeah. So?"

"Then you killed her. And I swear, you're going to fucking pay. Do you hear me?"

Carver ignored the threat. The kid's rage, though weak, unsettled him slightly.

"Angelica Pulaski knew," he said.

"Yeah. So that's it. Wherever the tapes are, they're just going to sit there."

Carver got sidetracked by this. "Was she one of his women?" he said. "Was he fucking her, too? Jesus, was there anyone he wasn't fucking?"

"Shut up," Cal said.

"Oh, so you were the one fucking her. Quite a coup for a grease monkey like you, banging a woman like that. It's been all over the radio today, by the way. 'Prominent local woman found dead, killed in an early morning motorcycle crash.' That's how we found out who she was. The good news is, you seem to be in the clear so far. The bike was unregistered, so there's no way to trace it back to its owner. The scene clearly shows that there were two people on the bike, though, so they know she wasn't driving the thing. Of course, the cops will search the thing for prints, take it apart if they have to, dust every scrap of it. Once they lift a print, all they have to do is get a print of yours to match it to. Plenty of those at the garage, right?"

Cal said nothing.

"Of course," Carver continued, "no reason for the cops to come to the garage at all. No reason to connect you to that bike. Yet. All the more reason to tell me the truth, Cal. She was beloved in this town, friends with all the right people. I'm no lawyer, but you might be looking at a charge of negligent homicide. I know how you feel about cops. Do you really want to put your future in their hands, trust that they'll do you right?"

Cal remained silent. Carver looked at him for a moment.

"So you're telling me, Cal, the one person who knew is dead."

"Yes."

"Something this important to Lebell, and he only told one person?"

Cal nodded.

Another pause, Carver studying his friend's face.

It was Cal who broke this silence.

"What are you doing?" he said. "With these people? What are you doing?"

"What I have to do. To get myself out of the hole I'm in. The hole I got put in when the town wouldn't let me tear this fucking place down. Let's just say 'these people,' as you call them, know how to reward a favor. They came to me, told me about Lebell, what he used to do, that he was a fugitive, said they'd help me if I helped them. I figured there were certain men in town who'd be pretty pleased when they learned I got rid of our cock-happy friend. The kind of men who could open certain doors for me, you know. So it was a win-win all around. Who could walk away from a deal like that?"

Carver leaned back in his seat, looked at Cal for a moment more, then said, "I know he was like a big brother to you, Cal. I know he was like getting back the brother you lost. But don't forget who took you in when your real brother was killed. Don't forget who gave you a job and a place to live when you needed it, when you had nothing and no one. I think I deserve a little loyalty, too, don't you? Help me help them, and we all win. Don't you understand that? There's still a way for you to walk away from this."

"I'm telling you, the one person who knew is dead. You guys win."

"You're certain Lebell didn't tell anyone else?"

"I only know what he told me. He said she was the only one who knew. He had a lawyer retained, but Angel was the only one who knew."

Carver nodded, then stood up and said, "Is that good enough?"

Cal realized quickly that his boss wasn't talking to him but rather someone else, someone standing behind the chair.

Another light came on, a bare bulb overhead. *Yet more pain for*

Cal's eyes. Looking around, he saw the chair Messing had been bound to. It was an office chair, just like the one he was in. The detective, though, wasn't anywhere to be seen.

Then, on the floor nearby, Cal saw a body wrapped up in a clear plastic tarp.

Through the plastic, blurred by its layers, was Messing's battered face.

Staring, dead.

Cal looked away. Tierno was standing beside him.

"Maybe he's lying, maybe he isn't," he said to Carver. "We'll know either way in a little bit."

Carver nodded, looked down at Cal, and said, "I'm sorry, Cal. I really am. I tried to help you." He took a breath, let it out. "Man, this is going to suck for you," he concluded. "Bad."

"I need something to eat," Tierno said. "C'mon, let's go."

Tierno was climbing the stairs, hadn't even looked at Cal. Carver turned finally and followed the FBI agent. The door was closed, but the lock didn't turn, and the lights remained on.

Cal tried to squirm free, but this motion, desperate and futile, only served to set his broken hand on fire, and he gave up.

There was nothing to do now but wait.

Eve was sitting on the edge of the bed, looking toward the window, when she heard footsteps coming down the hallway.

Janssen's footsteps, she'd know them anywhere. He opened the door. A little bit of light spilled in from the hallway, laying an oblong shape across the floor.

"How do you feel?" Janssen said.

She looked at him, smiled, and nodded. *Fine.*

"It's time," he said.

She stood and picked up her mechanic's bag. She felt nausea, needed to concentrate to maintain her balance, but hid this from him. "What do we need to know?"

"If everything he has told us is true."

"And after?" she said.

"No loose ends."

So, a torture and a kill.

"We in the clear?"

Janssen nodded. "It looks that way."

"So this is it?"

"If he's told us the truth, yeah."

So, her last torture and kill.

"Where will we go first?"

They would, he'd promised, be free to make use of his wealth when all this was done. Free to travel, free to live. No more hiding, no more jobs, no reason for them to ever be apart again.

"Wherever you want to go," Janssen said.

"I'm thinking Amsterdam."

"You'll like it there."

"I want to smoke hashish for days. Just forget everything. Erase it all and start with a clean slate."

"Then let's take care of this," he said.

She nodded, smiled. "Okay, let's."

Following him down the long hallway, Eve lost the vision in her left eye. Suddenly, as if she had closed it. But by the time she reached the ornate stairs it was back.

In the kitchen, Tierno and the other man, Carver—the man who owned this building, had stocked her room for her and provided the Ford sedan—were waiting.

Carver looked at Eve, his eyes quickly moving down to the canvas bag in her hand. "I think I might wait outside," he said.

"Why don't you go and get us something to eat," Tierno said to him. His tone was casual.

"Yeah, all right," Carver said.

"Any good pizza out here?"

"Depends. What's good to you?"

"Greek."

"Yeah, there's a place in Bridgehampton, actually—"

Janssen told them to shut up, that they weren't out of this yet, and that no one left till it was done. The men instantly went silent, though, Eve noticed, the FBI agent's demeanor didn't change.

No respect for the work, Eve thought. She'd gotten that sense from him the first time they had met. A man interested only in shortcuts, arrogant and devoid of patience. She felt sorry for his wife, had even indulged herself, as she had waited for days in her room upstairs, in fantasies of going to work on him.

Janssen led Eve past them and to the basement door.

He opened it for her, and she looked down the stairs, wincing at the bright light.

Hiding from all these men the effort required, she took the first step downward.

Thirteen

He heard her at first, moving down the stairs, and then, as she approached the bottom step, he began to see her.

Feet and legs—boots, black jeans—and then the rest of her, dark sweater tight on a long torso. It was a gradual unveiling during which his heart began to race and, despite the cold around him, he began to sweat.

She was, when he finally was able to see her face, exactly what Lebell had said she would be: beautiful. Stunning, regal—even the bandage on the side of her head couldn't take away from that.

Walking toward Cal, slowly, she looked to him like a woman who had just emerged from a deep sleep. Her mouth was turned up by half-smile—a contented smile—and there was a twinkle in her eyes.

She was carrying a green canvas bag, which, once she reached him, she placed on the cement floor. Pushing aside the chair Carver had sat in, she stood over Cal, looking down at him, saying nothing.

Finally, she got down on both knees, just a foot from him, and unzipped and opened the bag. She was, as she did this, still looking at him, maintaining a kind of lover's eye contact. *Lingering, intense, intimate.*

"It's Cal, right?" she said.

He heard the same accent he'd heard on the phone two nights ago. Her voice was low and calm, like before, but her tone was more friendly now, more casual.

Cal said nothing.

She took in a breath, through her nose, slow and deep, and waited for a response to her question. When it became obvious that she wasn't going to get one—this realization only took a few seconds—she let the breath out, then, her smile growing just a little bit more, nodded decisively and said, "Okay. So let's get started, then."

He watched as she laid out a hand towel and began to place the contents of the canvas bag upon it one by one.

A revolver was first. Pulling the release pin located under the thick barrel, she pushed the hinged cylinder from the frame, confirming that the weapon was loaded. Replacing the cylinder with an expert flip of her wrist, she laid the gun down.

Next was a pair of large scissors, and, after that, vise-grip pliers.

The last item she removed from the bag was a cell phone, and Cal recognized it immediately.

Heather's old phone. *With her new number stored in its memory.* One of the few numbers, in fact.

This phone was his only means of contacting her, since he didn't know what motel she and her sister had run to. More than that, though, it would be a way for Janssen to contact her as well, should he for some reason decide to do so.

Cal wanted to step on the thing, felt an overwhelming urge to smash it to pieces with his bare foot.

Like his arms, though, his ankles were held by duct tape to the chair, so there was no chance of getting at the phone.

"It's amazing," the woman said then, "the history of inflicting pain on a person." Her voice was like a coo. "There have been so many elaborate ways over the years, so many machines constructed for that purpose, and yet it is the simple methods that remain the best. In the Dark Ages torturers used to focus on the hands and the feet, not only because our extremities are made up of small, easily broken bones and nerve clusters, but because without the use of them, you simply couldn't survive. With beaten feet, you couldn't walk, had to crawl, and with mangled hands, you couldn't feed yourself, never mind apply your trade, tend crops. The best torment is always a combination of physical and psychological. I came across in my studies a method that really intrigued me. It involved binding a person's fingers together tightly and forcing arrowheads between them. Genius, really, because all you need is some twine or strips of leather and a single arrow. Easy enough to come by back when this technique was devised, right? And you could do it all day and the subject wouldn't even come close to dying. Apply some pressure to those cuts and they would close, so you could control the blood loss. And then, if you wanted, you could start over again, make new cuts or just open up the old ones."

She paused, then continued. "So, you have the physical pain but also the psychological element of knowing that, with each finger that is mutilated, your day-to-day life will only get more and more difficult. Who wouldn't confess to stop that, right?"

Cal said nothing. His heart was pounding so hard he almost couldn't breathe.

"Today," she said, "we're going to be working on your hand. I understand one is already broken, so we'll focus on that to start, see where that gets us."

Still kneeling, she reached for the oversized scissors, did so without severing eye contact. Her half-smile didn't for an instant diminish.

She saw the look on his face when she picked up the scissors.

"Cutting off pieces of you is a last resort," she assured him. "I'm pretty certain we'll know whether you're telling the truth or not before it gets to that, though. These I use for something else."

She began to cut his jeans, from the cuff of the right leg up to his thigh, and from there, carefully, all the way to the waistband. Then she did the same with the left leg, again all the way up to the waistband. With a bit of doing, she pulled his jeans off him, then cut his underwear, removing that, too.

His shirt was next—one cut up the center, then one up each sleeve. She cut with care, but when it came time to remove the shredded garments, she wasn't shy about manhandling him.

Strong hands, powerful arms flexing. Within a minute, he was naked.

Kneeling still, she moved closer to him, to the point where her shoulders were squarely between his knees. She was just inches from his groin now. Laying the scissors back down on the towel, she picked up the pliers. During this her eyes shifted once, and she looked at his manhood. A quick glance, and then, her smile unbroken, she looked at his eyes again.

Sitting back on her heels, she rested her elbows on his thighs, holding the pliers with both hands as though it were a wishbone.

She wanted him to see it, get a good look at it. She wanted, no doubt, to call attention to his utter vulnerability—her position between his knees, his exposed genitals just inches away.

"It works better if I tell you first what I'm going to do," she said. "Normally, I'd start by crushing the first joint of your little finger, then move on to the next finger, and then the next one, and so on. After that

I'd go back to your little finger again and work on the second joint, move on from there. That's eight fingers and two thumbs, two joints in the fingers and one in the thumbs. And when I say crush, I mean it. I grind each joint to splinters. The little ones I have actually turned to dust. But, like I said, since your hand is already broken, I'll just go ahead and make use of that. For starters, anyway."

She placed the pliers in her back pocket, then put her palms on his thighs and pushed herself up. Rising to her feet, she stood up straight but seemed, suddenly, to lose her balance. Closing her eyes, she held still for a moment, or tried to, ended up, despite her efforts, wavering just a little.

Cal watched her. After a moment, she opened her eyes again, took a breath, then another, eventually regaining her composure.

Whatever that spell had been exactly, it was behind her now.

Looking down at him again, displaying that same almost loving smile, she bent forward without warning and pressed her palm on top of his hand, leaning all her weight upon it, crushing it against the wooden arm of the chair.

He screamed and flailed against the restraints but got nowhere. She held the pressure for several seconds, then let it up just a bit, only to press down again, even harder than before. She repeated that procedure about half a dozen times—pressure, relief, then more pressure—before actually stopping.

"That hurt, didn't it?" she said. She made no effort to hide the fact that she was pleased with his reaction so far. "And to think, we've only just begun."

"Please," Cal said.

"Did you tell us the truth?"

"Yes."

She went at it again, this time grinding her thumb into one of the broken bones itself, twisting back and forth as she drove into it with all her strength.

Another scream broke from Cal, tearing his dry throat as it rose to his mouth. He flailed again against his restraints, jumped as if a current of electricity were moving through him. His muscles flexed, every one, but no matter how hard he tried he couldn't get away from the pain.

As before, she pressed down, then released, only to press down again, harder. Many more times, though, this time. He lost count when they got up to around a dozen. After that, all he could do was flail and twitch, wait for it to end, if it was ever going to end.

Then, finally, it was over.

She stood up straight and looked down at him, giving him a moment. A glance at his genitals, then back to his eyes.

"One man actually got an erection during his session. Can you believe that?"

Cal said nothing. Slumped in the chair, he tried to breathe. Tears had welled in his eyes. There was nothing he could do about that.

She was quickly becoming a blur towering over him.

"Have you told us the truth, Cal?" she said.

"Yes. I've told you everything I know. I don't know anything more."

She reached for her back pocket then, removed the pliers, folded her arms across her stomach.

"Have you told us the truth?" she repeated.

This time, however, she slurred her words.

There was no pretending that didn't happen. Blinking his eyes, Cal looked up at her. Something was wrong, he could see that. Her eyes fluttered, and she wavered again.

"Have you—" She stopped short; the slurring had become worse.

Leaning down before he could even respond, she drove the blunt ends of the metal pliers handles into the same already broken bone.

Two points of pain this time, and no fake relief, just a steady application of pressure.

He was screaming now through gritted teeth, expected them at any moment to shatter under the pressure of his clenched jaw—somehow, through the chaos and fear and pain, this thought existed. She let this session go on for the longest time yet, maybe a good half minute.

Agony with no promise of an end, and an endless supply of screams interrupted only by a few gasping pleas for her to stop.

She ended this assault, at last, as suddenly as she had started it.

Pausing, she watched him, then decided quickly, "This just isn't painful enough, I guess."

No slurring this time, but she still sounded strange, her words drawn out and monotone, as though she were a deaf person trying to speak.

Cal blinked the tears from his eyes, or tried to; he could still, for the most part, only see a blur of a woman above him. He watched as she knelt down again, fitting her shoulders between his knees once more.

She touched the little finger of his broken hand, and even the slight movement her contact caused set off a spasm of sharp pain.

"How will you work," she said, "with hands that don't?"

There was definitely something wrong. Her voice sounded even stranger than it had sounded seconds ago. Again, Cal blinked his eyes, tried to clear his vision. After several attempts he was able to see her face with a degree of clarity, and what he saw made no sense at all.

One side was drooping, the corner of her mouth looking like it was being tugged downward by an invisible string.

His eyes quickly went to the bandage on her temple. From his wrestling years he knew enough about the dangers of head injuries, and the potential aftermath of any kind of brain trauma, to realize what was happening.

She was stroking out.

Struggling to maintain her focus, she took hold of his little finger, brought the pliers to it, and was lining up the first knuckle between its ridged jaws when her hand went limp and the tool dropped to the floor.

She grabbed onto his thigh with her other hand—the hand that was still good—to keep herself from falling over, but his leg was slick with sweat, and anyway, it was too late. Her head tipped forward, acting like a dropped anchor and causing her to lean against him with all her weight. She lingered there for a bit, then slid along his inner thigh and, within seconds, was in a heap at his feet.

It was then that the seizure began.

Cal looked down at her, almost asked if she was okay, but caught himself before he spoke. She had landed on her side, and he could see that the half of her face that had twisted horribly was now frozen that way. Her still-good arm was raised, held out in midair and shaking; it looked to him like the arm of a puppet. From her misshapen mouth was coming a dreadful sound, the worst Cal had ever heard, part old person moaning and baby crying and dog whimpering. Not a loud sound at all, compared to his own howling screams a moment ago, but still loud enough that those upstairs might be called by it to investigate.

If he was going to make a move, he needed to make it now.

He looked at the tools she had laid out, his eyes quickly landing on the large scissors.

They could cut the tape that was holding him.

He would have to tip himself over, though, and make himself fall to the cement floor to reach them. Even if he did that, there was no guarantee he would land close enough. He tried to scoot the chair closer by bucking his torso, but his tormentor was in his way.

It would be impossible, with her there, for him to make it to the scissors. He frantically looked for something else, something closer, a piece of glass or broken bit of cement, something, anything. He saw nothing at all—and then something caught his eye.

A flash of silver, clipped to the hip pocket of her jeans.

A folding knife.

His heart soared. Quickly he turned the chair so his left hand—his unbroken hand—was directly above her. To lean in a way that would cause him to fall onto his left side meant pulling up against his restraints with his right hand, but what choice did he have? Each jerking motion sent pain rattling through him. It was like a spike was being driven through his palm. Even so, he kept at it and finally got momentum enough to upend himself. He lingered for a second on the edge of balance, then fell over, landing on top of her, close to his target but not yet there.

He needed to wriggle his torso and buck with his legs to bring her hip pocket within reach of his bound hand.

Her seizure was ending; she was making almost no noise now. Still breathing, but not regularly, and not without having to struggle. Every exhalation now carried a wet, raspy sound. Faint, from deep in her lungs.

Her face was just a few inches from his; there was no avoiding that if he was going to position himself properly. They were eye to eye, but hers were, thankfully, closed. He found the edge of her pocket, dug his fingertips in, and pulled her closer still. Her breath now, when she breathed, touched his face, and his hers. Grabbing the knife at last, he pulled it free, carefully but quickly turned it in his hand. He expected that at any moment the door at the top of the stairs would fling open. Looking down at the knife, he saw that there was a hole in the exposed back edge of the blade that would allow for one-handed opening.

Pressing the fleshy tip of his thumb into it, he pried open the blade till he heard it lock into place. He turned the handle again and began to work the blade between his sweat-soaked skin and the tape clinging to it.

It took some doing, but finally he was cutting through it.

Still, it took him a good minute to free his left hand. All that time, he was face-to-face with her. She was dying, there was no mistaking that. By the time he cut his right hand free, she had stopped breathing altogether, and by the time he cut the tape holding his ankles to the legs of the chair, her dark, flawless skin had begun to pale.

Tossing the knife aside, he stood, looking toward the stairs and listening. He heard nothing, not even the sound of people moving around above. *Could they have left?* Bending down, he grabbed Heather's cell phone, but since he was naked, he had no pocket to put it in. His clothes had been cut to useless rags, so he quickly looked around for something he could cover himself with.

Nothing.

Out of desperation he looked at his tormentor. Maybe her clothes would fit him. Then he thought of Messing, rolled up in layers of clear plastic. As desperate as he was, as vulnerable as he felt, he didn't have what it took to strip a dead body of its clothes.

He looked for his Schott jacket and Sidi boots—they had been removed, so maybe they were here somewhere—but he didn't see them. Giving up his search, he cradled his right hand against his chest and placed the cell phone between his elbow and his ribs, holding it there, then bent down again and picked up the revolver with his left.

His palm was sweaty, making the grip slick, but he didn't think too much about that. All he cared about was getting out of there, putting this place behind him.

He moved to the bottom of the stairs, lingered there for a moment, looking up at the door, then finally started to climb them. He moved as slowly and as quietly as he could; it took all he had not to just bolt. Near the top of the stairs he paused again, listening through the door, hearing still nothing. He needed to turn the doorknob, did so with his broken hand, wincing but forcing himself to keep silent. Just as the latch was released and the door began to move from its frame, Heather's cell phone started to slip from under his arm. Catching it in time with his left hand, while still managing to hold on to the gun, he placed the phone between his teeth. What else could he do with it? Nudging the door open with his shoulder, he looked through the widening gap into a dark kitchen. The door swung silently for a foot, and then another, and then, suddenly, the upper hinge creaked.

He probably wouldn't have seen the figure on the other side of the cluttered kitchen if not for the sound the door hinge had made. Seated, its back to the door, the figure instantly stood, knocking the chair over in the process, and, turning, reached under its jacket for—there was no mistaking this, even in the confusion—a weapon.

Panicked moves, though.

Cal calmly raised the revolver and, aiming at the dark figure, pulled the trigger once.

Instantly the figure folded, dropping as though a trapdoor had opened beneath it, landing with a solid *thump* on the floor.

The sound of the gunshot was like a slap to both ears. Cal heard now only a dull ringing, but he ignored that and stepped away from the basement door, from where he'd been standing when he fired his shot. He seemed to know to do this. Moving around an island counter located in the center of the room, he took cover in a corner and aimed the revolver down at the fallen man, watching for any sign of movement but seeing none.

He realized then that this kitchen was a professional kitchen, the kind he and his brother had worked in years ago, back when Heather had been their boss, back in the *good ol' days*. This gave the room, then, a degree of familiarity, and that, in turn, gave Cal the confidence to try to make his way around it in the dark.

Just as he thought this, though, a second figure appeared, stepping into the kitchen through a wide entranceway to the left of the basement door. This figure reached out and flipped a nearby light switch, and the row of fluorescent lights overhead began to flicker.

Visible in this blinking light now was Janssen. Standing just twenty feet away, he quickly looked down at Tierno's body, then at the naked kid standing in the nearby corner, gun in his hand and cell phone clenched between his teeth.

The flickering stopped, the overhead light glowing steadily now. Before Janssen could even speak—before he could do anything more than display a look of angry surprise—Cal calmly took aim and fired another shot.

The bullet entered Janssen's chest, and he was dead before his body hit the ground.

Cal displaced again, stepping over Tierno and moving to another corner, this one on the opposite side of the room. He took cover beside a stainless steel refrigerator, didn't have to wait there, though, for long.

Carver entered through the back door. He took one step inside and then froze when he saw the two bodies.

Leaning around the refrigerator, Cal raised his left arm and aimed at his boss.

His hand, to his surprise, was remarkably steady.

They looked at each other for a long moment.

Finally, Carver said, "Jesus, Cal." He waited for some kind of response, a word, a nod, something, anything, but it must have dawned on him that there would be no such reply, that there was no talking his way out of this, because suddenly he broke for the door, backing toward it, his eyes, wild with desperation, fixed on Cal.

Carver had started a step, but he did not complete it. The bullet Cal fired shattered his forehead, exited the back of his head, and what had begun as a step quickly turned into a stumble.

He fell dead just inside the doorway.

It was minutes later that Cal emerged from the back door of the Hotel St. James. He was dressed in his boss's jeans and boots and Belstaff jacket, nothing on, though, beneath that. It had been difficult enough—between his having one good hand and the fear rushing through him—to remove even those articles of clothing.

Holding the revolver, in case there were others he didn't know about, he saw five vehicles parked in the unlit driveway. Around the property on three sides were trees, some bare, others not, and beyond them, fields. There were no neighboring homes, so no one was close enough to have heard the gunshots, or to glimpse him scrambling now to leave. Or so he hoped.

The first two vehicles that caught his eye were Carver's Corvette and a black Town Car, but the very fact that they were the first he noticed meant they would be too conspicuous. He thought the same about the two unmarked sedans—Messing's and Tierno's, he assumed. The fifth vehicle, a basic four-door Ford, was the only option left, so he hurried toward it.

The keys were in the ignition. Cal wasted no time getting behind the wheel and turning over the engine. At the end of the driveway he paused, uncertain which way to turn, left or right. He still had no idea where in the world he was—the road ahead of him was a secluded two-lane road, probably a stretch of Montauk Highway, but which part, near which village? He decided to turn left, and in a matter of seconds saw a familiar landmark.

A landscaping business, closed for the season.

So, he was in Bridgehampton—just past the village itself—heading west on Montauk Highway.

Maybe all of two miles from his home.

He decided he would drive through Water Mill, and from there follow the back roads till he connected with Scuttlehole. An instinct, this blind urge to return to a safe place, or what had been once, for so long, a safe place.

He quickly thought better of that plan and pulled into the landscaper's empty lot, parking in the shadow of the building and killing the lights and the motor.

He knew that he had left traces of himself back in that place. He didn't have to think too hard to come up with a list of them. Footprints on the basement and kitchen floors, fingerprints on the knife, sweat and skin and probably hair on that chair, certainly on the tape that had held him to it.

There was also the matter of his cut-up clothes and missing boots and jacket.

What choice did he have?

He exited the vehicle and doubled back to the hotel on foot, careful to stay off the road—and out of sight—as much as possible.

Inside the kitchen, he went straight for the industrial dishwasher, identical to the one he'd used back when he had worked for Heather. Using the cuff of the Belstaff jacket like a glove, he pulled off the lower panel and found exactly what he was looking for.

A near-full container of liquid dishwashing detergent.

Removing it, he headed down to the basement. On the cement floor was the dead woman, and, not far from her, in the sheets of thick plastic, Messing.

Stepping to the chair in the center of the room, Cal looked for the knife he had used to free himself, spotted it, and picked it up. Wiping it clean against the designer jeans, he folded the blade closed and slipped it into his hip pocket. Turning the container upside-down, he poured the blue liquid over the chair, then picked up the pieces of his clothing and, using a segment of his cut-up jeans, wiped the chair down. Finally, after recovering and pocketing all the pieces of duct tape, he began walking backward toward the stairs, spilling as he went dashes of the liquid onto the trail he'd no doubt left with his bare feet. Dragging the same segment of his jeans with the toe of Carver's boot, he smudged his markings.

When he reached the stairs, he picked up the soiled piece of jeans, wiping the steps as he climbed them. Every movement, every step and every bend, triggered tremendous pain in his hand, but he couldn't care about that right now.

He retraced his movements through the kitchen as best he could, wiping away his footprints just as he had downstairs. Placing the now empty container on the center island, he wiped down the handle with a piece of his T-shirt, then paused to make certain he had covered everything.

It was at this moment that he realized something.

The second man he killed was, he had assumed, Janssen—but no one had ever said his name, had they? Cal remembered now what Lebell had said when he warned him about that man. *A monster. The fucking Antichrist.* Best, then, to be sure this was him.

Stepping to the body, Cal crouched down, covering his hand with a piece of his T-shirt as he searched the man's pockets. Finding a wallet, he opened it and removed a driver's license.

Holding it to the light and examining it, he saw the man's photo and, printed beside it, the name he was hoping to read.

He'd got them all, then.

Good.

Dropping the wallet, he stood and was about to leave when something in the next room—the room from which Janssen had come—caught his eye.

This was, apparently, a dining room, and on a long table was another body wrapped in plastic. Cal hesitated, then took a few steps toward it, getting as close as he dared, seeing through those sheets the face of the man whom Angelica had struck and killed with a ball peen hammer.

It was only now that Cal realized traces of this man's bone and blood were likely all still at the garage.

As he was turning away to leave, though, one more thing caught his eye.

At the man's feet, on the far end of the table. Several items.

A closer look revealed a helmet, motorcycle jacket, and boots.

His helmet, jacket, and boots.

Grabbing them, making a bundle of all his collected items, and tucking it under his one good arm, Cal fled that place, walking as quickly as he could back to the Ford.

He sat behind the wheel, his heart pounding, his hand throbbing, each out of sync with the other. A numbing pain, the kind that interrupted thought, caused confusion, but he willed himself to focus through all that. Studying his surroundings, looking in all directions, he was fairly confident that no one had seen him come and go. He'd left footsteps, a trail from that hotel to this lot, and in the lot itself, tire marks. That didn't matter. He would discard Carver's boots eventually, and ditch the Ford, too, as soon as he could.

So, then, one more thing to do.

A hulk of a building, made of rotting wood and set on a dark Bridge-hampton back road, the only indication of possible use visible from the outside a small security keypad mounted near the office door.

Holding the helmet, into which he had stuffed his torn jeans and shirt, Cal entered the garage through the office, moving quickly into the first work bay. Switching the circuit breaker back on, he flipped on the lights, saw right away the cloud-shaped stain of blood on the wooden floor and the ball peen hammer not far from it. Leaving them for now, he laid the helmet down and removed the heavy revolver, hold-ing it ready and checking every corner, every possible hiding place, as he made his way through the work bays and to the plank stairs.

Up in his apartment, he proceeded with the same caution, only daring to relax, and even then only slightly, when he was positive he was alone. Putting the revolver back in the outer pocket of the Belstaff jacket, he paused in the doorway of Heather's room and looked at her bed, did this for a long moment. Finally, though, he entered and re-moved the pillowcase from her pillow, filling it with her few belongings—the thrift shop clothes he had bought for her, her vial of jasmine rose oil from her bureau top, her decks of playing cards and tarot cards, her few toiletries.

He stepped into his bedroom. There, of course, was the bed he had, for a few hours anyway, shared with Angelica. After everything that had been done to him tonight, that he had done, all he wanted was to hang on to the memory of her beside him, the stillness he had sensed from her. He would have given anything to put himself back there. He looked at his bed till he simply couldn't look at it anymore, then went to his bureau.

He removed a thermal shirt, put it on, then the jacket over that. Every move, because of his hand, needed to be made carefully. Carver's jeans didn't fit very well, were too long, so he changed into a pair of his own—his second and only other pair. Putting Carver's boots back on, he took Heather's old cell phone and Carver's wallet from the jeans he had removed. He decided to check Carver's wallet, found in it five hundred dollars. *His five hundred?* It had to be. The cash went into the right hip pocket of his jeans, the cell phone into the left.

There was something else in the wallet, too.

Cal's driver's license. He pocketed that as well.

Hurrying to his closet and lifting the loose plank, he reached under the floor for the metal cashier's box. Opening it, he grabbed all of his cash and stuffed it into the jacket's inner pocket, did the same with a roll of quarters he kept for emergencies. After that he picked up the vial of morphine, studied it for a moment before finally pocketing it, too. He'd be a fool to leave it, considering.

Instead of replacing the floorboard, he carried it with him as he stepped into the middle of his room. Placing one end on the floor and holding the other, he stepped down onto the center of the plank, snapping it into two pieces.

Back downstairs, he placed the pillowcase with Heather's things in the office, then hurried back into the first work bay, heading this time straight for his tool chest. He removed a roll of duct tape and pulled off several foot-long strips of it, hanging each strip in a row from the edge of his workbench. Sitting on a stool, he made a splint of the two pieces of wood, securing it to his wrist as best he could with the tape. A crappy job of it, but it would have to do for now. As he did this—no easy feat, indeed—he looked at the Russian's bloodstain just a few feet away, and the hammer resting not far from that.

It was too big a stain to simply wash away, and throughout this place were the Russian's footprints—as well as those left by whoever had taken his body from here. Too many footprints to account for. Anyway, it was the presence of his own fingerprints—on every tool, every part of this place—that he was concerned about now.

When the splint was done, he removed a large screwdriver from his tool chest and stepped to the rear of the Benz, got down onto his knees, and, with one thrust, punched a hole in the gas tank, letting the fuel pour out onto the already oil-saturated floor.

In the next stall he did the same to the Citroën's gas tank, then picked up his helmet and emptied it of the torn clothing, dropping each piece to the floor. Tearing the liner from the helmet—it contained, no doubt, strands of hair, flakes of skin—he dropped the helmet, too.

He paused to be certain that he had covered everything, thought immediately of the Lexus parked out back. There was, though, nothing he could do about that—beyond the wiping down he'd already done. The presence of that vehicle here was a connection between this place and Angelica Pulaski, but it was one that could be explained. She was from Southampton, Carver was from Southampton, and this little side business of his catered exclusively to the wealthy and their luxury cars.

Anyway, really, what did that matter? Angelica no longer needed Cal's protection. He had already failed to keep that promise.

He looked around quickly. Not an easy thing to do, setting fire to one's home, even a home as makeshift as this. Barely, really, a home at all, but the only one he'd known for four years.

A long time, for a kid like him.

Cal kicked the ball peen hammer across the floor till it landed in the growing puddle under the Benz, then returned to the office and opened the top drawer of Carver's desk, grabbing a book of matches.

Back in the doorway—the garage already reeked overwhelmingly of gasoline fumes—he lit the liner and threw it toward the puddle.

The fire, of course, was instant; it rose to the height of a man in seconds and began to spread with a menacing speed that made it seem no less than alive.

Cal didn't look back as he burst through the door and ran for the Ford parked a few hundred feet down Scuttlehole Road, in the shadow of a tree. It wouldn't take long at all, he knew, for that place, and everything it in, to burn to ash or melt to scrap.

A fire trap, indeed.

So there was no need for him to look.

Still, as he drove away, he glanced once into the rearview mirror, saw behind him the tree-lined horizon glowing deep red, a broad rim of sky lit as if by a sunset.

He parked the Ford at the Bridgehampton train station, on the dark edge of the lot, and retrieved Heather's new cell phone number from her old one, making a point this time to commit it to memory.

Breaking the roll of quarters open, he selected six and, as he walked toward the platform, wiped them down on his thermal shirt, placing each coin, once it was clean of his prints, onto the palm of his taped-up hand.

At the station pay phone—the platform was empty at that moment, not a soul anywhere in sight, which was why he had chosen to come here and use this phone—he grabbed a scrap of paper from a nearby trash can and covered the tip of his finger with it as he punched in

Heather's number. Then he used the paper as a glove as he deposited the number of coins requested by the prerecorded voice.

Back at the Ford, he waited behind the wheel, watching as the 7:30 eastbound eventually arrived and its passengers disembarked and headed toward their cars. When the last vehicle had left the parking lot and was gone from sight, stillness and silence resumed.

It became more and more difficult for Cal to ignore the steady pain of his brutalized hand. No, not just steady, *growing*. His hand had swollen so much that his flesh strained the makeshift splint. The motor was off, so there was no heat, and he had hoped that the cold gathering around him would help somewhat, but it didn't. He knew that he needed to apply ice soon and get the swelling under control.

Finally, though, as his wait continued, the pain got to be too much to bear, so he reached into his pocket and removed the vial of morphine.

He looked at it for a moment, then twisted the cap and withdrew the eyedropper. A third of the way up the glass tube was a white line. A dosage marker? Probably. He reinserted the dropper, pinched the rubber nipple, then pulled the dropper out again.

Even in this dark the fluid was clearly visible. It reached just past that white line.

Close enough.

Tilting his head back, he put the dropper in his mouth, felt the fluid spill onto his tongue. Surprisingly sweet, this stuff. Swallowing it, he recapped the vial and returned it to his pocket, then resumed watching through the windshield for the cab that would bring him to Heather and Amanda.

Fourteen

———◆———

The numbness began in his lips and spread quickly to his face, and soon enough there was a lightness in his chest that was a powerful mixture of both indifference and bliss.

He could think only of Aaron's girlfriend, and the smile on her face whenever she got high. He knew, though, that he wasn't smiling at all.

The cab, driven by an old, withered black man with a Jamaican accent, took Cal to a motel on the western edge of Southampton Village, just past the movie theater. A smart choice, he thought—everything they would need was within walking distance, and the police station was only a block away. Heather and Amanda, waiting for him at the door of their room at the far end of the motel, immediately rushed to him and helped him inside, where he lay down on one of the two twin beds and they placed a bath towel filled with ice on his broken hand. Heather, desperate to understand what had happened to him, asked many questions, but then, when it became clear that he had taken morphine—Amanda was the first to realize that—allowed him to rest quietly.

He could have talked to them, could have made an attempt to answer at least the first few of the many questions that were thrown at him, but there was nothing he could say to them that wouldn't lead to his having to reveal what had been done to him and what he had done. He wasn't ready to speak those words yet.

Anyway, it had to be obvious enough—by his hand, yes, but also by the look in his eyes, the combination of terror and sorrow that even morphine couldn't mask—that he had been through some kind of hell or another.

His eyes were closed, but his mind raced. He felt like he was on a train that was moving just a little too fast, on the verge of flying off its rails. All he could do was sit tight and wait.

He wasn't aware of his body, only the absence of it. He was simply consciousness now. Active, alert, gushing. He thought of the claims of those who had experienced near-death—the floating, the looking down upon themselves from above, the feeling of euphoria. He could see himself as clear as day stretched out on that motel bed in the dark, could even see Heather and Amanda in the next bed over. The grip that terror had on him was loosening; he could feel himself about to slip away from it, be rid of it for good.

Then the parade began. Faces moving past. His father, his brother, Lebell, Messing, Angelica—all the dead, all those who had been killed. It wasn't long, though, before a second parade came along. Tierno, Janssen, Carver—those Cal had killed.

Then, the face of the woman who had hurt him, tortured him. To gain knowledge he did not possess. What was it Tierno had told him? *I feel for the person who has nothing to make them stop.*

It was some time after this that Cal remembered what Lebell had told him.

All that matters is that the people I leave behind are safe.

All the rushing thoughts were gone suddenly, and only this one remained. Cal hung on to it, looked at it and only it with his mind's eye, wouldn't let it go away, till the effects of the morphine began at last to fade and the sense of having a body—a body in pain, no less—began to return.

Sitting up, laying the towel full of ice on the other side of the bed, he moved to the edge of the stiff mattress, lingered there for a moment, adrift, then finally stood. The painkiller had faded but hadn't left him, not yet. He felt lightheaded, clumsy, but he focused through it and was able to move with a degree of skill.

He stepped to the desk, where all his gear lay. He found the Belstaff jacket, removed his cash from its inner pocket. It was too dark to count the bills, so he thumbed through them and divided the stack roughly in half, returned one pile to the jacket and laid the other on the desk.

Then he dressed, as quietly as he could. Carver's boots, not his own, and the Belstaff jacket, the revolver in one of its outer pockets.

He placed his Sidi boots inside the Schott jacket and zipped it closed.

Standing between the beds, he looked down at the girls, knew by their breathing that they were asleep. He remembered the dream Heather had—what was it, all of two nights ago?—about the unknown man, like a shadow she had to shake but couldn't, following her through dark city streets and across empty fields, and all the while, cupped in her hands, a candle she could not—she dare not—let go out.

He wondered if she was dreaming that now, or if maybe she was dreaming something else, something pleasant. *Like the dreams he had of her.* His daily life, the routine he followed, obeyed like church doctrine, was all about doing what was right, what was expected and, therefore, safe. It was in his dreams that he indulged in the inappropriate, the risky, the downright dangerous.

That was, at least, till now.

He thought of leaving without waking them, without a word, but he couldn't bring himself to do that. He hadn't known that the night his brother left—to get morphine for his girl, so she would stay with them—would be the last time he'd see Aaron. He had lived in fear of all kinds of abandonment since, big and small. There was no way that he could just disappear on Heather without first telling her why.

Without knowing they were saying good-bye.

He sat on the edge of her bed, and this motion alone woke her.

Cal quickly glanced at the clock on the table between the two beds. It was just past ten.

"You okay?" Heather whispered.

Groggy, she reached for him in the dark, her hand finding not skin nor the material of his thermal shirt but leather.

She propped herself up on her elbows. "What's going on?"

"I need to go," Cal said. He didn't want to disturb Amanda, whispered even more softly than Heather did.

"What do you mean? Where?"

"Away."

"What's going on?"

He paused, wished he could think of a way around having to say it, but there just wasn't one.

He needed her to let him go, for her own good.

"I killed some men tonight," he said.

"What?"

"One of them was an FBI agent. He was on the take, but I don't think that matters."

"Cal."

"He was going to kill me, but I don't think that matters, either."

"Jesus. Is this because of Lebell?"

He nodded, then said, "He's gone, too."

"What happened?"

"The cabdriver, he knows to keep his mouth shut, right? You trust him."

"Yeah. He's a friend."

"It's important that no one knows I came here tonight."

"Cal, talk to me. What happened?"

"One minute I was working on a car, and the next thing I know . . ." He was still stoned, he realized, his mind not nearly as settled as he'd thought it was prior to getting up and moving around.

He fought through it, though.

Heather switched on the bedside lamp. All its light seemed to pour right into Cal's eyes.

Sitting up, Heather grabbed the lapel of the Belstaff jacket with her one good hand, hung on to to it, onto *him*.

"Cal, you're not making any sense."

On the other side of the bed, Amanda stirred, rolled onto her back. Cal looked at her, saw that she was watching him through squinted eyes.

Still, Cal maintained his whisper. It felt . . . safer.

"I don't know enough about disappearing yet for all three of us to go. Anyway, if they find me, you guys can't be with me. They'll send you to jail, and your son will end up with his father. That can't happen. None of it can."

"They'd send me to jail for what, exactly?"

From behind her, Amanda said, "Aiding a fugitive." She was up on one elbow now.

"We'll figure this out, Cal," Heather said. "Amanda knows all about hiding. She does it to me all the time. Between the three of us—"

"You have to listen to me, Heather. Okay? I need you to listen. No one knows you were staying with me. The few who did are dead now. But you and Amanda will still need to lay low for a while. If what's about to happen is going to work, you guys need to stay out of sight. Do you understand?"

"What do you mean, 'if what's about to happen is going to work'?"

Cal said nothing.

"Cal?"

"I can fix this," he said. "I have to."

"Fix this how?"

He shook his head. Decisive, authoritative. *No time, subject closed.*

"I need to go, Heather. I need to know you guys are safe. You deserve that much, at least. And a son needs his mother. Trust me on that, okay?"

"We can get a lawyer. If it was self-defense—"

"It doesn't matter. Anyway, I don't have what it takes to sit in jail and hope it all works out. I guess I have too much of my father in me after all. I can't put my life in the hands of the police, sit still and hope that they do right by me. I can't do that."

Heather said nothing.

"I left you some money. It should be enough to last a while. You won't hear from me for a long time. It has to be that way. You'll understand why. Keep your new number, though. If I ever think it's okay, I'll get in touch."

She was still hanging on to his jacket. He placed his one good hand over hers, held it for a moment, then gently pulled it away.

He said to Amanda, "Take care of your sister for me. Do that and we'll call us even."

She nodded, smiled slightly. "You got it, Cal."

He stood. It took a moment, then, "I'll see you guys."

He grabbed the Schott jacket, his boots bundled inside, and tucked it under his right arm. He didn't look back, simply headed for the door, opened it, and moved through.

He left them then, a man in a hurry.

Meeting House Lane was just a few blocks east. It took less than five minutes for Cal to make it to Lebell's apartment. He didn't pass another soul the entire way there.

Just down the street from it was the Mustang. Walking to it, Cal took a quick look around, then crouched down and reached under the front bumper. He found the magnetic Hide-a-Key box almost right away. Pulling it free from the frame, he stood, opened the tiny metal container, and removed the spare ignition key.

Inside, he leaned over the seat and opened the glove compartment. It held a rag for checking the oil and a pair of work gloves. Cal put the work gloves on, and less than a minute after arriving, he was gone, en route to Sag Harbor.

There was no reason to speed this time. He had hours still before the last ferry of the night departed Shelter Island.

At the Sag Harbor pier, he paused to look across the dark water. Difficult, standing there, not to think of Angelica, not to remember her approaching him, and her comment, strange then but making more sense now, about how young he was.

Eventually, he removed Heather's old cell phone, scrolled through the incoming calls. The only number it contained was Angstrom's. *The only remaining concrete connection between her and him.* If Angstrom had called from his personal cell phone, then there would be a record of him contacting Heather, but if it had been a prepaid cell—didn't dealers use those?—then there would be nothing to connect the two of them.

She would be free and clear.

As he had with Heather's new number, Cal memorized Angstrom's, then shut the phone off and removed the battery. He flung the phone as far as he could out onto the water, heard the distant, gulping splash as it was swallowed by the chop. As he made his way toward a pay phone at the adjoining marina, he wiped down the battery and then dropped it into a trash can.

He dialed Angstrom's number, waited to hear the amount required to complete the call, and dropped these coins in with the same precautions he had used back at the train station phone. When this call was done—*if Pamona wants his wife so badly, meet me in the parking lot with a thousand dollars and I'll tell you exactly where she is*—Cal returned to the Mustang and drove over the bridge to North Haven. Turning right, he headed down that long, unlit decline to Tyndal Point.

As he waited for the ferry to make its return crossing, he removed the revolver from the jacket pocket, did what he had seen his tormentor do back in that basement, and what he had seen his father do so often enough all those years ago.

Release the pin under the barrel, push the cylinder from the frame.

Inside, three unfired rounds remained.

Returning the cylinder to the frame, feeling through the cold metal the click of the pin locking into place, he wiped the gun down with Lebell's rag, then pocketed the weapon again and watched through the windshield as the ferry chugged slowly nearer.

By the time it reached the dock, Cal had the vial of morphine out and was placing another dose on his tongue.

He needed it to do more now than simply mask the pain growing once again in his hand.

Only a half dozen or so vehicles were in that beachside lot tonight, significantly less than half of what Cal had counted when he was last there two nights ago. Among them there wasn't a single Town Car, so he didn't have to worry this time about drivers-for-hire watching as they waited and smoked. Still, he studied each vehicle there—luxury cars all—to make certain there would be no witnesses.

We have to think that way, Lebell had said. *Like criminals.*

It was, for Cal, more now than a simple matter of just thinking like one.

He waited behind the wheel, watching the entrance to the path that curved through the thick wall of trees separating the lot from the old monastery. Invisible when he had first arrived, but he could see it clearly now. Angstrom and Pamona were supposed to be there, that was what Cal had instructed, but there was no sign of them, no sign of anyone.

Then suddenly, through the trees, a flickering light in motion.

A flashlight.

Cal climbed out of the Mustang, heard the water off to his left, kept his eye, though, on the light. It wasn't long before two figures were standing in the path's entrance.

By then, Cal was feeling the full effect of the oral morphine.

He approached them, his hands in the pocket of the Belstaff jacket. His good hand, his left, held the revolver, his finger covering its trigger.

Neither man was in costume tonight. Pamona wore dark slacks and a silk shirt, black shoes, and a wool jacket; Angstrom, jeans and a hooded Baja pullover. White, it made him, unlike Heather's husband, something of an easy target.

Angstrom was holding the flashlight. He shined it on the pavement between them. The light reflecting up was enough for each of them to see the other by.

Cal felt his palm begin to sweat. The walnut grip quickly grew slick in his hand. Pamona, he noticed, was staring at his face. Cal had yet to reach the two men, was still a good ten paces away when Pamona spoke.

"I know you," he said. "You were the dishwasher. Your brother was that wise-ass punk. Rakowski, right? What was your name? Cal? You enjoy fucking my wife, Cal? With my kid inside? You enjoy that, you piece of shit—"

Cal removed his left hand, aimed the revolver at Pamona's chest, and fired. The man folded and dropped, and before Angstrom could do more than flinch, Cal sighted him.

The single gunshot was less loud here—less loud than back in the kitchen of that abandoned hotel. Distilled by the open sky and swept off quickly by the wind, it was, nonetheless, a gunshot. There was no time to waste.

"Give me your cell phone," he ordered.

Angstrom was frozen. "What the fuck?"

"I want your cell phone."

Angstrom dug into his jeans pocket and removed it, holding it up.

"Put it on the ground, slide it over to me."

Angstrom did. The phone came to a stop at the toe of Carver's snake-skin boot. Cal glanced at it, saw no logo, no brand name.

"Is that a prepaid phone?" he said.

"What?"

"Is that a prepaid phone?"

"Yeah."

"And that's what you used to call Heather."

"Yeah."

Cal smashed it with the boot, grinding it to several pieces with the hard heel. He then kicked the larger of them into the woods and scattered the smaller ones among the bits of sand at the lot's edge.

Just one more thing remained.

He held his aim, his hand steady. Angstrom had both hands up in surrender. Cal noticed the rabbit's foot hanging around the guy's neck.

"Please don't," Angstrom said. "Just don't shoot, okay."

Cal's mind raced. It was more than the spinning of a brain under the influence of morphine, though. He knew he had to fire, just like he had done a moment ago, just like he had done back in the kitchen of that abandoned hotel. With Angstrom dead, there would be no one to connect Heather to Cal, and no way, then, for anyone to see this for what it really was.

A young man killing the husband of the woman he loves, for the woman he loves.

With Angstrom dead, there was no proof that Heather hadn't simply disappeared on her husband two months ago for parts unknown, nothing to indicate that she had anything at all to do with the kid with the leather jacket and busted hand the ferrymen had seen twice now, first on Halloween, then again two nights later.

Yet Cal couldn't close his finger around the trigger.

"Please, man," Angstrom said again.

Cal's hand was steady, Angstrom's rabbit's foot right there in his sights, *but he just couldn't fire.*

It was then that Cal detected motion directly behind Angstrom. Someone was emerging from the path. Someone with a weapon drawn.

It was a man in a suit.

The man who had inadvertently prevented Pamona from tripping over Cal as he hid at the other end of the path.

Cal was in this man's sights, but this man was moving—not running, that would have made too much noise, but in motion nonetheless, walking steadily both forward and to his left. *Clearing the path, looking for a clean shot.* He was, Cal sensed, just seconds from pulling the trigger.

Out of reflex Cal stepped to his right—*displace, like he had back in the kitchen*—and dropped low. That, dropping low, was the wrestler in him. As Cal moved, Angstrom was placed for a brief second between him and the man in the suit. It was at that instant the man in the suit fired.

Just like Pamona had, just like Tierno and Janssen and Carver had, Angstrom folded and fell.

A man falling through a trapdoor.

As Angstrom fell, Cal, in crouch, extended and raised his arm, to aim at the man standing over him. Whatever emotion had caused his trigger finger to freeze was long gone now. He squeezed once, and this fifth shot hit the man in the face.

He, too, folded and fell.

Cal stayed down, waiting, his eye on the path. Would another man emerge from it? Were there more? He heard and saw, though, nothing. It took a moment, but eventually Cal was able to stand. It took another moment, but finally he was able to think.

Despite the morphine, or maybe because of it, he realized what he had to do.

That was his gift, always had been. He could look at something— something mechanical—and just know what to do.

It wasn't till recently that he realized this natural ability of his extended beyond the intricacies of all things automotive.

He hurried to Angstrom, knelt down, and picked up Angstrom's right hand, fitting it around the grip. He knew that for this to look the way he wanted it to look, the cops would need to find powder burns on Angstrom's hand. *Yet another drug deal gone bad, perhaps—anything but what it really was.* Placing Angstrom's finger over the trigger, and his own gloved finger over Angstrom's, he aimed the revolver out over the dark water and fired off the final round.

This shot, like the ones before, dissipated quickly, might have been, to the remaining partygoers inside the monastery, the crack of nearby fireworks.

Or maybe not.

Still, Cal didn't stick around to find out. He ran to Lebell's Mustang, got in behind the wheel, and drove to the north end of the island, where another ferry landing was located, this one connecting Shelter Island to Greenport, on the northern fork of Long Island.

As he made his way through those dark streets, Cal kept his eye on the rearview mirror, watching for some indication that he was being pursued. Often he would realize that he was holding his breath, tell himself to breathe, only to find a moment later that he was holding it again.

He continued to watch what that narrow mirror showed of the world behind him as he parked the Mustang at the bow of the empty ferry and waited for this crossing to begin.

PART FOUR

November 2–5

Fifteen

———◆◆◆———

He ditched the Mustang, along with the Belstaff jacket and snake-skin boots, in Connecticut, where, like the Rakowski he was, he boosted an old Pontiac and in it made his way to eastern Ohio. There, at a walk-in clinic, he had his wrist set and put in a cast. He paid in cash, giving the name Adam Pulaski to the admitting nurse because it would be easy enough in his current state to remember, and because Cal Rakowski simply no longer existed.

The only document to contradict that fact was his New York State driver's license, which he cut up and flushed down the toilet in the clinic's rest room.

At a bus station ticket counter a few blocks away, when asked for identification, he claimed to have lost everything in a recent mugging. One look at him and there was no reason for the ticket agent to doubt his story. A woman Angelica's age, though nowhere near as well-tended, she took pity on the boy and issued a ticket anyway, even wished him luck.

His destination was a town a thousand miles from everything he knew. A college town, it was a place his brother had often mentioned, a place where thousands of people his and Cal's age walked around every day and there were plenty of restaurants and bars in which to find off-the-books work. It was the town, in fact, Aaron's girlfriend had come from. She had filled Aaron's head with stories about it, and he had filled Cal's.

Upon his arrival, Cal found a cheap hotel to stay at, checking in with the same story about having lost his identification. Then, after allowing himself a few hours' sleep, during which he dreamed of being followed by some faceless shadow, he began to search around for long-term accommodations.

The right accommodations.

He began to seek out, too, news coverage of all that he had left behind. Reports were limited at first to the New York papers—the headline of the *New York Post* read BRIDGEHAMPTON BLOODBATH—but the story was picked up within days by the national press. It was a report in *USA Today* that first referred to a connection between those murders in Bridgehampton and an apparent drug deal gone bad on Shelter Island. The gun that had killed three men in Bridgehampton—one of which was an FBI agent—also killed two of three men murdered on Shelter Island on the same night. It was the next day that an article in *The New York Times* connected those murders with an apparent suicide in Southampton that had taken place in the home of a "prominent and beloved town matriarch" who herself had been killed in a suspicious motorcycle accident and the murder of a seasoned detective.

For days and days it went like that, each paper Cal opened offering newly disclosed details—revelation upon revelation, connection upon connection, yet each new piece seemed to only add to what had become a state of confusion. In none of the articles, however, appeared the name Cal Rakowski—and, more importantly, neither did the name Heather Pamona. Even when the stories focused on the violence that had occurred on Shelter Island—one of its victims, Ronnie Pamona, was connected through the sale of a restaurant to a South American gangster that had recently gone missing—even then there was no mention of Pamona's estranged wife.

Eventually, though, Cal knew, someone would make that connection. On the day that the names of the Shelter Island victims were reported, he'd felt an overwhelming urge to call Heather. He didn't dare write down her number, so he repeated it countless times a day like a mantra, got to the point where he could have dialed it in his sleep. But he knew better than to risk it, to risk her. He'd gone through hell to remove from that nightmare all trace of himself and her, all the things that connected them.

It was best to leave everything as it was, for now anyway.

Still, the time was coming when Heather would be able to emerge from hiding. The articles were setting that up nicely. Cal had no doubt that she'd know what to say and what not say about where and with whom she had been for the past few months. Who could blame her— now that it was coming out exactly what kind of man her husband was, the life of decadence he was drawn to—for having taken off in the first place?

All that remained, then, as far as Cal could see, was what might be recovered from the old Triumph motorcycle. He usually wore gloves when he worked on the thing, but perhaps on one of the engine parts, something small that had required a dexterous touch, awaited a perfect print. He had to be careful from now on, not that he wasn't careful by nature. But, now, even more so. The last thing he needed was for his fingerprints to be entered into the nationwide database. The one thing that could bring this all down around him was something connecting Adam Pulaski with Cal Rakowski, and Cal Rakowski with what the press was now calling *The Halloween Murders*.

It was three days before he found a sign that interested him. ROOM FOR RENT, in a window above a little breakfast and lunch place. INQUIRE WITHIN. He watched the restaurant for much of the morning from a coffee shop across the street—it was that kind of neighborhood, lots of places to eat everywhere you looked, so maybe he'd find work that he could walk to, which would be helpful since he couldn't buy a vehicle, at least not till he was officially someone else.

But where to look for someone like Lebell's friend Pearson?

First things first.

He waited till the lunch rush was over and the only waitress inside was alone, then crossed the street and entered.

The room above was gloomy but big, had a kitchenette and a small table set beside a window that overlooked the busy street. High ceilings, a bed twice the size of his old bed, and, directly above it, a wooden fan.

The waitress was a tall woman, in her fifties, Cal guessed. Curly red hair, a deep voice, blue eyes that looked at him with a degree of skepticism. He was getting used to that, though, had been getting such looks from more or less everyone now. *Did it show? What he had done? The man he had become?* The woman told him that she owned the building and the business below, seemed to want him to know that she wasn't just a waitress in some coffee shop.

"Do you have a job?" she said. She was standing in the open doorway, watching him as he moved around the room.

"No, but I'll be looking once my hand heals. I can pay in advance, though. For as many weeks as you want."

He looked out the window, saw barely any vehicles on that narrow street. Foot traffic only. Voices, footsteps, a flow of people.

"It's a hundred a week," the woman said.

"I can pay you for ten."

She looked him over. He just stood there.

"Yeah, okay," she said finally.

He reached into his jacket and pulled a grand from his wad of bills. Crossing the room, he held out the money for her.

She didn't take it just yet, though.

"You'll have to share the bathroom with the other tenants," she said. "A couple. They have the back room. I should warn you, they argue a lot. If it gets to be too much, just let me know."

"It's all right. I'm pretty good at minding my own business."

The woman nodded, gave him one last look, then took the bills from him.

"Good for you," she said. "So what's your name?"

"Adam."

"Adam what?"

"Pulaski."

"What kind of work will you be looking for when you start looking again?"

"Anything I can get."

"Ever work in a restaurant?"

"Yeah."

"I'm looking for a busboy-dishwasher. Would you be interested?"

"Maybe."

"We'll talk about it when the time comes." She folded the money, stuffed it into her apron. "I'm Corita, by the way."

They shook hands. He noticed there were no rings on her fingers.

"Do you have a lot of things to carry up?" She glanced at the cast on his hand. "I can maybe get my cook to help you."

"No, this is it, this is me. When do you think can I move in?"

She shrugged. "Looks to me like you already have."

Later, stretched out on his bed in the dark, he listened to the sounds coming up from the street. They lasted well into the night. It was very different here from what he was used to, from the silence of Scuttle-hole Road, but he didn't mind it. Getting up at one point, he looked out his front window, saw, again, people his age moving about. Couples, here and there; small groups; the occasional solitary soul heading some-where. Pulling up one of the chairs from his small table, he sat and watched them all.

It wasn't till midnight that he heard his neighbors arrive. He lis-tened to the noise of them coming up the stairs, moving down the hallway, entering their room. There was nothing unusual for a while, and then, suddenly, he heard raised voices. An argument—like an explosion—that lasted for several minutes, a man cursing and a woman crying. Finally, a door slammed shut, the voices stopped. There were footsteps in the hallway and then on the stairs. A single set of footsteps, angry.

The downstairs door closed, and from his window he saw a man walking away in a hurry.

Tall, dressed in jeans and an army field jacket, storming off. Cal couldn't see the man's face but didn't really want to. Within seconds, his neighbor had disappeared from sight.

Cal waited fifteen minutes, then decided it was time for sleep. Step-ping out of his room, into the narrow hallway, he saw that the bathroom door was closed. Before he could turn back, though, the door opened and a woman appeared.

Young, maybe even his age, with shoulder-length dark hair—black hair, really. She was dressed in a T-shirt that was several sizes too big. There were tears in her eyes, one of which—Cal saw this and immediately wished he hadn't—had a half-moon bruise beneath it. A black smudge that stood out even in the darkness of that hallway.

She saw him, and he saw her, so no turning back for either of them. Nervously, she brushed her long bangs behind her right ear, leaving her left side alone, no doubt to hide her blackened eye.

"You must be our new neighbor," she said.

Cal nodded. "Yeah."

"I'm Lily."

"I'm Adam."

"Listen, sorry about the noise before."

"Don't worry about it."

She smiled. It was, at best, a forced smile. "He wasn't like that before we got married. He's having a hard time finding work, like everyone else these days. It's a world gone mad, you know. He'll probably keep it down now that we have a neighbor again."

"I'm a heavy sleeper," Cal lied. It seemed the thing to do. "Speaking of, time to wash up and go to bed."

She realized she was blocking the doorway, smiled that same smile again and stepped aside. "Sorry."

"It's all right."

"Good night."

"Good night."

In the bathroom he ran the water, washed his face, brushed his teeth, looking as he did at his reflection in the mirror.

He was still taking the morphine for the pain, and it showed in his eyes. Glassy but burning, distant but fierce, too. How could his new landlady have looked at him in a way other than skeptical?

Stepping back into the hallway, he noticed that his neighbor had left her door open. He could see only a portion of her room, but it was enough to tell that it was no different from his.

Turning, he walked toward his door, was almost there when he heard her say, "Hey."

She was standing in her doorway, had put a bathrobe on over her T-shirt.

Cal thought, of course, of Heather.

Lily said, "Would you like a drink, maybe?"

He looked at her, saying nothing.

"He'll be gone for a while, if that's what you're worried about. A couple of hours, at least. I could use the company, unless you're too tired or something."

She was a bundle of nervous tics. Cal looked down at the length of floor between them.

"I have cards," she said. "We could play a couple of hands, get to know each other. I mean, we're going to be neighbors, right? Share a bathroom and all that."

He didn't make a move, in one direction or the other.

"C'mon," she said, "just one drink. No harm in that, right?"

No, he thought, *probably no harm in that.*

He said, though, "Maybe another time. I need to get some sleep."

She offered another nervous smile, absentmindedly curled her bangs again behind the one ear.

One side of her face showing, the other concealed.

"Okay," she said.

He heard disappointment in her voice—*the sting of rejection, even, maybe*—but he didn't care.

Back in his room, he sat at his window for a while, watching the people, then stretched out again on the large bed. He wondered if he would dream that dream again, *Heather*'s dream of being pursued from town to town, across the vast stretches of nothingness between, through a dark maze of unfamiliar streets.

By some faceless shadow that could not be shaken, Cal all the time holding a candle he very much needed to keep from going out.